FINDING YOU

12/21

ALSO BY JO WATSON

Burning Moon

Almost a Bride

FINDING YOU

JO WATSON

FOREVER

NEW YORK   BOSTON

Copyright © 2017 by Jo Watson
Excerpt from *Burning Moon* copyright © 2016 by Jo Watson
Cover image from Shutterstock. Cover design by Elizabeth Turner.
Cover copyright © 2017 by Hachette Book Group, Inc.

Forever
Hachette Book Group
1290 Avenue of the Americas
New York, NY 10104
forever-romance.com
twitter.com/foreverromance

First edition: May 2017

Forever is an imprint of Grand Central Publishing.
The Forever name and logo are trademarks of Hachette Book Group, Inc.

The publisher is not responsible for websites (or their content) that are not owned by the publisher.

The Hachette Speakers Bureau provides a wide range of authors for speaking events. To find out more, go to www.hachettespeakersbureau.com or call (866) 376-6591.

LCCN: 2017934095

ISBNs: 978-1-4555-9554-9 (pbk.), 978-1-4555-9552-5 (ebook), 978-1-4789-6731-6 (audio)

Printed in the United States of America

LSC-C

10 9 8 7 6 5 4 3 2 1

This book is dedicated to everyone who's ever felt like they didn't belong. And DM.

FINDING YOU

PROLOGUE

⌒

The day of my mental breakdown was a Wednesday.

And when I say "mental breakdown," I don't mean the kind that celebrities have when they check into a luxury spa for medicated mud wraps and mojitos. I'm talking about the other kind. The messy kind.

It was a normal Wednesday. An unspectacular, uneventful, run-of-the-mill, *not* Monday, *not* Tuesday, but *Wednesday*. There was nothing special about the day.

So why was I feeling like this? *Like what exactly?*

Well, that's the million-dollar question, isn't it?

Because I couldn't quite put my finger on it. The feeling wasn't fully formed yet, but it had gripped me nonetheless. Embedded itself like an arrow in my back or a virus in my bloodstream— invisible, but *deadly*.

Something was wrong. Very wrong.

A mild pressure in my solar plexus. A slight heaviness in my head and a feeling of total disconnectedness. Everything around me screeched that I did not belong here, and suddenly I felt like an alien in my own home.

I rubbed the sticky sleep from my eyes and glanced around my room. The chair in the corner that Mother had insisted on having reupholstered in *Toasted Granola Sunrise* suede, and the walls she had insisted I paint in *Mystical Song of the Gray Dove*, looked odd. (Sidenote: Who the hell is coming up with the names of colors these days, anyway?)

I climbed out of bed apprehensively, stalked over to my bathroom, and looked at myself in the mirror. My features were the same—large and distinct. Olive complexion, unruly curly black hair, that "signature" mole on my cheek that I'd always hated, and then there are my eyes...one dark brown, one light hazel.

But somehow everything looked different. I looked less like myself and more like someone I didn't know. If that makes sense?

But of course it doesn't make sense. Because nothing about this so-called normal Wednesday was making any sense at all (hence growing suspicions of imminent mental breakdown).

Perhaps I was still asleep and dreaming. That was surely the only possible explanation for these feelings.

I pinched my cheek. *Nothing.*

Splashed water on my face. *Nope.*

I stood in the strange bathroom, looking at this strange person in the mirror. Her name was Jane. Plain Jane Smith. Dr. Plain Jane Smith.

Well, that's my name *now*; it wasn't the name I was born with. But that had nothing to do with the way I was feeling, *did it*?

Kitchen. Tea. *Now!*

A soothing cup of tea was surely the antidote that would rid me of these feelings. I walked into the kitchen, turned on the kettle, and waited. I felt out of place here, too.

Tea—one bag.

Sugar—zero.

No milk in sight.

I stirred the liquid that I was pinning my hopes of normality on and sipped. It tasted bitter. Did it always taste like this?

The so-called soothing tea only seemed to intensify the feelings and gave rise to a humming anxiety, which crept slowly like a growing evening shadow.

What was going on with me? I could phone one of my friends. But what would I say?

Help! I think I might have been sucked into the Twilight Zone.

Nothing had changed really, nothing significant enough to explain this feeling anyway. I'd just graduated and had started my new job. But no surprises there. It certainly wouldn't be the thing shaking me to my very core. The job had been planned for and organized, and it was inevitable—I was going to be taking over my father's dental practice.

It was my birthday in a few days, but birthdays came along every year. Again, nothing out of the ordinary. I needed to stop this feeling. I needed to stop obsessing.

Drive!

That always cleared my head. I got dressed and brushed my teeth for precisely two minutes—no excuse for bad dental hygiene, even in the face of a total nervous breakdown.

I climbed into my car and started driving through the sleepy suburbs. Then I veered left, away from the little houses and toward the city.

The mall. With shops and people and breakfast. That would surely make me feel normal again.

It was early, so most of the shops were closed and the mall looked like an empty school hall: depressing. Like it was waiting for kids to rush in, and without them was just a sad shell of what it had once been. A washed-up carcass on an empty beach.

The pressure in my solar plexus was back. The feelings intensified into a painful stab. I grabbed my stomach. *What's that?* This time the feeling was somewhat familiar.

Loss.

A deep sense of loss washed over me, loss like I'd experienced only one other time in my life. *But what the hell have I lost?*

I took in a deep breath and filled my lungs to capacity and then I walked. I walked as fast as I could.

Past the banks, past the hardware store, and past the shop where I'd bought the exorbitantly overpriced scented candle that I had absolutely no use for (but I'm a people pleaser and the shop attendant had been so nice). I passed a coffee shop that had just opened its doors to a solitary customer in need of an early-morning fix.

And then...*I saw it.*

I stood outside Flight and Travel Center, looking up at the electronic display of all the holiday specials. And there it was. At the very top.

GREECE

A special.

Round-trip ticket $800.

Almost sold out.

Buy now. Complimentary beach bag and

sunscreen included.

Terms and Conditions apply

And that's when the mists of confusion started to evaporate and the picture finally came into focus.

This *was* about my name. This *was* about my job and this was definitely, *definitely* about my birthday. This was about the day I was born and the circumstances in which I was born.

I slumped down against the wall and pulled out my credit card. I clutched it tightly and waited for someone to open the shop so I could buy the only thing that could furnish me with the answers I'd been seeking my entire life.

CHAPTER ONE

I've always known I was adopted. It's not one of those closely guarded family secrets that makes its way onto a TLC reality show: *My mother is actually my father's Siamese twin's second cousin's daughter's lover twice removed.*

Besides, it's pretty damn obvious. You would have to be seriously visually impaired not to notice.

My family—Mom, Dad, and twin sisters Janet and Jenna (my mother has a thing for the letter *J*)—all look alike. They're short, fair skinned, with strawberry blond hair, blue eyes, and cute little button noses.

They're also all terribly attractive, looking like one of those happy families that appear in TV ads for fiber-rich breakfast cereal or *get up and go* multivitamins.

Me? I'm none of these things. I'm tall, *freakishly so*. I'm also dark, with a complexion that goes the color of a cappuccino with too much sun—I avoid it at all costs. My features aren't delicate, either: nose more pronounced than most, lips fuller than usual, and I seem to have large, furry caterpillars masquerading as eyebrows. Thank God those are back in fashion now, so I no longer have to endure hours of root-ripping torture.

You could quite literally call me the black sheep of the family. And for all this, I suspect I am my mother's greatest disappointment. Maybe that's why she overcompensates with me so much. Not that she would ever admit that out loud. I was adopted after she and my father spent years trying to get pregnant. But six months after I arrived, she was miraculously pregnant with perfect twins. I often wonder if she regrets adopting me...

Standing out wasn't easy. It made growing up even harder than it should have been. During middle school I went through a particularly awkward stage where my limbs seemed too long for my body and my facial features too large for my face.

"Maybe she'll grow into them?" I once overheard a classmate's mother say.

"She's a big-boned girl," someone else once said. *"You know, sturdy. I bet she'll never break a bone."*

It was true; I've never broken a bone. But I would have gladly traded a little snapped femur or two for the joy of not being likened to the foundations of a house. Kids teased me for not looking like my family. For being too tall, having a big nose, and anything else the snot-nosed schoolyard bullies could think of.

And then there was that one boy who told me my parents didn't really love me because I wasn't their *real* child. And I took it all in. I internalized every single cruel word, each one feeding off the other, until I was carrying around a dark, twisty, cancerous growth inside.

Luckily, when I hit eighteen, stuff started falling into place. That is to say that things weren't so disproportionately big, long, and full. I still don't look like my sisters, though. I envy them so much, sometimes, that I struggle to like them. *Does that make me a bad person?*

I've always felt like the perpetual ugly duckling, waiting for her swan moment that never seemed to come. The wallflower that never bloomed. And believe me, I've tried to bloom. I fight with a hair straightener most mornings, and I've probably watched every YouTube makeup tutorial on the contouring craze. But each time I tried to make my nose look slimmer and cheekbones higher, I just ended up looking like a zebra, and no amount of blending changed that. And as of today, I officially own precisely thirty-three lipsticks. I got it into my head once that somehow the perfect shade could save me from myself and transform me like Cinderella's glass slipper. I try them all on once, but none of them seem to do the job. So I put them all into a giant makeup bag and close it, and each time I do, I close off a little bit of hope inside myself, too.

There was nothing I could do to change. I was just...different. I have since accounted for that difference, though.

At the age of eighteen, I was legally allowed to reach out to my biological mother through the adoption agency. I wanted answers and was desperate to meet her and know who I was and where I came from.

She, however, did not want to meet me—which broke my heart

more than I can ever describe. She had rejected me at birth, and now done the same thing to me eighteen years later. She did pass on a few breadcrumbs, though.

She told me that she'd named me Tracy, that I'm half Greek, and that she was only eighteen when she'd given me up. As if her young age were some kind of excuse, or explained away any accountability she might have had in the act. I wrote back asking for information about my father—maybe he would want to meet me—but all she told me was that I was the product of a youthful holiday fling with a tour guide named Dimitri. That was it. And then she slammed the metaphorical door in my face.

I thought finding out about my birth parents would have made me feel better. But it didn't. In fact, it made me feel worse.

Greek. There it was: the reason I wasn't blond and had to pluck a stray chin hair by the age of eight. I didn't want to be different. Why couldn't I be blonder and prettier, with size 6 shoes and ballerina limbs?

Why couldn't I be *not-me.*

I remember crying myself to sleep that night and wishing I could have the part of me that made me different, the Greek part, surgically removed. The next morning I woke up and two things happened.

I decided that if I couldn't change the color of my skin, shrink my features, or radically shorten my limbs with dramatic, experimental plastic surgery (I really did Google this), I would become the poster child for "normality." So I rejected everything about myself that was different and went about trying to blend in.

Plain Jane Smith. Polite, run-of-the-mill, average. I strove to be that person you couldn't pick out of a crowd if you tried. That person that at your ten-year school reunion no one even remembers. I flew under the radar like a stealth plane in enemy territory. Stealth Plain Jane. *If they can't see me, they can't tease me.*

The second thing I did was start building a wall that kept me somewhat separate from the world around me—only allowing access to my select group of friends, each one of us outcasts in our own special way.

That was also the last time I cried…

I stared up at the electronic display once more. GREECE. I'd rejected and denied my Greek heritage in every possible way. In fact, you could go as far as saying I'd developed some kind of psychosomatic allergy to anything Hellenic.

And now I want to go to Greece with every fiber of my being?

Not only that, but I was overcome by a desire—no, a *need*—to find my biological father. Maybe meeting him would finally give me the answer to this drowning confusion I felt. Maybe it was time to tackle my Greekness head-on.

But I couldn't embark on this journey alone. I grabbed my phone, opened WhatsApp, and quickly created a "Jane goes to Greece" group.

Then:

Lilly added

Annie added

Val added

Stormy added

Jane: Guess what?

Annie: You know what time it is here in LA?

Val: What?

Jane: Where is everyone? Hello?

Annie: Lilly is probably (a) staring at her engagement ring, (b) having sex with Damien, (c) staring at her ring while having sex with Damien.

Lilly: I saw that! And you're wrong, it's (d) postcoital cuddling while staring at my ring.

Annie: Nympho.

Val: Hang on…YOU'RE GOING TO GREECE? Did I read that right?

Annie: What?

Lilly: You hate Greek food!

Annie: You hate anything Greek!!!! WTH

Lilly: Hang on, Stormy is phoning me. She's probably confused about how to use the iPhone Damien bought her again.

Annie: I can't believe she even agreed to use it.

Val: She's named it "Tumor" and refuses to hold it to her ear when talking.

Annie: LOL that's dramatic!

Lilly: She's freaking out because green speech bubbles have invaded her screen.

Val: hahaha

Lilly: I've tried to explain to her how to join.

Stormy: aml Here's ?

Val: Welcome to 2017!

Annie: OMG it's going to snow.

Stormy: wHose is talks ing ?

Jane: I have to go. The shop is opening.

Annie: What shop?

Lilly: ? Wait.

Val: ARE YOU GOING TO GREECE?

Stormy: wHY os is rhis THIS going so gast ?

Stormy: gast

Stormy: DUCK this. FAST?

Stormy: Fuck this!

CHAPTER TWO

$\smile$

$\mathcal{O}$ne round-trip ticket to Greece please, the special." I pointed at the board, unable to contain my excitement.

The woman looked slightly irritated with me. I'd barely given her a chance to open the shop and slide a high-heeled toe inside. I'd been waiting so impatiently that I'd practically cartwheeled through the doors the second they were opened. Not my usual style. I always waited patiently and let the elderly and the women with children go in front of me. But today, if there'd been an elderly lady with a walker, I may have actually used the thing to catapult myself inside.

"Sure thing." She smiled sweetly. "Just give me a moment, please."

She turned on the lights, fired up the computers, and fiddled with some knobs and switches.

"Right." She started typing with her excessively long, glitter-tipped nails.

"Mmmm." She looked up at me from the screen. "You're lucky. There's one last ticket available. When would you like to go?"

"How's tomorrow?" The words caught me completely off guard as they flew out of my mouth.

The woman looked as surprised as I felt. "All right." She sounded reticent but tapped away on the keyboard. "Ah. Lucky again. One more space on that flight."

"Great!"

"And accommodation, where will you be staying?"

I paused for a moment. This was a very good question. I had no idea where I was going to stay and certainly no clue where to start looking for my father.

"What's the most popular holiday destination?" My birth mother had been on holiday, so I reasoned it would have been somewhere touristy.

The woman looked at me and blinked slowly. Her makeup was fresh and thickly applied. Her mascara was so heavy and moist that some of her lashes stuck together like large fat worms.

"Mykonos, I guess." She slid a pamphlet across the table. "Very nice there. Hot men," she added with a wink of her sticky lashes.

"Mykonos, Mykonos, Mykonos." I repeated the word out loud a few times, stretching it out as I went: "Myk...o...nos." I was hoping for some kind of inexplicable psychic feeling, or an Oprah aha moment that told me that I was on the right track. But nothing came.

"Any more you can recommend?"

"Corfu?"

"Corrr...fu. Cor...fuuu. Corrr...fuuu." But the more I said

it, the stranger the word sounded and the less I wanted to go there. "Another one?"

"Um, Spetses."

"Spet...ses...sss." It sounded like something you might find floating in formaldehyde. "No. Definitely not there. Another one?"

"Rhodes?"

"Doesn't sound Greek enough."

"Zakynthos."

"Perhaps a little too Greek. Anything else?"

Glitter-Talon was officially looking at me strangely. She narrowed her eyes as if she was trying to bring a faraway object into focus. "Santorini?" she finally proposed.

"Santorini. Santorini. Santorini, SAN...tor...ini." I'd obviously heard of Santorini. I said it some more, and this time I felt a little something. Nothing mind-blowingly Oprah-ish. No heavens opening up with a chorus of trumpeting angels. Just a tiny little tug in my gut. Under normal circumstances I never would have based a decision on a barely there gut feeling, but these were not normal circumstances. And I certainly wasn't my normal self today.

"Perfect. Santorini it is," I said quickly. She went back to typing and just as she was about to hit enter...

"Wait!" Self-doubt suddenly gripped me. "Just give me a moment."

"*Hello, I am Dimitri from Santorini,*" I said, role-playing in a male voice. "*Dimitri from Santorini.*"

Now she was really looking at me strangely. I pulled my phone out.

WHATSAPP GROUP: Jane goes to Greece

Jane: What do you think of when you hear Santorini?

Val: WTF is going on?

Annie: Sunburn.

Lilly: Hot tour guides and tropical seas and parties and sex and love.

Annie: LOL Lilly. She said Santorini. Not Thailand.

Jane: Hot tour guides? Really? OK perfect. Bye.

Val: Wait!!!! Are you really going to Greece????

Stormy: how uou type oon thiS thjng ?

I pocketed my phone and looked at Glitter-Talon again. "Santorini it is then."

"Uh, you sure?" she asked, voice still dripping in sarcasm. "Maybe you'd rather go somewhere else? Somewhere closer to home?"

"Why?"

"Well, do you even know anything about Greece?"

"Of course I do!"

She looked at me expectantly. I reached into my brain to retrieve everything I knew about the country. What was there to know anyway? Their flag is blue and white...then there's the Parthenon and...lots of other ancient ruins and pillars and rocks. Olives and the Olympics and dipping your pitas into sauces and there's that famous dessert...balaclava?

"So?" she said with a sigh that screamed irritation. This woman had a bad attitude, not to mention a slight gap between her central and lateral incisors. I hoped she flossed properly. She was really starting to piss me off.

"It's not like you have a million customers today," I heard someone snap.

"There's no need to be rude."

I looked up and glanced around to see who she was talking to. But there was no one there. And when I saw her glaring at me, that's when it dawned on me...

I'd said it.

I slapped my hand over my mouth. *I said that?* I had actually spoken my mind. Clearly the filters in my brain that stopped stuff like that from tumbling out of my mouth had completely malfunctioned.

What the hell is wrong with me?

"Santorini. Please." I tried to smile sweetly at Spider-Lashes.

"And can I book you a tour guide? There are lots of reputable ones we use and lots of great tours," she asked, grabbing for some additional leaflets.

"No. I don't need any guiding." I raised my hand and blocked the oncoming bits of paper.

She looked at me curiously again. "So no sightseeing then?"

"No."

"No island-hopping? No wine tasting? No tours of the ancient ruins?"

"No. No and no. Thanks." I was still trying to sound polite.

She half grunted to herself, "Fine. I'll just organize for someone to fetch you from the airport at least."

"Fine."

"And how long will you be going for?" The fake pleasantry returned to her voice. She reminded me of one of those call center workers trying to sell you a death and disability insurance policy but sounding like they're telling you that you'd just won the lottery.

"As long as it takes!" I replied.

"No, seriously. I need to put in a return date."

"As long as it takes," I repeated.

"As long as it takes for what?" she asked slowly and deliberately, as if she were talking to a child.

"To find the answers."

She put down the pen that she had been grinding between her teeth and folded her arms. She sat back in her chair, and her eyes came up and met mine.

"Um...are you sure you should be, you know, traveling? Alone? I mean, you seem...kind of sick?"

"Sick?" This woman was treating me like I was trying to make a quick escape from the asylum, all the while tapping her stupidly long glittery nails and blinking her judgmental lashes at me. Something about this whole scenario struck a nerve deep inside.

And then it snapped. The elastic band inside me that had been stretched to the breaking point over the years finally broke. And whatever it had been holding together and keeping neatly in place all fell apart in one surreal moment.

"Look! I'm having a really *weird*, bad day today. And I don't need you making it any worse than it already is. So I would really appreciate it if you would do your job and put your glitter nails— *which you should really consider trimming by the way because it's incredibly unhygienic*—back down on the keyboard and type up my ticket as fast as possible. And while you're at it you should really stop chewing your pen, you're going to get hairline cracks in your tooth enamel, which can lead to all sorts of oral health issues not to mention bad breath if debris gets stuck in them."

Her bottom jaw fell open. "Who do you think you are?" She shot me a look that could murder kittens.

"Sorry... here." I quickly slid my credit card across the counter.

She picked it up and glared at it. "Dr. Jane Smith." She looked up at me suspiciously. "Doctor?"

"Dentist."

A smirk washed over her face slowly. "Well, that explains a lot."

When the whole encounter was finally over, I walked out clutching my ticket. I was leaving for Greece tomorrow; it was almost unbelievable. This was not how stealth Plain Jane behaved. How the hell was I going to explain this to my friends and family?

How was I going to explain to everyone why I had just made the most bizarre, uncharacteristic decision of my entire boring life— one that not even I fully understood?

CHAPTER THREE

Did you know that chalk and cheese actually have something rather significant in common? They are both very high in calcium.

So to say that my family and I were like "chalk and cheese" would be totally incorrect. To say we were more like pterodactyls and turnips would be far more accurate. They all seemed to be on the same page and I seemed to exist in an entirely separate book. That one lonely, dusty, neglected book at the bottom of the shelf.

My mother enjoys lazy champagne-laced days at the country club. Trips to the spa for the latest breakthrough in cellulite treatment, wrinkle decreasing, lip upsizing, and lash extending. Her greatest ambitions in life are to have the eyelids of a newborn baby and Madonna's upper arms. And when she's not spending all her energy on looking at least two decades younger, she's meddling in my life. She's been meddling since I can remember and over the years has managed to turn it into something that resembles an Olympic sport.

Being an ex–beauty queen, she places a lot of importance on outward appearances. She still has an old photo of herself winning Miss Johannesburg 1983. Despite the helmet-sized perm, blue eye shadow, and shoulder pads you could land a Boeing 747 on, she did look beautiful.

But no matter how hard I tried, she despaired at my posture, held her head at my ungainly manner of walking, and recoiled at my overbite. She was practically heartbroken the day she discovered that my eyebrows were migrating toward each other. That could be fixed, though, and I was shipped off to a waxologist *tout de suite*. As a result, I've been waxing strange and unusual places for as long as I can remember. Which is a good thing, because these days it seems that having any form of body hair is about as sinful as letting your six-year-old smoke a cigarette while poaching rhinos. Everyone is obsessed with removing as much of it as possible. I made this shocking discovery a few months ago when the waxologist very crassly asked me if I wanted an anal wax—just like that.

She also very kindly educated me on the new trend in male grooming…*crack and sack*. "Even the men are doing it these days."

I still declined politely.

What couldn't be fixed, though, was how much I let my mother's "constructive criticism" and "helpful suggestions" break down my self-esteem. And to make matters worse, male admirers were pretty scarce on the ground, just confirming my suspicions about myself and fueling my mother's relentless interference in my love life, or lack thereof.

During my almost-twenty-five years on this planet I have had exactly two sort-of, almost, borderline "boyfriends." Neither relationship went well.

The first one was the kind of guy whose secretive nature gave me images of bunny boiling, or maybe a creepy serial killer wall covered in voyeuristic photos. Turned out, though, that his general sneakiness was due to the fact that he had a girlfriend back at home. The embarrassing scene that transpired outside my apartment one night confirmed that. The scene then went from embarrassing to crushingly humiliating when she screamed, *"He says you're shit in bed anyway!"*

As for number two, the guy was obsessed with *Star Trek*. His claim to fame was that he could speak in both Klingon and Ferengi. I suspected it wasn't going to work when he met my friends for the first time and greeted them with the Vulcan finger salute. My suspicions were only solidified when during sex that I really wouldn't write anywhere about, let alone home, he grunted into my ear . . .

"HISlaH, HISlaH, HISlaH." (Translation from the Klingon: "Yes, yes, yes.")

No. No. No. Naturally the relationship did not "live long and prosper."

And when a vaguely normal guy does pay me any kind of attention, my crippling shyness kicks in, leading to many embarrassing and less-than-desirable responses on my part. The last time a guy tried to kiss me, I told him that the adult mouth contains five to ten thousand different types of bacteria. Needless to say, we didn't swap any.

It would be accurate to conclude that my love life has been a rather lackluster affair to date. My heart is probably the most under-utilized organ in my body, even more so than my appendix, which serves no medical function whatsoever. It's not that I don't like guys and sex; I like them very, *very* much. They just don't seem to like me as much as I like them.

So at the age of almost-twenty-five, I know absolutely nothing about this crazy little thing called love. I've heard it's supposed to make the world go around and conquers all, and apparently it finds a way and is blind . . .

It wouldn't really matter if it were also deaf with bad skin and a limp, because I wouldn't be finding it anytime soon. Correction, it probably wouldn't be finding me. Love got lost years ago and clearly didn't have a GPS.

"*You just need to meet more guys!*" my friend Lilly was always telling me.

But the only time I met men was when I had on a white mask and was preparing to plunge a sharp needle into their gums—not exactly conducive to romance. I did get a marriage proposal once, although he did make it when the laughing gas had kicked in.

And let's be honest about something while we're at it: *Everybody hates the dentist!* I was already a person with naturally low self-esteem, and this job didn't exactly boost it.

But becoming a dentist just seemed like the right thing to do. I'd practically grown up in my dad's practice. While my sociable sisters were being rushed around to extramurals in the afternoons, I sat in my dad's office diligently doing my homework and reading the Guinness book of records.

But had I even wanted to be a dentist? Let alone take over his practice so he could play golf full-time.

Well, that's what my whole wacky Wednesday was all about. I actually had no real idea who the hell I was. I had no idea where I came from and, as a result, had no idea who I was meant to become. All I knew for sure was that there was only one place on earth I would find all these answers.

Greece.

WHATSAPP GROUP: Jane goes to Greece

Jane: I'm going to Greece tomorrow guys.

Annie: What's going on?

Val: In detail!

Jane: I can't really explain it. I just woke up with a really strange feeling, and I NEED to go and find my biological father. I know. It's weird.

Annie: As in hot tour guide Dimitri?

Jane: It's been 25 years, I'm sure he's not that hot anymore.

Lilly: George Clooney! Hello!

Val: Colin Firth! Mmmmm.

Lilly: Pierce Brosnan.

Val: David Duchovny.

Lilly: Oooh, hello Mulder.

Annie: GUYS! We are getting off track here.

Lilly: Sorry ☺

Annie: How are you going to find him?

Jane: I'm formulating a plan.

Lilly: Hang on, I'm with Stormy (she came over for another iPhone lesson). She says she's having a premonition about this.

Val: LOL.

Annie: Do share?

Lilly: She says she feels the fates colliding (or some such thing) and says that something really strange is about to happen . . .

Val: Like Jane going to Greece. That's really strange.

Jane: Yep. I feel like I've lost my mind a bit here.

Lilly: No, she says something really big is about to happen to you. Something totally life changing! Something that will fundamentally change everything . . .

Chapter Four

*S*tormy's words stuck with me all night. Usually the things she said went in one ear and out the other, but for some reason these didn't. They resonated deeply within me; it was certainly time for a change. But a change into what? Her words were still playing in my head later that day when the plane had taken off.

I thought about my biological father, too. Would I recognize him if he walked past me on the street?

I was sure it would be easy enough to find him. How hard could it be? Anyone can be an amateur detective thanks to Google and Facebook. All I had to do was Google all of the tour guides named Dimitri and then meet up with them. I was confident I would know who he was the second I saw him, because we would share some kind of connection.

It hadn't been like that with my birth mother. When she'd refused to meet me, I'd written her a long letter in which I'd poured my heart out, and still…nothing. She'd rejected me once when I was an infant in desperate need of a mother's touch and love, and then she'd done it again. She finally did write back to me. She really shouldn't have. It was short and emotionless.

She told me that she had a whole new life now, with new kids and a husband who didn't even know I existed. As if I were some kind of dirty secret. She also said that dredging up past "mistakes" would do no one any good. And then she simply signed off with:

P.S. I will always be grateful to your mom and dad for being your parents.

> *Regards,*
> *Phoebe*

I remember turning the note over in my hands and looking for more. After all these years, was that all she had to say to me? But there was nothing. That was it. No explanation. No *I still think about you and wonder what you're doing. I think about you on your birthday. I wish I had never let you go.*

I was a mistake.

The initial pain of her rejection eventually gave way to anger. Maybe anger is easier to deal with? It certainly felt better to hate her than to long for her love and acceptance. This thought always made me feel like I was choking, so I reached for the in-flight magazine in the hopes it might distract me. It was written in Greek, and not in a metaphorical sense. I flipped through the pages quickly, not really absorbing anything at all…Beach…sunset…umbrellas by the beach…sunset…romantic couple on the beach…romantic couple eating by the beach under umbrellas at sunset and…*and then I stopped flipping*. I stopped dead in my tracks and I stared.

It was a full-page advertisement. I swallowed hard. *What is the ad for?*

Who the hell bloody cared, because staring back at me from the pages was a Greek god.

He is an Adonis. I stared, unblinking. How could anyone be *that* good-looking? Clearly he'd won the genetic lottery and inherited just about every attribute that made a man handsome. He was nearly too good-looking. It was almost unnatural; a genetic abnormality. Like those rats that go down into the sewers and emerge years later with three eyes and a taste for small pets.

I glanced around quickly to see if anyone was looking in my direction; the last thing I wanted to do was get caught perving. But no one was looking, so I pulled the magazine closer to my face.

The Greek god was shirtless and emerging from the azure blue sea. He was flicking his wet hair back with one hand, and in the other hand he was holding a large fishing spear that looked decidedly phallic. Under normal circumstances one might call this photo "cheesy," but I challenge any woman on the planet to overlook the fact that his clenched fist was causing his arm muscles to bulge and ripple in all the right ways. That his perfectly chiseled chest was accentuated by the glistening drops of water running down it, and that the setting sun behind him was casting shafts of light and dark on his torso that highlighted those two lines running down… down…down…

Mmmm? The water was *just* covering that general vicinity, hinting at the possibility of total nudity. With one more step he would be standing in front of us in all his glory. And he looked like the kind of man with the confidence and swagger that came from knowing he's well endowed, not to mention well versed in using those endowments, too. Clearly he knew how to use a spear. In more ways than one. He was probably the kind of guy that speared you some dinner and then bent you over the kitchen counter while you cooked it. My eyes moved north and finally settled on his face. His face was so damn perfect that it wouldn't matter if he had a potbelly and a third nipple.

Perfectly proportioned. Chiseled, strong jaw darkened ever so slightly with a five-o'clock shadow. It was hard to tell the color of his eyes, but it wasn't hard to read the messages that they were sending all the way through the pages of the magazine...

"Have sex with me. Have sex with me! Now! Sexxxxx."

I swallowed hard at the mere thought. But when the air hostess walked past, glanced down at the magazine, and gave me a kind of knowing smile, I decided to close it and put it back where it came from. So with nothing else to entertain myself, I put my head back, closed my eyes, and drifted off to sleep.

* * *

I woke up and was lying in the warm sun. The sky above me was clear and there was a slight breeze in the air. I sat up and looked around. I was on a beach, but the sand around me was completely red. I recognized the beach immediately; I'd seen it in the Santorini tour guide. *How am I here already?*

I looked out over the water; it looked so blue juxtaposed against the red pebbly beach. A splashing sound caught my attention, and I swung around to see what it was...

Oh. My. God. It was *him*. He was emerging—in slow motion—from the sea, and this time he was completely naked. I gaped. My mouth fell open and my breath got stuck somewhere between my lungs and my throat. It was large. It was large, and it was coming toward me.

He flicked his head back, and drops of water flew through the air. He reached up with both his hands and tussled his hair, causing his stomach muscles to do something almost hypnotic. Something that should very possibly be illegal. He strode steadily through the water. I glanced around. The beach was totally deserted.

Why is he walking toward me?

He stepped onto the beach and his eyes locked onto mine...

"Have sex with me. Sex... Now! Sexxxxx."

I wanted to get up and run, but I couldn't move. His intense gaze froze me to the spot. Seconds later he was kneeling next to me.

"Jane." He whispered my name in the sexiest accent I'd ever heard. *Wait... How does he know my name?*

"Jane, you're so beautiful."

"Take me," I thought I heard some strange version of myself say.

"Oh, I will. And in more ways than one."

He leaned in and pushed me back into the warm pebbles. His eyes traveled up and down the length of my body, and then his fingertips. I let out a small breath of anticipation before he lowered his body onto me.

He rubbed his lips against mine. His skin felt rough, and he smelled sweet and salty. I closed my eyes and threw my head back to feel his lips on my neck…my ear…my chin…and then he came up to kiss me. I heard myself moan against his mouth as the kiss deepened and became more frantic. His hands trailed down my body, coming to rest on my breasts. Suddenly I was naked. One hand went farther down until I felt it between my legs, pushing them apart and then—

I moaned at the intense feeling and closed my eyes. I could feel all my usual control melting into the sand beneath me as he slid inside me. Some version of myself brazenly grabbed him and pulled him farther into me. Hard and deep. I wrapped my legs around him and clawed at his shoulders and…

"*Oh God!*" I shouted the words. The sound jolted me up and, *wait*…I was in a seat. *The plane seat.* I looked around and a few eyes were on me.

"Hey!" My neighbor sat up and rubbed his elbow.

"Sorry…I didn't mean to, I just…" I couldn't finish the sentence and quickly turned away from him before he noticed the luminous red color of my cheeks. What the hell had just happened? I'd just had a sex dream. Me? Of all the people in the world. And it had been better than anything I had ever experienced in real life.

After that the rest of the flight felt torturous. It was almost impossible to stop thinking about the dream and him and his eyes…

"*Have sex with me. Subconscious dream sex…yes, sex…Now!*"

By the time I landed, I was exhausted from trying to push thoughts of him out of my mind. I was desperate to get to my hotel room and crash. I collected my bags, walked out into the airport, and looked around. People were holding up placards with names on them, but mine was nowhere to be seen. We'd landed early, so maybe my tour guide wasn't there yet.

My shoulder was breaking under the weight of my handbag, and I was forced to put it down. It weighed a ton what with all the things I'd put it in: hair straightener for emergencies, another hair straightener (battery operated) in case there was no power, hair gel, sunscreens of varying SPFs, electric toothbrushes, flosses, and mouthwashes for convenient brushing after meals, hand disinfectant, a little medical bag for minor cuts and scrapes, hairbrush, comb, lipstick-stuffed makeup bag, books, deodorant (spray-on and roll-on), pens, notebook, and more. I like to be prepared.

I rolled my shoulder a few times, trying to loosen the knot, and then stood still and scanned the crowd. I studied them carefully, taking in their faces and features. Complexions here were darker. So was the hair, and many of the women had hair like me! Thick black curls were everywhere. Suddenly it felt like I was looking in some kind of a mirror. There was something familiar about these people. My eyes kept drifting over them . . . and that's when I saw it.

Him!

There he was. *Or am I dreaming again?*

CHAPTER FIVE

⌒

*T*he Greek god, or a man who looked exactly like him, was standing to the side of the crowd, leaning against a pillar. I glanced behind him, and even in my shocked state the sheer ridiculousness did not escape me. There, wrapped around the top of the very pillar he was leaning on, was the ad. The azure-blue sea, the sand, the *have sex with me now* eyes, and the not-so-subtly suggestive spear.

I glanced from him, to the ad, and back again. Was that really the same guy? It seemed too much of a coincidence, but then logically, medically, genetically the probability of two such good-looking people existing on the same planet seemed highly unlikely—if not impossible. It had to be the guy from the ad!

This was one of those moments that seemed orchestrated and rehearsed. The ad was perfectly placed above him. *He* was perfect. In fact, he was so damn freakishly perfect that he looked like he'd been Photoshopped and professionally lit and everything around him—the people and the airport—was just the backdrop for a

Ralph Lauren shoot he was currently starring in. *There must be photographers hiding somewhere.*

I could see that all the women in the general vicinity thought the same thing. Several of them were gaping, and one husband hurried his wife away when she ran her tongue over her lips and looked as if she was about start licking him like a giant lollipop.

Oh. My. God. Suddenly he was moving in my direction. Quickly. Smiling. This was exactly like my dream, and I couldn't stop my cheeks from turning crimson. Thank God humans aren't capable of telepathy, because the only thing going through my mind right then was...

"Sex! Have sex with me. Airport sex...now! Sex!"

I turned around to ascertain who he was walking toward, but there was no one standing behind me. *Is he walking toward me?* Strange waves of panicky embarrassment almost knocked me off my big feet. He held his hand up and gave a tiny wave. I turned around again to see if I'd missed someone lurking behind a potted plant or something...but there was no one.

He didn't walk, either, *no*; he sort of strode. Prowled. Stalked. He looked like a man who was about to hunt something large, wrestle it to the ground with his bare hands, and then make a key ring out of its paw. And he was prowling in my direction. But with each approaching step, I was becoming more and more nervous. This was what the awkward morning after must feel like, only it was imaginary sex and he didn't even know that we'd had it. And I'd seen his penis! Well, an imagined version of it. And with that thought, my eyes automatically drifted down to his crotch. When I realized what I was doing, I flicked them up again.

I quickly picked my ten-ton bag off the floor and rummaged through it for my trusty sunglasses. I put them on; this was something I did regularly when I wanted to disappear, and it also saved me having the inevitable *Wow, what happened to your eyes?* conversation. I glanced back at him again . . . *still walking toward me!*

He was way too hot to be walking in my direction. I turned around and glanced off into the distance meaningfully, as you do when trying to avoid a person you know but don't want to talk to.

"Jane Smith?" The words were coated in a delicious accent and wafted toward me seductively. His voice was even hotter in real life. I froze in panic. *Why is he looking for me?*

"Jane Smith? I'm here to fetch you. Sorry I lost my sign but I recognized you from your passport photo."

Act normal, Jane. Act natural. Act . . .

I plastered on a smile and turned to face him, trying my best impersonation of a cool-casual person. Only it didn't work. Because in that moment something terribly unfortunate happened.

I'd misjudged his closeness, the size of my bag, the wildness of my overcompensating swing; I'd misjudged everything. I was neither cool nor casual . . . *I was crazed.* My bag collided with his arm, it popped open, it fell to the floor, and it vomited its contents everywhere. Things bounced and slid and skidded in various directions. A hair straightener hit the floor and cracked (luckily I had the other one); a can of deodorant rolled off at breakneck speed. Everything dispersed violently and quickly, like the mushroom cloud of an atom bomb. And it was just as disastrous. I glanced down and to my absolute horror, horrendous horror of horrors, I saw it. And then another.

Two boxes of condoms. Boxes I'd never seen before in my life.

I feel like this is an appropriate time for some more backstory about my mother.

When I say my mother is a meddler, I really mean that. While other mothers are telling their daughters *not* to be dating, flirting, or having sex, my mother is encouraging it. So adamant is she that I am incapable of finding myself a man and doing my own dating that she has taken over my love life. She's even created an online dating profile for me. Just the other day—she told me with great excitement—LonelyGuy28 sent me a smile and a photo request.

"Don't worry, though, I put your photo into that editor program and shaved off at least a pound around your jawline. I also told him that you weren't into the kinky spanking stuff, but you weren't entirely vanilla, either. Winky face."

I didn't even know what that meant!

She's always forwarding me interesting articles about "How to Marry a Man in 60 Days," "Flirting Your Way into His Heart," and the current—and most inappropriate to date—"How to Break Your Sexual Dry Spell." So these condoms were definitely her doing!

I watched in jaw-dropping horror as the *ribbed for extra pleasure* variety skidded all the way across the floor and disappeared, but the scented ones, *well* ... let's just say those were the ones that caused all the issues. The little box skidded across the shiny polished floor until *bang*, it finally came to a complete stop next to his sexy sandaled foot.

I bit my lip. It was all I could do to stop myself from throwing up in the agony of sheer humiliation. I glanced down at the offending box that was touching his sandal. I stared at it, willing it to reverse across the floor and back into the bag. *It did not.*

I looked up at Mr. Greek God to see if he'd noticed it yet, and just as I did, his eyes began to drift down, down, down. There was only one thing to do really. So as fast as the limitations of the human body would allow, I flung myself down onto the floor and grabbed the box by his foot. I then dove and darted back and forth with manic energy as I retrieved all my belongings. By the time I was done, I was out of breath and sweaty.

"Whew!" I exclaimed loudly and started fanning myself with my hand. "You know, it can often feel at least two to five degrees hotter inside than outside." I continued to fan myself and babble. "I'm thirsty. You know, the human body can lose about a liter and a half of water during a three-hour-long flight." My eyes were flicking around for something to focus on, and my brain was searching for something else to say. "You should really consider not wearing sandals, they can expose your feet to all kinds of bacteria and fungi, especially staphylococcus...not that I'm saying you have a fungal infection or anything."

Mr. Greek God smiled. It was a slow, curious smile. "I'll remember that." He sounded strangely amused, and although he spoke in a thick accent, his English was perfect.

"Sorry," I said in a defeated manner.

"No worries, no stress! Welcome to beautiful Santorini." His smile grew, revealing the cutest little dimples in his cheeks. God, he was hot. And he totally terrified me. "You're going to fall in love with it."

"Huh? With what?"

"This is the island of love and romance. It's where anything and everything is possible. You're never going to want to leave." He flashed me another killer smile. The kind of smile that made you think you should be holding on to your panties. We were close enough now that I could finally see his eyes. And they were breathtaking. His irises were a pale-green color—not your standard green, either, but one that looked like it had been mixed with a dollop of gold. The mesmerizing green-gold got darker as it radiated outward until it turned almost black at the edge. They were smoldering bedroom eyes that oozed sex.

"Have sex with me now. Sex, sex, sex."

I was staring. I could feel my jaw starting to slack. I had to snap out of this, but clearly he gave off some kind of invisible scent or pheromone that was intoxicating. Like a silent whistle that only dogs were drawn to. Perhaps he was well versed in the dark arts, able to cast a spell over all the three and a half billion women on the planet.

"Shall we?" he suddenly said, breaking my stare.

"Shall we *what*?" The words came flying out of my mouth, but as soon as they did I realized how off the mark I was. My filthy, gutter-swimming thoughts were influencing me badly.

"Go. Shall we go, Jane?"

"Go where?" I asked, feeling very confused. Why was this hot model—or hot model look-alike—picking me up from the airport?

"To your hotel."

"Are you really here to fetch me, I mean . . . you? Are you really a tour guide?" I pointed at him. "How do you know I'm the person you're supposed to be fetching?"

He reached into his pocket, pulled out a folded piece of paper, and opened it. "Jane Smith, Flight South African Airways A-One-Oh-Seven from Johannesburg, arriving at eighteen forty-five, booked through Flight and Travel Center, Rosebank Mall." He lowered the paper and looked at me.

I nodded. "Sounds right. Fine." I started walking after him but we managed to get only a few feet before a man intercepted us. He stretched his hand out, and my heart plummeted.

"I think you dropped this." The other box of condoms beamed up at me from his outstretched palm.

I shook my head. Hard. "Nooo. Not mine, never seen them before," which was actually the honest-to-God truth. The man gave me a little knowing wink and turned the box over in his hand. *Oh God, what was that?* It looked like my mother had pinned a little note to it. He opened it and read.

Jane, in case you decide to let your hair down. Mom X

A strange, shrill laugh pushed its way through my lips. "Hahaha…Mothers, hey…hahaha!" The laugh continued for a little longer than I would have liked it to. The man said something to the Adonis in Greek and handed him the box.

"Oh no! No!" I gestured frantically and shook my head even harder. "We're not, I mean, I would never. It's not like that, it's…" The man gave me one more amused look before walking away. I looked over at Mr. Greek God; he was holding the box of condoms in his hand with a strange smile plastered across his face.

"Jane, here's a condom and have sex with me. Have sex with me now!"

He extended his hand, the bright-red box almost glinting in the overhead lights. I was going to kill my mother for this! Or maybe this was one of those incidents I would laugh about in years to come. "Remember the time...hahaha."

I doubted it.

I cringed as I reached out and took the box from him and slid it into my bag. I looked up at him briefly, and he smiled.

"I can see you're really going to love it here, Jane."

CHAPTER SIX

I'd read enough travel brochures on the plane to know that I should have been looking out the window at the unsurpassed beauty that is historic Greece. But all I was thinking about was the unsurpassed beauty that was sitting next to me in the car, and how a few moments ago he'd been handing me a box of condoms, and a short time before that I had been having wild sex with him on a beach. Awkward.

It had been completely silent since we'd started driving, which I was grateful for. Had he asked me a question in my current state, I might have said something about head and brain injury being the most common type of injury caused by car accidents or that the most dangerous road in the world was in Bolivia or that—*Stop it, Jane, get a grip.* I was also still trying to figure out why a model who was also a tour guide, or so it seemed, had just picked me up at the airport?

"So pleasure?" he finally asked.

"What? I beg your pardon?"

"Business or pleasure?" He glanced at my bag, and if he had X-ray vision I'd say he was staring straight through to the box of condoms. "Pleasure I presume." His smile was dazzling. Stunning. Despite the fact that I wanted to crawl under a rock or fling myself from his car, I couldn't look away. But I had to get his mind—and mine—off condoms.

"I am definitely not here for any pleasure. I can assure you of that," I said firmly, making sure I set the record straight. It's funny how boxes of condoms kind of send the wrong message to people.

"So business?" He sounded slightly amused still.

"What? No! No!" *Does he think I'm a working girl?* "No, it's not that kind of business at all. Not at all."

"So what kind of business brings you to Santorini that is so important you aren't here for a little bit of pleasure, too?"

Again with that loaded word! And the way he said it certainly didn't make it sound like he was referring to innocent frolicking on the beach, sightseeing, or eating meze in the sun. I was suddenly feeling very hot again, so I proceeded to fan myself with my passport.

"It's hot in here," I exclaimed.

"At least two to five degrees hotter," he said with a smile in his voice as he began opening his window. "The air conditioner is broken."

I attempted to do the same, but the button didn't seem to be working. I pressed it a few times, but the stubborn thing didn't budge. And then suddenly, without any kind of warning, I felt his big muscular arm reach across me.

"There's a trick to it," he said in a playful tone. "You have to jiggle the switch." He jiggled it and his arm brushed my stomach lightly and then the worst thing imaginable happened: His whole hand fell into my lap as the car went over a bump. I jumped, letting out a little gasp as he pulled away quickly.

"Sorry. Bumpy road," he said casually, as if nothing out of the ordinary had just happened. But I felt anything but casual. In fact, my entire crotch was now on fire and felt like it was melting into the seat beneath me.

What the hell was wrong with me that one touch from this guy had me feeling like I was losing all control of my body? (We've established that my mind was already lost.)

I felt I needed to say something in an attempt to act casual and unperturbed. "Yes, did you know that in Ireland there are some potholes that are so big you can actually swim in—" I stopped myself midway. "Never mind."

He looked at me sideways and flashed me a small smile. *Why is he smiling so much?* "So what is your business then?"

"I'm looking for someone."

"Who?"

"A man." I kept my responses brief. I wasn't going to tell this stranger my whole life story.

"Mmmm," he said knowingly. "I think that all the beautiful women who come to Greece are looking for a man."

"What?" He'd just called me beautiful and for a second I almost let my imagination run away with me, but I quickly reeled it in, because this was obviously a blatant lie. I was not beautiful. He was obviously in default charmer mode. The quintessential Greek cliché: hot, romantic, charming playboy. He probably called all the women he drove around beautiful. I wondered—was this the kind of guy my biological mother had fallen for?

Well, not me! I would not be charmed by this Greek playboy. His act reminded me of that freshly polished floor in the mall—it was too smooth, and if you weren't careful about watching where you walked, you might slip and break something. Or at least leave with a large, painful bruise.

"It's not that kind of man!" I finally said after I had gathered myself.

"Oh?" he turned and arched his brow in query. "Not romantic?"

"Not all relationships with men are romantic, you know. In fact, I read a fascinating study stating that it has been scientifically proven that members of the opposite sex can just be platonic friends. The study was conducted with eighty-eight undergraduate students and—"

I stopped when I noted he was *still* smiling at me. That devastating smile again, as if what I'd said had amused him. That smile, coupled with the eyes and the dimples and the perfect face and hair, was almost too much to look at, like the Greek legend of Medusa. But instead of being turned into stone, it was the opposite: You were turned to jelly. I turned away from him and looked out the window, trying to focus on my surroundings instead.

"So what kind of man is he then?"

God, he wasn't letting this go. He was like one of those children that kept asking *"Why?"* or *"Are we there yet?"*

"He's just someone who worked here a while ago."

"And where is he now?"

"I don't know. All I know is his name is Dimitri." I felt mildly irritated and frustrated at this stage and I wasn't doing a great job at hiding it.

The Greek god burst out laughing. "Everyone here is Dimitri. My name is Dimitri."

"I doubt that," I said drily.

He reached into his cubbyhole, pulled out his driver's license, and passed it to me.

The photo was obviously old—his hair was much shorter and he looked more clean-cut—but he was still deadly gorgeous.

"Dimitri Spiros," I read out loudly. "Oh. I see."

We fell into a silence again. I couldn't believe his name was Dimitri. The bizarre, uncanny coincidence did not escape me. Not that I wanted to draw any comparisons between myself and bio-mom. I was nothing like her. At all. Nor did I ever want to be. History was not going to be repeating itself; as far as I was concerned, this Dimitri was totally off the menu. Not that he was ever on it! The silence seemed to drag on, but this time I noticed him glancing over at me several times.

"What?" I heard myself asking.

"Do you always wear dark glasses in the evening?" He sounded amused again.

"Yes. As a matter of fact I do. They happen to protect your eyes against harmful UV rays, which I might add are still present at sunset, so..." I stopped myself again as my MIA took over: Male Induced Awkwardness. It's not a recognized disorder per se, but the symptoms are very real and if there was a pill I could take to stop it, I would.

"So you're not a celebrity hiding from the photographers?"

I *tsk*ed loudly. "Please. Do I look like a celebrity?"

"Definitely." His response was instant, and the word was said so deliberately that I had an abrupt case of arrhythmia.

"In fact, you look a bit like one of our local pop stars, Helena. She's considered to be one of the most beautiful women in Greece."

In one violent movement, my heart swapped places with my spleen. I sat up straight and adjusted my seat belt; maybe subconsciously I thought I was going to fall out of the moving vehicle in total shock.

This guy was a real pro. He probably told all women—no matter what they looked like—that they resembled some great beauty. Confirmation received (not that I needed much more)! He was, without a doubt, the local holiday fling. All those newly divorced women who went looking for themselves in Greece probably landed here and then immediately landed on his lap. I crossed my legs and angled my body away from him. My lap was sealed for business. We continued to drive a little more, until a small town came into focus.

"Welcome to Fira. This is where you'll be staying. It's one of the most beautiful towns in Santorini," he said enthusiastically.

"I see." I took in my surroundings. Everything was white—the homes, the hotels; even the streets were quaint little paths cobbled in light-gray stones. And because it was evening, the entire place was drenched in a warm golden glow. It looked magical, like something out of a fairy tale. We were forced to make an impromptu stop as a lazy donkey decided to cross the road.

"You will find the pace of life here is a bit different," he said, looking relaxed.

"Mmmm." I looked down at my watch, agitated by the holdup. I hated being late. I wondered what time check-in was?

"So, where're you from, Jane?"

"South Africa."

"Aaah," he said, "the beautiful rainbow nation. Home to the greatest leader that ever lived, Mr. Mandela."

I swung around and looked at him. *Aha!* The last bit of evidence that proved—beyond a reasonable doubt—that he was a "professional wooer of womenfolk." Say something intelligent and thoughtful about the person's country, and it reveals you as being not only sensitive but also knowledgeable and interested in the world around you. What a smart little addition to his seduction routine. I bet he had a "great" person lined up for every possible country. He probably Googled them regularly. Still, I wondered how many women had fallen for this particular little gambit. He was so good that he probably broke the air conditioner himself and orchestrated the bump in the road, not to mention the crossing donkey to give the women a chance to navigate their way onto his lap. The car finally started moving again as the donkey cleared the street. I gave it a once-over to check it wasn't animatronic. We drove a little more before finally stopping outside my hotel. The Luxury Aegean Villas.

"Are you sure this is your hotel?" It sounded like he was trying to be polite.

I pulled out the large plastic envelope that the travel agent had given me containing all the pertinent details of my trip. *Terms and Conditions* really had applied to the sunscreen, though; I'd received two small 0.05-ounce tester sachets of the stuff. I pulled out my itinerary and read it loudly.

"Luxury Aegean Villas."

"Are you sure it doesn't say Aegean *Sea* Villas?" he asked in that same strange polite tone.

"Why?"

"There're two hotels here with a similar name."

"Nope." I read the words once more, but the word *sea* was very clearly absent.

"Okay." He eased the door open and climbed out with über-cool confidence, as if he were starring in an ad for extra-strength Viagra and had the kind of rock-hard erection that had just brought an entire small village of women to their quivering knees.

Stop! Crapping hell, Jane. What had gotten into me? The only kinds of thoughts I seemed to have around this man were either of the dirty, filthy kind, or filled with irritation and disapproval. This was not a rational combination. I physically shook my head, hoping to dislodge them, and climbed out. It was getting too dark to wear my glasses now, and I took them off. Suddenly I sneezed. A cat skulked out of the shadows and walked past my feet. Dammit. I was completely allergic to cats. I hoped this place wasn't full of them.

"Well, Jane, it was a pleasure meeting you. I hope you find the Dimitri you're looking for."

And then, to my absolute horror, he leaned forward and kissed me on both cheeks. I caught a brief whiff of his scent—it was exactly like I'd imagined in my dream, only better.

"I...I...yes, thanks for the lift." I stumbled over my words while in my mind he was busy running his fingers through my hair and nibbling on my earlobe.

He nodded and strands of hair fell into his face again. It was as if all the fantasies about men that existed in the female collective consciousness had somehow coalesced and transformed into physical form. And its name was Dimitri Spiros.

"Do you know where you will look for your Dimitri?" he asked.

I shook my head. "No idea."

"So if you don't know who he is, or where he is, how do you know I'm not the Dimitri you came looking for? Maybe you were meant to find me." He flashed his deadly Medusa smile again, and my skeletal system liquefied.

I smiled politely, trying hard to ignore the insinuations in that line. "Good night, Dimitri, thanks again."

"It was my pleasure."

Again with that bloody word. I turned and started walking away.

"Wait. I almost forgot," he called after me. I turned and looked straight into one of the last shafts of sunlight.

"If you ever need anything, here's my card. Call me when you're ready for a tour of Santorini. I'm already taking a group around, so you can join us. Or maybe you want something more private?"

"Private?"

"Yes. If you don't like groups, I do private tours, too. We could go island-hopping, or see some of the beaches here. Santorini has the best beaches in the world, you haven't lived until you've walked on the red beach or—"

I cut him off. "Thanks, but I won't be doing any sightseeing while I'm here."

"You won't?" He sounded disappointed. I wanted to add, "*Especially not with you*," but didn't.

"None? You don't want to see anything?"

I shook my head. Why did everyone find this so hard to believe? I wasn't here to get swept up in an exotic island trip. I wasn't here to enjoy "romantic Greece and its red sands." Besides, I wouldn't like it even if I saw every beach and sunset and ate olives and sipped wine al-fucking-fresco! I didn't like Greece, and no amount of touring would change that. This was a business trip! Plain and simple.

"Why don't you just take it anyway? Maybe you'll change your mind."

"I'm not the kind of person to change my mind," I said quickly, tucking the card into my bag.

Dimitri smiled at me and started walking to the car. "This is Greece, Jane. This place has a way of getting under your skin and into your heart. Greece has a way of changing people." He shrugged. "Maybe it will change you?"

He climbed into the car and waved at me before pulling away and driving off.

CHAPTER SEVEN

$\mathscr{M}$istakes can happen. Like the time I accidentally told my mother I was a lesbian over text:

Jane: Mom, I'm lesbian now.

Mom: OMG. That's y u never have a bae.

(My mother has fully embraced texting language)

Jane: LEAVING. Leaving! Damn autocorrect!

So ... it could have been an honest-to-God genuine mistake. But the more I remembered the look on Glitter-Talon's face, the tone in her voice, and the snarky little look she'd given me, the more I began to think that this was very intentional.

But how could I have predicted that the absence of a tiny three-letter world like *sea* in the hotel name, Luxury Aegean Villas, could have had such a devastating effect?

The first thing I noticed when I walked into my hotel room

was the thick blanket of moist and terribly uncomfortable heat that smothered me and coated my skin with a vile stickiness. The second thing was the smell, *musty locker room jockstrap* mingled with subtle aromas of moldy cheese. The carpets were in desperate need of a cleaning—*no, correction*, they needed to be ripped up and burned. The curtains looked tattered, like someone had ripped them into shreds in a desperate attempt to escape. I took a brave step forward. The smell only intensified, and I was now aware of a strange dripping, banging, growling, hissing noise.

I heard a loud thud behind me as the doorman, *although I doubt you call him that at an establishment like this*, dumped my bags on the floor. Dust billowed up from the carpet, and I coughed. He glared at me for a moment or two before extending his pudgy paw. His palm was sweaty, and there were some glistening beads of moisture collecting on his upper lip.

"Sorry, I haven't exchanged any currency yet," I said, trying to force a polite smile.

He curled his lip up, revealing a particularly coffee-tarnished incisor. "Humph." He turned on his heel and headed out the door.

Oh God, what's that sound? There was a tiny door at the other end of the room and the noise was definitely coming from there. Note to self: Never walk toward strange noises coming from behind doors. Wasn't this how all the slasher horror movies started? Except the first victim was usually a hot blond teenager with big boobs. But I did . . .

Hissing cockroaches and dripping tap? Gurgling sink and mice nibbling on steel showerhead? Donkey trapped in bathroom?

I would have put my money on any of those, because the last

thing I expected to see was the "activity" that two people were "doing" in the shower with that peculiar "item" that looked like an inflatable pool chair.

I couldn't even scream I was so shocked. It wasn't normal. It wasn't natural and it wasn't right! I rushed out of the room as fast as my legs could carry me, grabbing my bag on the way out and slamming straight into the greasy-looking doorman.

"Humph," he mumbled again as if he didn't give a Continental shit that I would never be able to look at inflatable objects in the same light again. Another key was thrust into my hand and I glanced down at it. ROOM 5. I looked up at the door next to me. On closer inspection you could clearly see that the "1" that was meant to be next to the "5" had fallen off.

I rushed down the corridor, located my *real* room, and barged in. The first thing I did was peer into the bathroom...empty. I was finally alone and I was completely exhausted and traumatized. I had hardly slept in over twenty-four hours. I looked at the bed. The duvet had debris on it. The once white pillow had a yellow smudge on it that looked like a Rorschach test—the more I stared at it, the more it started to look like the gates of hell. Tomorrow morning I would definitely go online and find a new hotel, but tonight I would have to stay here and brave it and pray that small mammals wouldn't arrive in the middle of the night and carry me off. I put my bags down on the floor next to the bed—and that's when the glossy magazine on the bedside table caught my attention. I reached for it and started flipping through the pages until his familiar face was once again staring at me. This time he was with a woman.

I examined it further. He and the woman in question were

tangled up in each other's arms, implying some kind of postcoital thing. Both looked naked, and their perfect bodies were silhouetted against atmospheric lighting. In arty black and white, I might add.

The only things they were wearing were large, designer wristwatches, as one does during sex. Because it makes perfect sense that you would wear a bedazzled timepiece while bonking just in case you needed to time your foreplay or, better yet, the nine-hour-long orgasm you gave her before she passed out from sheer pleasure due to the size of your manly spear.

They were also lying in the sand together, which I've never understood. Sand gets into strange hard-to-reach places under normal circumstances, let alone these kinds of circumstances.

I flipped through the rest of the pages and a familiar name caught my attention. *"Greek pop sensation Helena on what it's like to get engaged."*

Never! This couldn't be the woman he said I looked like. We looked nothing alike. I had more in common with one of those blue things from *Avatar* than this voluptuous beauty who looked like she ate men's hearts for hors d'oeuvres.

I closed the magazine and tossed it to the floor. I was relieved that I had the letters *DR* in front of my name in case I needed to prescribe myself emergency medicines for tetanus or rabies. Perhaps it wouldn't be so bad if I slept on top of the covers, fully clothed and wearing my shoes and a hat? Unfortunately, I hadn't thought to pack a full hazmat suit.

Oh God! I looked around and let out a loud sigh. This place was more depressing than the latest Adele song. And way too hot.

WHATSAPP GROUP: Jane goes to Greece

Jane: If you don't hear from me again it's because I've been murdered in my bed or died because I caught dysentery from the bedsheets. This hotel is a total dump! You wouldn't believe it.

Annie: Take some photos and send immediately.

Val: That's why you should never book online.

Jane: I didn't. I went to a travel agent.

Val: Travel agent must have hated you then.

Jane: Funny you say that…

I started taking some photos of the hotel and quickly sent them to the group.

Val: What's that on the duvet?

Jane: I'm not sure. And I don't want to know.

Lilly: Eeeewww…seen any hot guys yet?

Jane: No. None.

I responded quickly. I wasn't going to admit to them that I had actually just met the hottest man on the planet. In fact, I would rather pretend that I'd never met him at all.

Jane: I'm going to try and get some sleep. Bye.

Annie: Good luck.

Lilly: Don't die on us. We'd miss you. XXX

* * *

I was soaking wet when I woke up. I was also dizzy, dry mouthed, and felt absolutely disgusting. The heat in the room was unbearable and the long-sleeve sweater, jeans, and sneakers that I'd slept in hadn't helped much, either.

I stumbled out of the bed and peeled my clothes off. I looked at myself in the dirty, half-cracked mirror. My chest and forehead were wet with sweat. My hair, as usual, had a mind of its own—hanging in a thick, heavy mop behind my head. My underwear looked great, though. Black-and-pink Victoria's Secret balcony bra and thong set. I always bought sexy underwear, although I never had an occasion to use it. The only living thing that had seen me wearing it was Fishy, my goldfish.

Sudden thought: I hoped my mother was feeding him.

Another sudden thought: I hoped she hadn't taken it upon herself to redecorate my flat. About a year ago she had pulled up my old, out-of-fashion carpets and put laminate wood flooring in.

She was worried that my ugly, out-of-date décor was scaring off potential husbands and giving them the wrong impression about me (i.e., that I was dowdy, boring, and destined for a life of spinsterhood). And when I'd protested and reminded her I wasn't looking for anyone, she'd reminded me that my eggs were shriveling and dying as we spoke.

"Tick-tock-biological-clock, dahling."

The sun was streaming through the crack in the curtain and highlighting the horror that was my hotel room. I could almost hear my mother's concern about the type of men I might bump into here. I reached for my phone and did a double blink in case I was seeing incorrectly. The phone said two thirty p.m. As in, the afternoon.

I'd slept the entire day away; no wonder I felt so bad. I had that hangover feeling one gets from totally oversleeping. I'd wasted an entire day when I could have been out there looking for my father. I quickly scraped back my wild hair, which was made even wilder by the humidity in the room. But no amount of hair gel and painful scraping seemed to flatten it sufficiently today. I grabbed my computer and went online to look for the Aegean *Sea* Villas. Before booking, though, I decided to leave this one a little review...

Liked: That I made it through the night without catching a dreaded disease

Disliked: The fact I could have caught a dreaded disease

Tips: Make sure you're up to date with all vaccinations when staying here

CHAPTER EIGHT

I stood outside on the street with my bags feeling a little like a homeless person. I'd just had one of the most unsuccessful conversations of my life trying to arrange a taxi. And after what felt like a tragic game of Pictionary combined with charades, during which I'd been reduced to making loud *vroom*ing noises and miming a steering wheel, I'd called it a day.

I surveyed my surroundings and sneezed again. *Cats!* Had it been daytime when I'd arrived, I might have noticed the subtle clues that indicated that this was the *wrong* place to stay. Two flowerpots flanked the door, both containing the brown, dead remnants of the flora that had once occupied them. One of them also looked like it was frequented rather often by the local felines and also used to dispose of beer cans. I sneezed again. Why were there so many cats here? Luxury Aegean Villas. *Luxury.* The only luxury here was that I'd left with my life intact. I took stock of my situation. Now what?

"If you ever need anything, here's my card."

His chiseled face pushed its way into my brain once more. I could almost hear his business card whispering to me, *"Call me, call me now and then have sex with me."*

Urg. The last thing I wanted to do was phone Zoolandimitri. *Yes*, I'd thought of that rather terrible nickname while teetering on the brink of sleep last night somewhere between the time he'd kissed me on the neck and the moment he'd whipped my bra off. Okay, fine, I'd had another sex dream. A sex dream with the last guy I should ever have any sort of sex with!

"Call me. Sex. Phone sex. Let's have it ... Now."

His card whispered a little louder this time. I huffed a very audible resigned sigh as I reluctantly fished it out of my bag. I took a moment to study the card. *The arrogant thing!* The back of the card was perfectly normal: name, address, basic info. But the front...

Was it really necessary to have his face plastered across the front of the card? And with that big, cheesy, self-satisfied grin? It was the grin of a real estate agent trying to sell you four-bedroomed happiness, except he was trying to sell you sex in all four bedrooms and then bent over the balcony rail, too. Possibly in the shower, not to mention against the freshly painted walls...

My mind began to conjure up images of him showing me around the granite-topped kitchen and then fucking me alfresco.

Stop it! God, I had to snap out of this.

I dialed Zoomitri's number. (*That nickname works a little better, I think?*) I really didn't want to see him right now, or ever. Tour guides named Dimitri were bad news. In fact, it was a tour guide called Dimitri that had landed me in the situation I was currently in.

"Dimitri Spiros." His voice sounded husky and terribly dreamy.

"Hi…it's a…"

"Jane. I was just thinking about you."

"You were?" I forced down the bubble that rose up from my stomach. Fucking hell, I hated myself for having this illogical reaction to him.

"*I don't like him,*" a loud voice shouted inside my brain.

"*Oh yes you do!*" another part of my body replied seductively.

"*You're wrong!*" the voice in my logical brain screeched back defensively.

"*Well. I wouldn't be feeling all tingly if you didn't,*" it cooed seductively.

"Shut up."

"What?" Dimitri asked.

"Nothing. I was just…you were saying?" I deflected quickly.

"I woke up thinking that you should be in the *Sea* Villas and it's some kind of a mistake."

"Mmmm, I think you're right, only I'm not so sure it was a mistake. I've actually checked out and made a reservation at the Sea Villas and—"

"I'll fetch you now." And with that, he put down the phone. He was coming to fetch me. I felt almost hysterical with panic and my pulse started pounding a technobeat.

"*See…you're totally in lust with him,*" the voice mocked me one more time before I managed to muffle it and tried to distract myself with my phone. I was sure my friends were all worried about me.

WHATSAPP GROUP: Jane goes to Greece

Jane: I'm not dead. I made it out alive.

Lilly: Yay!

Annie: Ditto. I don't look good in black so I was dreading wearing it to your funeral.

Stormy: Of coursess u Not. Dead. U 're only GoinG to dies ins 2076

Jane: Huh? How do you know when I'm going to die?

Stormy: the Nnumberss

Lilly: LOL

Annie: Haha. Numerology tells you when you are going to die?

Stormy: alSo sayss whe.n you will get Married.

Jane: Also in 2076 I'm guessing.☺

Stormy: Noo you 're gettling married in 2019

I burst out laughing at the mere suggestion. Me married in two years. The notion was ridiculous. To marry someone, you actually had to mingle with and then date a member of that elusive thing called the opposite sex. Not only that, but you had to fall in love and have him love you back and want to spend the rest of his life with you. Where the hell was I going to find someone like that?

"Hi."

"Aaah." I jumped at the sound of Dimitri's voice and suddenly realized he was standing right there in front of me as if he were the answer to my rhetorical question.

I froze. My stomach knotted, and the familiar nervous nauseous feeling rose.

I told you so. You want to marry him and have his babies. That voice was mocking me again and I wished I could shut it the hell down.

He was smiling at me in that unnerving manner again. "What was so funny?"

"Uh…" I quickly slipped my phone back into my pocket, feeling the desperate urge to say something. Some interesting facts about horses or marsupials or Tibetan singing bowls or…

"You know, the length of a shadow is constantly changing as the Earth rotates on its axis," I said, pointing down at the shadow he was casting over my feet.

"Really?" He sounded amused again. "That's good to know. I took your advice, by the way." He smiled and looked down at his feet. My eyes drifted down to where he was looking. "Closed shoes."

"I see that." I was stunned. Had he really changed his footwear because I'd suggested it? *Wait*…had he actually listened to my ramblings? No one else ever did—except my friends, and that wasn't guaranteed.

"Shall we?" He grabbed my bag with one hand and tossed it into the trunk as if it were full of feathers. He'd probably had a lot of practice tossing things around so expertly, like women onto beds for example. I walked over to the door but just as I was about to open it, I noticed the bright-red writing across it.

DIMITRI'S ISLAND TOURS

How could I not have seen that last night? Had I known his name was Dimitri, I might never have left with him in the first place.

I climbed into his car again and tried to make myself comfortable. It was hard. Everything about this guy made me feel as comfortable as if I'd swallowed a cactus and it was now stuck in the back of my throat. In fact, since meeting him it felt like I'd been ripped out of my comfort zone like a baby pulled kicking and screaming into a brand-new world. *Hey, good analogy there, Jane.* Because like a baby, I seriously lacked any kind of tools to deal with the feelings I was currently experiencing. This guy struck both lust and total fear into my heart, simultaneously.

When I was around him, I felt my control slipping. I could always rely on my control, but lately it had been letting me down. The mere fact that I was in Greece was a sign that it was failing miserably. Failed. *No*, it had definitely failed. Past tense. And truthfully, I feared what would happen if it failed in front of him. I could never give in to any physical feelings I was having for Dimitri. Ever. If I did, I was no better than my biological mother. And I didn't want to be anything like her.

Zoomitri climbed into the car, and I made sure to avert my gaze as quickly as possible. My phone suddenly buzzed and I glanced back down at the screen to see a WhatsApp message from Stormy.

Stormy: corrections…! its actually 201 8. Youll get MaRried mext year !

Another laugh escaped my lips, and out of the corner of my eye I saw Dimitri turn to look at me. It made me feel so uneasy that I wanted to jump out of my skin. I angled my body away from him, trying not to look too rude, and stared out the window. We drove slowly through streets that were lined with more potted plants than I'd ever seen in my life. Greens, reds, yellows, pinks: Flowers exploded out of every pot with such vibrancy. Pots of cacti and other things that looked like they could seriously injure you were also in abundance. But it was the bougainvillea that stood out the most. Pinky-purple and thick, it peeped out of every corner, casting a colored glow on the white walls around it. The color was so bright you couldn't quite believe it even existed in nature. It looked more like a color you might find in a box of children's crayons.

For the first time I also noticed the brightly colored houses peering at me from behind all the whitewashed ones. A bright-orange one, a pale-pink one, and a few terra-cotta homes decorated with bright-blue mosaics stood out against all the pristine, snowy whiteness. This place was an electrifying kaleidoscope of color. I was so deep in thought that I hardly noticed the sound until Dimitri embarrassingly pointed it out.

"Hungry?" he asked.

"What?" I was genuinely confused until I heard the loud gurgling sound emanating from my stomach, followed by the painful, acidy feeling that crept up my esophagus. *Great!* Nothing like sharing embarrassing bodily noises with a hot stranger. But hell yes I was hungry. No, starved. I hadn't eaten in more than twenty-four hours—something my mother would probably congratulate me on.

"I guess I am."

"I wouldn't have eaten there, either. Call me totally crazy, but I just have a thing about catching food poisoning."

I heard a small chuckle leave my lips, which I instantly regretted. My laugh only seemed to encourage him.

"I went onto TripAdvisor when I got home and read some of the reviews. One person actually said it looked more like a crime scene than a hotel room. I was so tempted to drive right over and save you."

Save me? In an uncontrollable instant my brain started conjuring up all sorts of images: shining armor and Rapunzel and breaking down the door with bare fists, lifting me and carrying me out of the room in his arms and then *having sex with me. Valiant savior Sex! Now.*

"Not that you seem like the kind of person that needs saving," he quickly added. He turned and smiled at me again. His smile was very different this time. It didn't have that crazy-sexy quality to it; instead it seemed friendly and familiar. And strangely, this smile unnerved me even more than the other ones. Those were predictable; this was not. I kept quiet and decided not to say another word. I didn't really want to encourage conversation. I was not here to become buddies with the model slash tour guide slash whatever else this man was. And certainly not anyone named Dimitri.

He stopped the car and jumped out. I opened the door and was immediately greeted by an onslaught of busyness. I was surrounded by narrow cobbled streets brimming with shops, restaurants, stalls, and throngs of mesmerized-looking tourists. I scanned the area, trying to look past the crazy mess spread out in front of me.

"Where's the hotel?" I couldn't see anything that resembled one.

"I'm taking you somewhere first." He flashed me another worrying grin before walking up one of the streets. It was rather comical actually. Heads turned, mouths gaped, and several women looked like they were about to take off their clothes and throw themselves into his path and onto his penis. I wondered what would happen if he walked around holding a sign that said FREE SEX. How many women would take him up on his offer? Probably all of them.

I followed Mr. Greek God as he parted the people on the street like Moses did the Red Sea. My heavy handbag was digging into my shoulder; I had to keep adjusting it. It felt like I walked past a hundred souvenir shops in the space of a few feet. They were selling everything from bags to hats, hand-painted ceramic plates depicting Greek scenes, and little statuettes of windmills. Racks and rows and walls of postcards lined the small streets, too—who could possibly buy that many postcards?

I'd never really understood souvenirs. They seemed like the wrong thing to give someone after you've come back from a holiday.

"Here, have a set of frosted shot glasses with the Parthenon painted on them to remind you that I was away sunbathing in the tropics while you were at home, working, in the bitter winter cold."

There is something vaguely antagonistic about them. *Mmmm, perhaps my mother would like that little plaster bust of Athena?* Dimitri wove through the crowd so stealthily that it was hard to keep up. "Hey. Where are we going?"

"It's a surprise," he said over his shoulder.

"I hate surprises!" I called after him. Which was true. Ever since I'd gone over for one of my family's usual Thursday-night dinners and found a young, upwardly mobile lawyer sitting across from me. My mother's doing.

The dinner had gone horrifically. In between my mother's hideously obvious attempts to get Gabriel, the upwardly mobile man in question, and me talking, he'd stared at my twin sisters all night. My mother had been about as subtle as Kim Kardashian's naked ass on a magazine cover. It would have been preferable if she'd just come out and told him she was already buying diapers for our firstborn.

"So you know Jane graduated cum laude."

Gabriel looks at my sisters and flashes them a smile.

"So you know Jane's just bought herself a darling little apartment in Rosebank, with laminate flooring." She winks at me.

Gabriel puffs his chest out in a manly display.

"So you know Jane is a very sought-after dentist."

Gabriel bites his bottom lip with lust-filled eyes. Gabriel is officially a pervert.

This was confirmed right after dinner when he'd asked both of my sisters out on a date. Both of them!

"You're going to like this surprise," Dimitri called out, snapping me back to reality. After what felt like another five minutes of arm wrestling my way through the crowd, ducking under canopies of bougainvillea, and nearly tripping over two cats, Dimitri stopped.

"We're here." He waved his hand and indicated a small street food vendor tucked between the shops. I looked up at the sign.

"Dimitri's Gyros?" I looked from the sign to Dimitri. "So you're a tour guide and you sell food?" (I wasn't going to let on that I suspected he was a model, too, for fear his ego might grow large enough to engulf the entire island and possibly the mainland.)

"I told you everyone in Greece is named Dimitri."

I seriously hoped that wasn't the case.

"Chicken or beef or pork?" he asked happily.

"What?"

He pointed at something and my eyes followed. *Mmmm*, I

wasn't so sure about this. Giant slabs of meat on large poles spun around while a man cut chunks off them with what looked like a pirate's knife. And then there were the bowls of hummus. There was enough of the stuff to use as cement and build a bloody mansion. It did have a similar texture, and I'm sure when it dried would be just as effective at holding bricks together in perpetuity. French fries bubbled away in oil to my left, large carby pitas were piled on top of one another to my right, and feta, fried halloumi, and little brown meatball-looking things were everywhere.

Illegal foods. All of them. My mother had suggested a diet at fourteen when she realized I was the kind of person who could convert lettuce into fat cells at a disturbing rate. Her greatest fear was that my reprobate fat cells might go ballistic and take over.

"Sorry, but I don't eat that kind of thing." I tried to sound polite. I didn't want to offend him, especially not when he looked so damn happy to have brought me here.

"But have you ever tried a gyro? You haven't lived yet until you've eaten a gyro on the streets of Fira!" He sounded so enthusiastic, I almost felt bad.

"No."

"Then how do you know you don't eat it?"

"Well, first, I don't eat fried foods or carbohydrates. I avoid gluten at all costs; we all know it's basically from the devil. And second, I don't eat Greek food."

"You don't eat Greek food?" He almost shouted that, and his brow furrowed in what could only be described as total confusion. "Are you sure?" he asked dubiously.

"Positive." I nodded.

"But you're in Greece!"

"Like I said, I'm not really here to sample the local delicacies and take in the sights and smells. I'm here to find someone."

"Dimitri?" It sounded like a very loaded question.

"Yes."

"How do you know that this isn't the Dimitri you're looking for?" He indicated the sign again.

"Because the Dimitri I'm looking for doesn't sell food, or whatever this is!" At least I didn't think he did. But a lot could have changed in twenty-five years.

"So what does he do?"

I really didn't want to have this conversation now. This had nothing to do with him. In fact, who the hell did he think he was asking me these kinds of personal questions anyway? Not even someone as good-looking as him could get away with this. I walked over to the counter in a deliberate attempt to kill the conversation, get this all over with so I could go to my hotel and start my search.

"Please can I have some lettuce and tomato in a pita? And two Coke Zeros." I hadn't drunk a Coke Zero in days and I could feel it. (I think they put something addictive into those things.)

The man behind the counter looked at me. Blank face.

"No meat?" he asked.

"No meat, thanks!"

"No hummus?" Confused face.

"No hummus!"

"Tziki?" He sounded desperate.

"No."

"Taramasalata?" Exasperated.

"Negative." (Now I was getting irritated.)

The man said something to Dimitri in Greek; it wasn't hard to figure out what he was saying from his tone. I took my salad-filled pita and watched as another one was being stuffed full of pork and grease. What followed was another embarrassing moment in which I'd forgotten I still had no local currency and Dimitri was forced to pay. I hated the idea that he'd bought me lunch; it felt way too friendly. Besides, I didn't want to feel like I owed him anything.

"Thanks for lunch," I said when we finally reached the car again.

"It was my pleasure. Besides, I wouldn't call that lunch." He looked down at my pita in a judgy way.

"Trust me. I can't afford to eat Greek food. You have no clue what will happen to my thigh . . . never mind." I went back to picking at the lettuce and tomato inside the pita.

It wasn't long before we'd arrived at my new hotel and were standing outside with my bags once more. My heart started thumping wildly at the possibility of another kiss on the cheek from him. I put my free hand behind my back in case it did something awful, like reach out and pull his clothes off.

"Can I help you with your bags?"

It seemed like a rather redundant question considering the porter that had already rushed to my side. So much more civilized than the previous establishment.

"No thanks. I think it's being taken care of."

"Oh. Yes." He almost looked disappointed? "Well, what about the one you're carrying? It seems very heavy."

I shrugged my shoulder. It hurt. "No thanks. I'll be fine."

"Okay, well, like I said if you need anything...*anything*." He took another card out of his pocket and started handing it over to me.

I blocked it with my hand. "I've already got one." I patted my bag.

"Take another...just in case."

"In case what?" I asked.

"In case you change your mind and decide to eat Greek food." He flashed me another smile.

"Wrap me in a pita and have sex with me. Sex. Now. Sex."

He stepped toward me. My heart stopped pumping. He leaned in close, pulled my hand from behind my back, and placed his card in the center of my palm. My nerve endings prickled, and the hair on the back of my neck stood up.

"Just in case." He repeated the words. They sounded so loaded.

In case what? In case I decide to lose all common sense, judgment, control, my mind (although that was already up for debate), and call you for a midnight beach romp? I'll be sure to bring my watch so I can take note of how long it takes you to make me start screaming your name in wild ecstasy...Oh God, that sounded good!

I took a large step back. He took a large step forward. Back. Forward. Then he leaned in again. Holy crap! He was coming in for that double-cheek kiss again, and I wasn't sure I'd be able to remain cool and calm and controlled this time. Only he didn't. He did something far, *far* more odd and unsettling. He pulled my sunglasses off, placed them in the same hand as the card, and then closed my fingers around them. He squeezed my hand shut while looking into my eyes in a way that rattled me to my very core.

My head started spinning and suddenly I felt a tad unsteady. I hoped to hell that I wasn't about to be knocked off my feet by my raging hormones and fall into his arms. He gave my hand one last squeeze, and then...he was gone!

What the hell did that mean? You can't just take off a person's glasses, put them in her hands, stare into her eyes meaningfully, and then mysteriously walk away without a word. What the hell was he playing at?

And why was it so hard to keep myself from falling for it?

CHAPTER NINE

I would imagine it's the same kind of joy you get from winning the lotto while simultaneously having the best sex of your life. That's what walking into the hotel room felt like anyway. Everything was carved entirely into the rock face and whitewashed. It looked more like a cave than an actual hotel room. All the other décor was blue, and everything looked so crisp and clean and sanitary. I put my handbag down and rubbed my shoulder, which was no doubt dented. This place was perfect. I could see why it cost at least five times more than the other place. But it was worth every single cent!

Two big blue shutter doors dominated the other end of the room, and I felt compelled to open them. And I was so glad I had, because when I did, I stepped into my own private paradise. A small, secluded balcony was covered in a riot of colors. Bright-pink bougainvillea wrapped itself around the pillars and dangled from the overhang above my head. A small rim-flow pool stretched out in front of me, and from where I was standing I could barely see where the pool ended and the sea began.

From my private terrace I could gaze out across the water. It looked like it stretched in front of me forever. I breathed in deeply, it was all so…and then I sneezed. I looked up and found a cat sitting on the wall staring at me. It made a hissing noise and then disappeared. Just when I thought this place was starting to grow on me, I was reminded of how allergic I actually was to Greece. I hated cats almost as much as I hated hummus. Cats were from the devil. Their eyes glowed at night, for heaven's sake. My phone rang and I went back into the room. I saw the word flashing on the screen from a few yards away and sighed.

MOM. MOM. MOM.

I hadn't responded to her millions of messages yet. I was actually impressed it had taken her this long to call me. Technology was just another weapon my mother had added to her armory for meddling in my life.

One of the worst days of my life was the day she got a smartphone. She'd mastered the art of texting, and that was still okay. But when she moved on to WhatsApp and emojis, and got herself a Facebook profile, my life came to an abrupt end. The last straw had been when she'd started sharing pictures of grumpy baby animals with me and sent me one of those "*1 Like = 1 Prayer*" things. She wasn't even religious…and she didn't even like animals!

"Mom," I said into the phone.

"God, Jane, where have you been? I've been sick with worry wondering whether you'd been kidnapped."

"That's a bit dramatic, Mother."

"Well, you never know. I mean look what happened to Lilly, basically assaulted in Thailand and rustled away to some debaucherous party."

"Mom, she wasn't assaulted, and she and Damien are engaged."

"Fine. Fine." She gave a resigned sigh, as if she was giving up, but I knew better. "So what's it like there? Are the men as gorgeous as they say?"

"Um..." I started to stammer just thinking about him.

"Because I've read so many romance books where some gorgeous billionaire Greek oil tycoon sweeps the heroine off her feet..."

"Mom!" I chided her. "Stop."

"Fine, fine." She was very fond of saying *fine*. "But promise me that just in case you meet a gorgeous Greek billionaire you will have a wax. You know how you can get. And a pedicure. You don't want him thinking you have hobbit feet."

"Mom, stop it!" I was very glad when my phone started beeping with another call coming in.

"Mom, hang on, I have another call."

"If it's your father please tell him that I put the roast on an hour ago and I expect him home on time."

I glanced down at the screen. It was Dimitri.

"It's not Dad."

"Who is it?"

"It's just...it's the tour guide. I'm sure he's just calling to check if the hotel's okay or something."

"He? Darling, please be careful of tour guides. Greek gigolos, all of them. Remember what happened to your biological mother. But a shipping tycoon…"

"Mom, I'm not looking to bed—or whatever else you think I'm going to do with the tour guide. And I doubt Greek shipping magnates would want to go out with me anyway."

"Maybe if you just put on one of those lipsticks you're so fond of collecting." She said it in that pseudo-sweet voice she used when she was trying to disguise the fact she was actually insulting me.

"Maybe I don't want a boyfriend," I snapped back. Thirty seconds into a phone call with her and we were already *there*. That place where she was complaining about some part of me and I was defending my right *not* to have a boyfriend. Why did we always have to go round and round in these circles?

"Everyone wants to be loved, Jane, even busy career girls like you."

Something about her statement ground me to a stop.

"I'll take it under advisement. I've got to go. Okay, bye."

"Wait!" she yelled. "I just wanted to say one more thing."

I sighed down the phone. "What, Mom?"

"Good luck finding him. I hope when you do, you'll finally find what you've been looking for for so long." Her tone was soft and, dare I say it, empathetic.

"Oh!" I was stunned by her statement. That was the last thing I'd expected to hear from her. I knew she and my dad had nothing against me seeking out my biological parents—it's what almost all adoptive kids do—but was she actually showing some insight there? Some actual *I understand what you're going through* insight? She'd never understood me. Or tried to, for that matter. The fact that I was adopted, never fit in, and stood out like a sore thumb was something that had never been spoken about while I was growing up. It was as if—to them, anyway—I'd never been adopted at all. The issue was totally under the rug.

"Okay, Mom. Bye." I hung up quickly, feeling awkward from the conversation we'd just had. At least I'd missed Dimitri's call now, probably a good thing.

All I wanted to do was have a bath. I peeled my clothes off, freed my mop of rebel hair, and stood in front of the mirror. There was nothing I liked about my body at all. I'd long since given up on the expectation that I might have a dormant gene lying in wait, ready to spring to life making everything a little smaller (especially my thighs) and blonder and blue eyed. Sometimes I looked in the mirror and was overwhelmed by this feeling that I was wearing some kind of disguise that I could take off to reveal my true self, only I wasn't.

I had no idea what my biological parents looked like, but clearly I hadn't inherited very favorable genes. I had the waist of a walrus and the tangled, matted, curly hair of a black poodle. My boobs were a large, good size, though. My mother was fond of pointing this out—they were my best assets, "it's just such a pity you don't dress to accentuate them." And I hated to admit it, but my mother was right: I could do with a little bikini wax. Another beep on my phone made me turn around. I reached for it.

Check the side pocket of ur bag. Just in case you change your mind. Mom X 😊 😊 😄 😉 😄

I rolled my eyes and reached in. I pulled out a package labeled CARE PACKAGE. Although I doubted very much that this care package contained tins of canned beef and dehydrated food rations for war-torn starving millions. *How the hell did she even manage to slip this in my bag?*

I opened it.

1 x pink bikini (Way, way too push-uppy in the bust area for my liking—and were those sequins?)

1 x romance book (*Stranded on Santorini: The Greek Billionaire's Virgin Bride*. Tamed by the Hot Greek Tycoon Series: Book 8)

I turned the book over in my hands. I wasn't sure what was more disturbing, the fact that my mother had packed this for me, or that there were eight books in the series. The man on the cover was hot, I grant you. But he didn't hold a candle, nay not even a tiny flickering matchstick flame, to Dimitri. My temperature rose at the sudden thought of him. I could really do with a swim, but I hadn't packed a bathing suit, since I'd had no intention of swimming, so I guess my mother's little gift would come in handy after all. And thankfully the plunge pool on the terrace was completely private, so no one would ever need to see me in this horrendous pink thing. I took my underwear off and maneuvered myself into the bikini; it took a lot of "lifting" and "separating" to get the girls to even fit into the cups. My stomach was still growling, though, so I quickly rang room service for a salad, which would be delivered in twenty minutes. Just enough time for a dip.

I caught sight of myself as I walked past the mirror. My boobs were practically sitting underneath my chin; it was a good thing that no one, *ever*, would see me in this bikini. Or so I thought.

CHAPTER TEN

ᴗ⌒

*E*ver seen a baby gazelle minutes after it's born? It attempts to stand on its never-used legs, and tumbles. It tries to jump, and topples. It falls onto its knees and crawls around on the ground until it can get up. It's pretty damn cute.

This was *not* cute.

It started with a knock on the door. Room service was clearly fast around here.

"Just bring it in and put it on the bed, thanks," I called out and waited to give them enough time to leave before emerging. I climbed out of the pool and shook the excess water off my hair in a way I suspected left me looking a bit She-Ra Wild Jungle Woman. I stepped into the room and froze.

"Dimitri!" It came out as a shriek. Thank God he wasn't looking at me. Hey, what was he looking at that was making him smile so much? And then he spoke...

"Then the hard, pulsing shaft of his manhood sought out her

most intimate part. The glistening pearl of her womanhood, moistened by the fiery furnace of unbridled passion. He impaled her on his—"

I could feel the smoldering heat rush through my body and soon it reached the boiling point.

"Okay. Stop. You can…enough!" I burst out laughing. This fake, strange maniacal laugh. "Besides, it's…it's not even my book." More fake, weird laughter that disturbed even me a little.

"Really?" he asked. Suddenly I saw little pinky-blue dancing dots of light playing on his shirt, his hands, and the book. A strange look scuttled across Dimitri's face as he noticed them on his hands.

I knew I hated sequins for a reason! My boobs were basically flashing at him. They might as well have been screaming at him, too. Could it get any worse? Oh yes it could. His eyes slowly drifted up from the book he held in his hand toward me, and that was my cue to grab the nearest folded towel.

Damn, a fucking hand towel! I had to choose: Cover the boobs, or cover the bottom half? I opted for the bottom half. I tried to wrap the towel around me but it didn't fit and fell to the ground. I went after it, bending to pick it up, only to feel the bikini bottom being eaten by one of my bum cheeks. I gave another shriek and shot up, maneuvering my ass away from his field of vision. But the floor was wet and I fell onto my hands and knees.

"Fuck!" I heard myself pant as I crawled across the floor in the most undignified moment of my entire life. The floor was slippery and every now and then my knee would shoot out to the side.

I finally managed to make it to the bed and launch myself onto it like a torpedo. I did it with such force that at some stage my entire body was suspended in midair. I collided with the bed, landed on my face, and bounced a few times until the bed finally came to a stop. I immediately reached for the duvet and rolled. I rolled as fast as I could until only my head popped out. I lay there and looked up at him, vaguely aware that I couldn't move my arms because they were so tightly wrapped against my body. I tried to act as casual as I possibly could.

"Dimitri." I smiled up at him through a crack in the wild hair obscuring my face. "What brings you here?"

He looked down at me, and a grin spread across his face. It seemed to keep stretching until I was sure he couldn't smile any more. I closed my eyes in sheer embarrassment.

"You left these in the car. I tried to call you." He held out his hand, revealing the two tiny sachets of sunscreen that had been bestowed upon me by Flight and Travel Center *Terms and Conditions apply*. I'd gone through all this for two tiny tester sachets of sunscreen?

He was still smiling. The smile radiated in his eyes as he kept his hand outstretched, waiting for me to take the packets. I tried to move my arms. No luck. I tried again. Still nothing. They didn't budge. I was totally stuck. I tried to move my body and swing my legs off the bed so I could at least extricate myself from the anaconda-like grip of the duvet.

Nothing.

"You need some help?" he asked, reaching toward me.

"No! No! I'm perfectly fine."

"Jane, unless you have a big knife in one of your hands and can cut yourself free, you're stuck."

"Well, it's a lucky thing I do, then…" I paused. "Okay. I don't."

He gave a small and ever-so-sexy chuckle as he bent down and wrapped his arms around me. This was the most embarrassing thing that had ever happened to me in my life—worse than the condoms. He fastened his arms around me and I had visions of him trying to lift me off the bed, then realizing that he was lifting a whale instead of a human and crashing down himself. I closed my eyes and waited for the inevitable big *boom!* Only it didn't come. Instead, I felt weightless for a moment or two, and then my feet were on the floor. Not just that, but I was standing right in front of him. Nose-to-nose. Our eyes locked, and a weird moment descended on us like a thick mist. Silence infused with a strange humming awkwardness that clung to me and sent shivers over my skin.

The shivers made a U-turn and ran back up my spine as he pulled my large bushy mane from in front of my face and his fingers grazed my cheek. Next I felt his fingers on my neck as he tugged on the duvet and finally loosened it. He gently turned me, as if we were dancing, and the first layer was released. I did a full 360 until I was facing him again. He gave me a small semi-smile and then turned me again, and again until I felt the duvet completely loosen around me and finally fall to the floor.

I floated in a moment of absolute bliss as I stood face-to-face with the world's most attractive man. But the bubble was burst in the worst way possible as I watched his eyes drift from mine to my lips, and then down. I saw a look flash across his face, it seemed to be a look of shock. Then his eyes locked onto something else.

I glanced down, and that was the start of my demise. If I

thought that this moment couldn't get any worse—it could. In all the rolling, my bikini top had done the most appalling thing. The fervent roll had caused one of the cups to wedge itself under my armpit, pushing my boobs together into something wildly indecent-looking. And yes, there was also the slightest nipple-peep.

I gasped and clasped my hands over them. And that was it. I ran into the bathroom and slammed the door behind me. I fell against it, out of breath from the mini sprint, while I adjusted the cups and tried to force the rebellious things back to where they belonged. I pushed my ear to the door and heard some shuffling sounds. He was still there.

"Um…you can leave the sunscreen on the bed. Thanks for bringing it. Bye." The words fired out of my mouth like bullets. I was mortified and never wanted to see Dimitri again in my entire life. Ever. *Never.* I heard more shuffling, and it sounded like he'd come all the way up to the door. I pressed my ear even harder and could make out the sound of his breathing.

"Was there something else?" I asked cheerfully.

"Yes. As a matter of fact. I was wondering if you'd changed your mind about Greek food?"

"No. Still don't like it."

"So you don't want to come out with me and my tour group later tonight?" he asked.

"No thanks. Thanks for asking, though."

There was a pause. I could still hear him at the door.

"Anything else?" I asked.

"Yes. You should really wear your hair down more often," he said.

I heard the hotel door close and he was finally gone. It took me a few moments to pluck up the courage to step out, and when I did, I could see he'd put my duvet and pillows back onto the bed and made it up perfectly. And there in the middle were the two sachets of sunscreen. I reached up and touched my wild mop of unruly curls.

"You should really wear your hair down more often."

CHAPTER ELEVEN

⌒

*D*espite the unpleasant events of the day before, I'd woken up the next morning feeling very positive about the day ahead of me.

WHATSAPP GROUP: Jane goes to Greece

Jane: Wish me luck. I'm off to find my father!

Lilly: Good Luck.

Annie: OMG. This is crazy. I can't believe you're doing it.

Jane: I know.

Lilly: So what's the plan?

Jane: Well...I Googled all the licensed tour guides and tour companies in Santorini. There were twelve. Three of the companies also had the name Dimitri in their title...

(I left out the part that I knew one of them.)

Jane: I've phoned them all and asked whether a Dimitri, approximately forty to fifty years old, was currently working there, or had worked there in the past. So now I have whittled it down to five companies and I'm on my way to see them all.

Annie: How are you going to know it's him?

Lilly: Exac. You just going to come out and ask, "Hey, did you have sex with a woman called Phoebe twenty-five years ago?"

Jane: I'll just know when I see him.

Annie: You'll know?

Jane: Sure. How could I not recognize my own dad?

Annie: Uh, I hate to point this out to you, but I think there are a few holes in your plan.

Jane: My plan is fine!

Val: Hey, just saw this. Cool news! I still can't believe you're even there. OK, gotta go. I see Matt's car pulling up to the apartment.

Annie: HEY! Stop stalking him and his girlfriend!!!!!!

Val: I'm not.

Lilly: You are!

Jane: Totally stalking him!

Stormy: LoVe = Poowerfull

Jane: Huh?

Stormy: Yourre staR Sign . t0day says is power.ful dAY for love/

Lilly: Stormy. Woo-hoo! You're getting better at typing!

Jane: Thanks Storm. But I doubt it.

I slipped my phone in my pocket. I donned the most comfortable pair of walking shoes I owned, grabbed my bag, and headed out the door. I figured it would be easier to navigate the narrow streets on foot to avoid the slow-driving tourists—and the bit of exercise wouldn't hurt, either.

But a few hours later, and four tour companies down, I began to realize the serious holes in my plan, which Annie had tried to warn me of. I think I'd shot her down so quickly because if I had thought about it, *really* thought about it rationally for more than a few seconds, I would have clearly seen the massive, gaping holes in this ill-concocted plan of mine.

First, one place employed two Dimitris, both of them in the right age bracket—neither of them looked right. Others said they *had* employed Dimitris, but had no clue where they were now. Most said they couldn't help me unless I had a surname, which I didn't.

As the day progressed I'd also become less and less confident in my so-called ability to recognize my own father. I'd stared at multiple Dimitris all day and none of them had jumped out at me. My enthusiasm began to wane, although the last Dimitri had suggested I go down to the port; there were boat tours there and he definitely knew of a Dimitri.

And that's when I saw him...

Growing up, my sisters were part of the cool crowd—no, they *were* the cool crowd. They defined what everyone was doing and wearing and what the latest buzzword was. Boys wanted them, girls wanted to be them. They oozed a gravitational force that was so strong, people seemed to take up orbit around them. Dimitri had that same kind of quality, only magnified. He was walking along the tiny-pebbled street, talking about something passionately. A smile illuminated his face, there was an urgency and excitement to his walk, and his gestures were large and uninhibited. He looked like an overexcited kid on the playground. This passion, mixed with that half-unbuttoned white shirt, made him obnoxiously good-looking. Surely no man had the right to be this good-looking. He radiated good-looking-ness from every single one of his tiny pores. I almost wanted to march up to him and prick him with a needle just to see if he was human and would bleed.

The women following him looked hypnotized. Although they were carrying little Greek tour books and maps, they were way more interested in looking at the way the wind was tugging at his loose-fitting shirt...*mmmm, so was I*...

Suddenly I imagined him plunging business cards into all these women's eager hands.

"If you need anything."

I crept a little closer. I didn't want him to see me, so I decided to stare at him rather psychotically from behind a bush. I was close enough to hear what he was saying now.

"...This island is like the Greek myth of the Phoenix that rose up out of the ashes." His voice had an excited quiver to it. "It was created from a massive volcanic eruption, and now it is the most beautiful place on earth..." He stopped for a moment, placed his hands on his hips, and looked around in awe, as if he were look-ing at it all for the first time. There was something so hypnotizing about him that for a moment I wondered if this was what my bio-logical mother might have experienced.

"Can you feel it?" He spoke again. "The magic of it all?" He turned and looked at the women, who all dutifully nodded their heads. But it was clear they weren't thinking of their magical surrounding but rather contemplating what magic might be lying under that shirt of his...or in his trousers.

I leaned in a little closer, and that's when I felt the buildup. No, no, no, no...*too late*. I felt the sneeze before I saw the cause of it lurking in the same bush I was in. "*A-chooo!*" I sneezed. Loudly. He turned and looked in the direction of the bush...

Fuck!

My first instinct was to drop to the ground. Perhaps try a military-style drop-and-roll slash leopard-crawl combo. But I'd done enough of that in the last twenty-four hours to last me ten lifetimes. My heart thumped. My head started to sweat, and my mouth went dry. *Think, Jane...think, Jane...be smart...use your doctor-y brain...what am I going to do?...think...*

So I threw myself at the ground once more. *Yes*, I did it again. Don't judge me. I was so embarrassed for myself that I didn't even care that a little boy pointed and laughed at me as I crawled across the ground. I just prayed *he* hadn't seen me...

"Jane?" A sexy leg appeared in front of me. I was assailed by feelings of panic, but I was also determined to remain cool this time. The most important thing to do in a situation like this was to relax, keep calm, breathe. Do. Not. Panic.

"Dimitri. Hi. I...hahaha. It's you." I looked up at him from the ground and realized that this was the worst impression ever of *surprised but totally cool, slightly aloof person*.

"Haha..." I nervous-laughed again. I hated myself. "Fancy seeing you here." *A+ for creativity there, Jane.*

I quickly scanned my brain for some valid excuse to be down there:

Looking for contact lenses. (Way too clichéd. Sounded like a lie.)

Studying the indigenous ant species. (Way too complicated.)

And then I saw it. My golden ticket out of the situation. My bag had opened and a can of Coke Zero had rolled out of it. I grabbed it in my hand and jumped up.

"Found it," I said triumphantly. "Sneaky little thing must have rolled away." And then to end my performance I decided to do it. If I'd been in my right mind I wouldn't have. It doesn't take a physicist to realize that motion and fizzy drinks do not go together. I opened the can, and it exploded.

It was the volcano erupting all over again. It exploded in a giant commotion of black fizzy liquid and we were both instantly covered. Through the dark, liquid veil now covering me, I could see that the stuff had coated his face as well as his shirt. Oh God. What had I done?

I heard a few snickers from the audience that had now gathered. A few who had been a bit too close were wiping the odd drops of Coke off their arms. I wanted to open my mouth and say sorry; I wanted to defy the laws of the universe and reverse time. But I froze to the spot as sticky Coke dripped from my face and ran down my neck and into my shirt.

I just wish I'd remained frozen, because it would have been preferable to what I decided to do next. I flung myself at Dimitri with a kind of mad panic and started wiping him. In a manic frenzy of hands I wiped his hair, his face, his shirt...*God, his chest feels hard.* But it wasn't working, so I grabbed some tissues from my bag and continued. The tissues disintegrated in seconds and left little clumps of whiteness all over his face.

"Dimitri, I'm sorry…sorry…I've…" My voice cracked and quivered as I continued to paw at his shirt in the hopes that both the white clumps and the soda would disappear. Dimitri reached out and grabbed my hands in his. I stopped my madness and sighed apologetically. Our eyes locked, and in that moment I realized my glasses must have fallen off at some stage, too. I sighed again.

"It's okay, Jane." He smiled at me, and I crumbled inside. "Look at you."

For the first time I acknowledged that I was also covered. I glanced down at my once white shirt—now brown and dripping. More sighs emanated from me.

"You can't walk around like that," he said. "Come. I've got something for you." He gestured for me to follow. "I'll be back soon," he called out to the pack of women who'd been following him. "Have a look around in the meantime, and if you have any questions about the area, I'll answer them when I get back." I looked over at the women, and their faces all seemed to fall. The only questions they probably had involved which page in the Kama Sutra he was willing to try with them.

I lifted my bag off the ground with great difficulty and hoisted it back onto my shoulder with a loud outbreath from the effort of it all.

Dimitri looked at it curiously. "Do you carry that with you wherever you go?"

"Well, I might need something in it," I explained.

"Like two hair straighteners?" He sounded amused but kept on walking.

"Excuse me." I stopped walking. "There is a logical reason for that, by the way. The one is battery operated and the other is not. So I have a backup in case I can't find a plug."

Dimitri stopped walking and turned to face me. "In case of a hair-straightening emergency?"

"Exactly."

"A life-or-death situation that requires you straighten your hair, or someone else's, immediately?" He smiled at me and raised a questioning brow.

"Uh...sure. Why not?" Actually, when he put it like that, it did sound ridiculous to be lugging two hair straighteners around in my handbag. Not to mention all the brushes and creams and gels and lipsticks and, and, and...

"Are you a hairstylist?" he asked.

"A what?" I burst out laughing. I could barely handle my own hair, let alone others'. "No."

"So what kind of hair emergency could you ever have?" He folded his arms in a slightly challenging manner.

"Well"—I folded mine, too—"in case my hair gets messy. Or in case..." I ran a hand over my head. My hair was perfect today; I'd managed to scrape it back this morning so all the curls were flat and my ponytail was silky and straight. "It's humid here, so it might get frizzy or extra curly or...I don't know. I just need them. Okay?" I was feeling somewhat irritated by this line of questioning. "Besides, why do you care if I have ten hair straighteners in my bag?"

Dimitri shrugged nonchalantly. "I was just wondering, that's all." He started walking again and I sighed. What was with all these questions? It wasn't like we knew each other well enough for this. I didn't want to get into a whole discussion with him about the ins and outs of my life and handbag and hair and Greek food or whatever else he was so persistent in trying to get out of me. This was how trouble started. I'm sure my biological mom had started with an innocent conversation, and look where that led. Knocked up. I stopped walking.

"Look, it's fine, I'm just going to go," I said quickly. "I have things to do today and I can't really afford this detour. But thanks, and all." I started to turn, and a hand reached out and stopped me.

"Come on, Jane. This will only take a second." He took me by the shoulder and started to lead me down the streets, and I, for some stupid reason that was really beyond me, let him. We continued to walk for a little way, down some small winding roads and up a little hill, until we reached a large parking lot. I recognized his car immediately. He opened the trunk and pulled out two T-shirts wrapped in plastic and opened them both. DIMITRI'S TOURS.

"Not glamorous," he said, handing me a red one and taking a green one for himself.

He smiled again. It had a languid, dreamy quality to it and for a second or two, before I mentally slapped myself silly, I glanced at his smiling lips. But then my eyes found themselves looking at something else entirely as he peeled his shirt off, tossed it aside, and stood there half naked. My eyes continued to drift down his body as if drawn there by some invisible force. The world immediately stopped spinning on its axis and that inconvenient voice came back.

You sooo want to run your tongue over his chest, don't you? You bad, bad girl.

My eyes snapped up immediately and tried to focus on his face.

"You can change in the car," Dimitri said, and opened the back door for me. The sudden terrifying image of me being half naked in the backseat of his car gripped me. No doubt he could see this on my face.

"I won't look. Promise," he said with a knowing smile. It was the kind of smile that said, *"Anyway, I've already almost seen it all."*

I climbed into the car with my massive handbag, half tipping it as I went, and then began trying to peel my wet shirt off and slip the other one on while trying to stay out of window view. It was a tank top, not something I would usually wear. Ever. I was far too self-conscious about my arms to consider wearing something like that. But it was the lesser of two evils at this point. I stepped out of the car. Dimitri gave me the once-over and stopped at my shoulder.

"The strap, it's..." He indicated the strap on my top, and I moved my fingers over it. My bra was twisted around it, and so was a strand of my sticky hair.

"Oh. Thanks." I tried to untwist it and couldn't.

"You mind?" he asked tentatively before reaching out toward the mess. As he did, his hand grazed my shoulder, and then at some stage, once the strand of hair had been loosened, he tucked it behind my ear.

The heavens and earth opened, the winds picked up, and the sea began to swell...*no they didn't*. But when his fingertips touched my ear ever so slightly, it did feel like the single most erotic moment of my life. I gazed up at him in total silence, trying not to look at him in a way that implied I was *freaking the fuck out*.

"Perfect," he said.

"Yes you are," I screamed back at him in my mind.

His face broke into a broad smile and for a moment I wondered if I had actually said that out loud and not in my head at all. We stood there for a few minutes. He stopped smiling at me and started staring strangely instead. It soon became so uncomfortable that I felt compelled to break the eye contact. His face immediately turned apologetic. "Sorry, I didn't mean to stare. It's just... your eyes."

I inwardly rolled those unnerving eyes of mine. *This again.* "Uhm ... well. Okay. I better be off. Lots of ground to cover still ..." I made a stupid hand gesture as if I was scanning my surroundings. "Lots to do, you know ... no rest for the wicked and all that." I tried to sound casual again. Epic fail.

"What have you been doing today?" he asked. Something behind him moved. I looked over his shoulder to see that all the women had appeared; they'd obviously decided not to wait for him, and they were attacking me with their accusing eyes and pouting in blatant disapproval.

"Oh. Nothing really, I've been looking for ... well, you know, Dimitri."

"Any luck?"

I shook my head. I wasn't any nearer to finding my father than I had been a few days ago when I was thousands of miles away on the other side of the world.

"Take a break and join us. We're going to the Cathedral of Saint John the Baptist."

I looked over his shoulder again. The cobras had all risen out of the grass now and were ready to spit their venom at me. I gave a small, polite smile. "No thanks. I've still got a lot to do." I started to walk off but felt a gentle hand on my shoulder again.

"It's one hour, Jane." His hand left my shoulder, and even though it had only been on it for the briefest moment, all my senses went into overdrive. I had to get away from him before I started to physically drool on him.

"I'll make it worth your while," he said with a perfectly sweet, innocent-looking smile, but all I could think about was…

"Have sex with me. Cathedral sex. Sex. Now."

"No thanks!" It came out almost like a panicked cry for help and I tried to give him a smile that wouldn't betray my feelings any further. I wiggled out of his grasp with a shoulder shrug and gave the ladies a tiny wave. "Bye. Have fun." I started scuttling away.

"But, Jane, you haven't lived until you've experienced the beauty and peace of standing inside it," he called after me.

"It's fine," I shouted over my shoulder, "I think I can live without that."

CHAPTER TWELVE

From that moment onward, my day went from bad to worse. In fact, the last good thing that happened to me that day was Dimitri giving me a new shirt. Because after that, it devolved into one of the worst days I'd had in a long time. With each passing moment, I came to understand just how futile the search for my father was. I came to realize that although I consider myself an intelligent human being, I had embarked on the stupidest crusade ever.

I hadn't thought this through. *At all.* I usually thought everything through. I always had goals and a plan. And a backup plan in case that plan went wrong. But this time I'd had no plan at all—not a real one anyway. I'd let emotions cloud my judgment from the moment I'd seen that stupid flashing sign in the travel agency. I wanted to kick myself.

I also started to wonder if perhaps my father wasn't a tour guide on Santorini at all. Santorini had been a total guess on my part. Perhaps he was on another island? Perhaps he was no longer a tour guide? The final nail in the coffin of my plan and my hopes of finding my father was hammered in after I had taken the six hundred steep steps all the way down to the port.

The port was lined with a wide variety of boats, from smaller fishing craft to yachts that looked like they were owned by a rapper; there were even two huge cruise liners docked there. Other than seafaring vessels, it was also lined with what can only be described as washing lines of dead octopuses drying in the sun. I discovered that when I walked into one. I screamed as my face was covered in slimy, slippery tentacles. Did you know that a very recently killed octopus is still capable of using its suckers? It's a muscular reflex. I discovered this the hard way when the thing attached itself to my face and head.

The scene I'd caused seemed to amuse the local fisherman. They'd all seemed even more amused when I asked about Dimitri, and one of them had said, "Everyone named Dimitri, raise your hand." Four hands had gone up, and one man asked if his dog counted. Dimitri the dog! I was forced to climb back up the six hundred steps in the blazing sun without my sunglasses—I couldn't find them—while still lugging around my bag, which now felt like it actually contained boulders. My shoulder was aching, my legs were shaking, I had a throbbing headache, and my back was killing me. My phone beeped in my bag and I hoisted the thing off my shoulder. It hit the ground with a thud that probably produced seismic waves as I pulled my phone out.

WHATSAPP GROUP: Jane goes to Greece

Annie: So? How's it going?

Jane: Not well!

Annie: I'm sorry. You okay though?

Jane: I'm not sure. Nothing feels right. I don't feel right. I don't know what's wrong with me.

Annie: There's nothing wrong with you.

Jane: Yes there is. Why am I like this then?

Lilly: Hey! Nothing wrong with you.

Jane: Then why do I carry two fricking hair straighteners in my fucking handbag?

Annie: LOL ☺ because you like neat hair.

Jane: Exactly. That's what I told him!

Lilly: Him? Told who?

Annie: Who is him????

A little bolt of panic flashed through me. I felt too ashamed to admit to having anything to do with a tour guide named Dimitri; I knew how bad that would sound. And how stupid and naive and ridiculous it would make me seem.

Jane: No one. Bye. Gotta go. XX

I slid my phone back into my bag and lifted it onto my shoulder again. An acute sense of misery descended on me, and I continued to walk through the streets in a kind of daze. Past the shops and happy tourists, past the quaint taverns and bars, until something caught my eye. I glanced up: SANTORINI INFORMATION CENTER.

There was a huge map plastered across the window. I approached it with a feeling of dark foreboding. I stopped in front of it, and that's when my body stopped functioning and wouldn't allow me to move. *What the . . . ?*

Greece had more islands than I'd thought. The mainland looked like it had once exploded and sent shards of itself floating across the sea . . . Ionian Islands, Saronic, Cyclades, Sporades . . . I rushed inside the shop and ran up to the first person I saw. She was busy with someone but I didn't care.

"How many islands are there?" I yelled at the top of my lungs. The whole shop turned and looked at me. I repeated myself when I didn't get an answer straightaway.

"Six thousand." The woman looked at me as if she wasn't sure if she should press the secret panic button under the desk.

"What?" I shrieked. I was frightening them now. I could see the terror in their eyes.

"But only two hundred and twenty-seven are inhabited," she quickly added with a smile, as if that were some grand consolation prize. "Are you interested in some activities on one of the islands?" She held up a pamphlet, and I stared at it in utter horror.

"Sorry, I clearly misheard you. You didn't say two hundred and twenty-seven, did you?"

"Two hundred and twenty-seven," she repeated slowly with a gentle nod, as if she was trying not to make any sudden movements, like I was a feral animal that had been backed into a corner. Everything went a bit blurry and whirly after that. I felt faint and strange. My head started to throb, and a buzzing noise was building in my ears. I stumbled out of the shop feeling like my head was about to explode. I caught a glimpse of a pharmacy across the road and managed to wobble into it.

For a brief and glorious moment I felt much better. There was a sense of familiarity about the place. Neat, ordered, sterile, categorized, and clear. I breathed in; the slight scent of disinfectant filled my nose. It was terribly soothing. I liked it here, until...

I looked up and caught sight of it in the men's cosmetics section. A poster of Dimitri hung on the wall above a fancy-looking fragrance display.

Ambition for Men. What's your next move?

This time he was wearing a full black suit and standing on one of those oversized chessboards. He looked like he was provocatively contemplating his next move while a woman draped in a transparent swathe of fabric suggestively straddled the castle.

I burst out laughing. I couldn't help it! It was completely cheesy and just all too much. Even when I wasn't bumping into him literally, I was still "bumping" into him in paper form. He was haunting me. Why was he everywhere I went?

My laughter began small and then it seemed to gain momentum like a snowball rolling down a hill. It grew bigger and louder and crazier as I backed away from the display. I bumped into something behind me, and it wobbled. I turned to grab it and the thing fell into my arms. I wrestled with it a bit until I managed to turn it around. And that's when I found Dimitri's suited crotch in my face. *You've got to be kidding me!* I was clutching a life-sized cardboard cutout of a sexy suited Dimitri Spiros. Was this really necessary? Did he need to exist in cardboard form as well?

His crotch was touching my nose and his head was somewhere down *there*. I quickly flipped the thing over so it didn't look like I was engaging in some strange sexual act in the shop.

"Why are you everywhere I go?" I moaned into his cardboard chest.

"Madame." A voice caught me off guard. I turned to see the pharmacist staring at me angrily.

"Please just get out," he said in a thick Greek accent. "I can't believe how many of you ladies come in here and steal this thing."

"Sorry, what?" I asked, still clutching Dimitri.

"I'm tired of phoning the company to ask for more," he said, trying to herd me out the door. "In fact, since you've already damaged it"—he pointed at the arm I'd accidentally bent—"why don't you just take it. Take it and go do whatever you girls are all doing with it."

"But I don't want it—" I tried to object but in one swift move the man pushed me out the door and closed it in my face. *Great!* Now I was standing in the street holding a life-sized cardboard cutout of Dimitri.

"How can this day get any worse," I cried out loudly. A few people turned and stared, and a couple of passing women winked at me. God, I felt like a dirty pervert. I could imagine what everyone thought: that I was going to take this thing home and show it a good time.

I put "Dimitri" under my arm and tried to walk as casually as possible. But the streets overflowed with tourists and I kept thrusting his head into someone's crotch, and then nearly decapitated a small child. *I need to get rid of it!* I shot up a deserted alleyway, found a trash can, and began shoving him into it. Easier said than done. The thick cardboard was hard to bend, and at one stage I found myself pushing him down with my foot.

"Get in," I said as I ripped off an arm. Oh wow, that felt kind of good. I pulled off his other arm and then ripped one of his legs into a thousand tiny pieces. I'd just ripped off his head when a door behind me opened. A man wearing a chef's hat with the word ZORBA'S across it started screaming at me. I didn't blame him; I must have looked like a wild woman. I ran from the alley and back into the street. It was only then that I realized I was still clutching Dimitri's head. "Fuck it!" I shoved it into my bag without thinking.

I hated this day, and the weight of it seemed to push down on me. The image of Atlas the Greek god holding the entire world upon his shoulders penetrated my bruised and hazy brain. I chastised myself for my utter stupidity: This was the last time I was ever going to let my emotions take over and govern a decision. I wished that I was a character in a book right then so that I could flip to the end—which I often do, as I hate not knowing—and find out what happens to me.

Does Jane find her father and do they live happily ever after?

*Does she not find him but, in a poignant twist, find herself instead? *Barf**

Does Jane have a complete meltdown and start eating carbs with reckless abandon until someone has to send for the firemen to bash a hole through the wall and drag her out of the hotel room she's been living in for the last ten years?

The sun was setting and I was thirsty. Without much thought I walked into a tavern and deposited myself at the bar. It was a whitewashed wooden thing—*surprise, surprise*. What was with all this whitewashing anyway? These people would probably white-wash night if they could. I glanced up at old fishing nets hanging from the ceiling. A very large taxidermied fish took center stage on the back of the wall, and beneath it was a name.

DIMITRI CHRISTOPOLULOS. 27 MARCH 1987.

Great! I'm sure *this* Dimitri was very proud to have pulled his worthy opponent from the sea. Good for him. Good for Dimitri. My brain had taken on a very cynical view of life today.

"What will it be?" the man behind the bar asked.

I shrugged. I wasn't a frequenter of bars; I had no idea what to order. "What do people usually drink?"

The man smiled at me. "That depends on whether their day has been good or bad."

"Bad. Very bad."

The man nodded knowingly. I wondered how many sob stories he'd been privy to over the years. He slid a drink over to me but there was no fizzy pink stuff and no umbrella or bobbing cherry. Instead, I was met by a glass of ice and whiskey. I hated whiskey. Nonetheless, I was determined to suck it down. It took me about thirty minutes to consume the two ounces of liquid, and by the end of the glass I was definitely more relaxed. The tension in my shoulders had dissipated, but now my bladder felt very full. I got up and walked over to the bathroom. The cubicle looked like a wall of graffiti. Clearly a hundred drunken girls had poured their hearts out on these very walls thinking they were poets. I started reading some of it...

There were a few SO-AND-SO WAS HEREs, one TRISTAN IS A DICK-HEAD, and one rather amusing LOSS OF VIRGINITY PROUDLY BROUGHT TO YOU BY JACK DANIEL'S. But there was also one...

PARTY LIKE IT'S YOUR BIRTHDAY EVERY DAY.

It suddenly dawned on me that tomorrow was actually my birthday. The irony made me roll my eyes. Twenty-five years ago tomorrow, I'd been given up...and so had begun the chain of events that had led me to this very moment in time. In a way, I was right at the very beginning, where it had all started.

When I got back to my miserable little seat at the bar, I noted that the one next to it was now very much occupied. A man—early thirties, not hideous-looking, a little too sunburned, a lot over-dressed for this kind of bar, and sporting a hairstyle that looked like it had taken a lot of time and gel—was casually sitting there.

"You looked like you could do with another." He slid the drink over to me with the kind of expertise that suggested he'd done this before.

"That obvious?" I asked.

"Pretty much." I accepted the whiskey from this stranger and wondered why the hell he even cared.

"So what's your sad story?" he asked.

"What makes you think I have a sad story?"

"Pretty girls sitting alone in bars usually do."

"Trust me, you don't want to hear mine."

"Why not?" He leaned toward me.

"It's very sad and sobby."

"Why don't you let me be the judge of that?" He looked genuinely interested. But I wasn't going to divulge my innermost secrets to this man.

Okay, so maybe it was the green drink with the swirly pink stuff floating on the top that he'd bought me after I'd polished off the whiskey. Or the two shots of creamy stuff I'd drunk after that, because about half an hour later I was telling him *everything*.

Every tiny detail. And he listened. He nodded at the appropriate parts, tutted loudly a few times, and shook his head when I wanted him to. He seemed interested.

Until I realized what he was really after, and what a dangerous situation I'd just gotten myself into.

CHAPTER THIRTEEN

*H*is hand came out and squeezed my knee in a lascivious, pushy manner. I tried to brush it off "accidentally," pulling my handbag onto my lap. It didn't deter him, though. He tried to slide his hand under my bag and up my leg. I quickly crossed my legs and started rummaging through my bag for nothing at all, trying to buy myself some time to figure a way out of this situation.

"If you're looking for this..." His voice was laced with vodka and sex. He pulled a shiny wrapper out of his pocket. It took my eyes a moment to adjust, but when the object finally came into focus, I gasped.

EXTRA-EXTRA-LARGE, STUDDED AND RIBBED FOR ADDED PLEASURE.

"No...no! I think you've got the wrong idea here." Wild panic-nausea was rising.

"No wrong idea here, baby." The guy leaned in again and this time made a beeline for my lips. I turned my head and felt his moist mouth smash into the side of my face. I could smell the overwhelming stench of alcohol and cigarette smoke. It made me feel sick.

"What's the matter with you?" he asked, trying to kiss me again, this time holding my head in place with his hand. His lips came down on mine and I felt sick. I pulled away again as quickly as I could.

"Nothing, I'm just not...I don't do this kind of thing. I'm sorry." Why was I apologizing to this awful man who was coming on to me in a bar?

He gave me the dirtiest look I've ever received in my life. "Do you really think I bought you drinks all night and listened to your sob-fucking-story for hours because I actually cared?" He made another move for my leg despite the fact that my bag was covering it. I jumped off the bar stool, bumping my drink and spilling it across the bar.

"You better pay for that." He spat his words at me like venom.

I started rummaging in my bag for my wallet. But as I did, he grabbed my wrist. The Coke Zero image from earlier that day flashed through my mind and without thinking, I grabbed a tall glass of beer off the counter and emptied it into his face.

"You fucking bitch," the guy hissed under his breath while wiping the beer off his face.

And so I did the only thing I could...I ran. I pushed my way through the crowd and stumbled out onto the streets. The uneven cobblestones and weight of my bag pulling me to one side tripped me up immediately and I fell. Red-hot pain shot through me as my knee connected with the hard ground.

I stumbled back up onto my feet, only now the world was

spinning and tilting and swirling and cruelly tricking me into thinking I was falling forward. I put my arms out in the hopes of steadying my balance, but it still felt like an invisible string was pulling me forward. I heard a noise behind me and turned. The door opened and *he* stepped out and looked at me.

Run. You have to run!

But my legs felt like they were unable to carry out my brain's commands. The man stepped through the door now and started moving toward me . . .

Run. Run. Run.

This time my legs obeyed. I ran out into the night as fast as I could. I had no idea which way to go. I couldn't even figure out if I was going up or down, my vertigo was so bad.

Up a narrow cobbled street. Turn left . . . *I think.*

Up or down the stairs in front of me? *Neither!*

Turn right and up another small alley. *Maybe?*

Left again. *Shit, shit, shit, be careful of all the potted plants!*

But it was too late. By the time I saw it, I'd already collided with it. My leg screamed at me as the pain of a thousand thorns dug into it. Fucking cactus bastard! Why do they have to have so many potted plants in Greece? And cats? I sneezed as one skidded across my path. I hated Greece!

I kept running. The streets seemed to be getting steeper and narrower as I went. I heard a noise behind me and turned. I shouldn't have. "*Ouch.*" I winced in pain as something yanked me backward. I reached up and my hair was twisted in the thorny vines of the massive, low-hanging bougainvillea I hadn't seen.

You've got to be kidding. Even the flora on this stupid island was out to get me. I was clearly allergic to Greece and as soon as I got back to my hotel, I was booking the first flight out of this God-forsaken place and back home. My fingers frantically pulled at the trapped strands of hair. The pain was unbelievable. I yanked. Hard. I heard some disturbing snapping sounds but I was finally free and carried on darting up the alley.

My heart was racing, my breath was catching in my throat, and I felt like I couldn't get enough air into my lungs. My body gave up and I couldn't run any farther. I backed up until I was resting against a wall. I was hot and sweaty, and the cool wall felt good against my skin. I looked down the alley; there was no sign of him. Relief washed over me as I slid down the wall and sat. I focused all my energy on my breathing and my pounding heart, willing them to slow down.

Get a grip, Jane. Breathe!

Slowly, after some very focused deep breathing, my heart rate started to return to normal. But I felt very far from normal. As the painful pounding in my chest calmed down, I became aware of the pain in my leg. I reached down and touched it. It felt warm and wet. I was bleeding.

My head also hurt; my scalp felt like it was stinging. A sense of total hopelessness started to rack my already-sore body. My life was falling apart right before my eyes, and there was nothing I could do about it but sit back and watch as one catastrophe opened the door to invite the next disaster in, which in turn paved the way for a further tragic event to unfold. It was as if someone was playing a sadistic game of dominoes with my life. In total misery, I dropped my head and held it between my shaking hands.

These kinds of dramatic emotions weren't me, *at all*. Maybe if I was more adept at expressing them, I would feel better now. Maybe if I could throw something, or kick or punch and scream. But that wasn't my way. My way was to take them all and turn them inside, where they'd obviously grown and fed off one another like a cancer. And now no amount of suppression could keep them down. They were out and they were rushing around with the destructive force of a hundred hurricanes.

And the dominant one was pain. I felt so alone. And that's when it hit me...

Where the hell am I?

I was lost. It was two a.m. and I had no idea where I was, or in which direction my hotel was. North, south, east...*where?* How did one hail a taxi here? Where was the main road anyway? I pulled my phone out and started trying to navigate Google Maps. But my fingers were shaking, my eyes were blurry, and I was in such a panic I couldn't think logically. So I did the only other thing, the simplest thing I could do under the circumstances. I pressed dial on my last dialed number.

"Hello." His voice sounded sleepy and sexy as hell.

"Um...hi...it's..." I managed.

"Jane. Are you okay?"

"Yes, I mean, *no*...I'm not sure." My voice cracked, and a betting man would probably have put money on me bursting into uncontrollable girlie sobs. But I knew better. Even when my life was falling apart, I still couldn't cry. I actually wished I could; I imagined it would be a massive relief.

"Where are you?" It sounded like he was moving around now.

"I don't know. I think I'm lost."

"Okay, look around, what do you see?" I heard more movement and a door shutting.

I scanned my surroundings. Everything bloody looked the same here. Whitewashed walls, whitewashed houses with little blue doors and potted plants and cobblestones and...something caught my eye. There was a trash can up the hill at the top of the alley. I ran for it, and that's when I saw Dimitri's cardboard arm sticking out of it.

"I know where I am. I'm in an alley behind a restaurant. Zorba's, I think."

"Stay where you are, I know the place." I heard a car start and a tiny scrap of relief crept in, but it wasn't nearly enough to douse the other emotions blazing inside me. I wanted the feelings out of me. They physically hurt. I closed my eyes, squeezed them together hard, and willed myself to cry.

Cry, Jane. Cry and let it all out. I opened my mouth and let out a loud crying sound, *"Waaa-aaahhh-waaa, waaaa."* But the noise wasn't inspiring the tears. It just wasn't working. I sat against the wall for what felt like forever until a noise made me jump up.

"Who's there?"

"It's me." Dimitri stepped into the light, and it gave him a glowing godlike halo.

"Are you okay?" He walked closer and his eyes scanned me as if he was taking stock of the creature before him. Then without warning he reached up, and I felt his hand on my head. He pulled away and held a piece of bougainvillea between his fingers.

"Thanks," I said faintly.

"You're bleeding!" In one swift movement he was kneeling on the ground examining my leg.

"It's nothing, just a scratch." I pulled away quickly.

He stood up and locked eyes with me. He looked more serious than I'd ever seen him look before. "What happened?"

I shook my head, which I shouldn't have as it felt very woozy again. "It's a sshhlong story." I was aware that I was slurring now, which was incredibly undignified.

"I have time." He stepped toward me and then in a move that almost made me squeal out loud, he gently took my face between his hands. "Jane? What happened?"

"Can we jushhst…" I stopped and moved my tongue around in my mouth in an attempt to moisturize it. "Can we *just* go," I managed to say without slurring this time.

He shook his head. "What happened?" He looked at me with such focus and determination that I knew I wasn't going to get away without telling him.

"It's just…there was this guy at a bar and he…He was trying to…he didn't, though. Anyway, I ran out and he followed but I managed to lose him so it's totally fine. It's nothing."

"*Nothing?*" The word came out so loud and firm that it caught me off guard and I flinched. "Which bar?" Dimitri reached for my hand and started pulling me.

I bucked against him. "No, no, leave it. It's fine. Just drop it. It was nothing…*really.*"

But he looked unmoved. "Which bar, Jane?"

"Please," I begged. "Please…I've already caused such a scene in there…please, Dimitri. *Please.*"

He scanned my face again, and the hard look in his eyes vanished. "Fine. I'll leave it."

Relief washed over me. "Thanks."

"Come." He held his arm out for me, and I stared at it. *Am I meant to take it?* I hesitated for a moment, and then he looped his arm through mine and started walking. I was secretly glad for it. The spinny, vertigo feeling wasn't entirely gone yet, and I stumbled ever so slightly.

"I've got something that will sort that out." He flicked his eyes toward me with a slight smile.

"Sort what out?"

"You ever had a cup of Greek coffee?"

I shook my head.

"It will sober you up quickly."

I felt a sudden thump of shame. What did he think of me—that I was some drunken tart that got herself lost in the early hours of the morning? I hardly ever drank. I couldn't remember the last time I'd been drunk, and I didn't think I'd ever been like this!

"I don't do stuff like this. I'm really sorry I woke you up," I said as we rounded a corner. "And anyway, I don't drink—"

He cut me off, sounding amused. "Greek coffee. I could have guessed that. But the thing is—"

I cut him off this time. "Let me guess . . . I haven't lived until I've drunk Greek coffee in the streets of Santorini while watching a sunset?"

Dimitri burst out laughing. It was warm and contagious and despite myself, I chuckled along.

"We know each other so well already." Dimitri said it playfully but his statement caught me off guard. Who the hell was this guy that I hadn't been able to shake since arriving on the island? And why were we now walking arm in arm and laughing and chatting and mind reading like we actually knew each other? We didn't know each other, and I certainly didn't want to know him!

I quickly pulled my arm away from him. "It's okay. I can walk on my own. Thanks." We finally reached his car and climbed in. I was relieved to be going back to my hotel so I could book the first flight out of here. I hated Greece, and I certainly wasn't going to find my father here. I just wanted to go home. My thoughts drifted off, and for a moment I was back home in the safety of my familiar four walls, standing firmly on my laminate wood flooring and getting ready to spend the day fixing people's teeth. The idea didn't appeal to me as much as I thought it would. *What is wrong with me?*

"Jane, are you sure you're okay?" Dimitri asked.

Maybe it was something to do with the safe confines of the car that made me open up. "I'm fine. But I'm really glad to be out of that place. I should have known it was fishy…literally." I laughed at my own stupid joke.

"Literally?" he repeated.

"Yes, there was a giant, hideous fish on the wall behind the bar. The whole thing's probably my fault anyway…I should have seen it coming. The guy was totally dodgy."

"Dodgy?" he echoed.

"Yes."

"Like?"

"Well, first he was totally sunburned…and I don't trust people that don't wear sunblock. It smacks of irresponsibility."

"Sunburned?" he said as he made a sharp turn up a road that looked like one we'd already driven up.

"Yes, completely, and don't get me started on that terrible earring!"

"Earring?"

"Revolting golden loop in his ear." I glanced over at him.

He made another sharpish turn, and everything looked familiar again.

"What a douche bag. I mean, who the hell wears a full-blown suit and tie to a casual seaside bar?"

"Full suit, hey?"

My elbow knocked against the side of the car as Dimitri made another sharp turn and started driving up a street I knew we'd already been up. He came to a sudden and very abrupt stop outside the bar and turned to me.

"I'll be a moment." He said it with a smile as if nothing was wrong, and then simply jumped out and walked toward the bar, muttering something. I leaned out the window in an attempt to hear what he was saying.

"Sunburned...earring...full suit," he whispered under his breath before turning back to me. "Wait there, Jane!" He sounded cheerful as he walked into the bar.

Oh shit! The realization hit me. Was he going to beat the guy up? I sat in the car and stared at the door in utter horror.

CHAPTER FOURTEEN

It felt like hours, but in reality it must have been a few minutes before he burst back out the door looking totally casual and cheerful. He even stopped to greet a man happily.

"Dimitri. *Kalimera.*"

"*Kalimera.*" The other man waved at him.

He climbed back into the car and without saying a single word started driving again as if everything was completely normal. Which it was not! He gave me a quick sideways glance and then flashed me a small, satisfied smile.

"What happened? Did you...you know?" Had he seriously just walked into the bar and beaten the guy up? I wasn't sure whether I should be completely flattered by this knight-in-shining-armor gesture, or whether I should be a bit scared of him. Maybe he was one of those guys who suddenly snapped?

"Of course not. But he did say he was very sorry."

"Did he?" I perked up.

"He said you didn't deserve to be treated like that."

"Really?"

"Yes... he said that when he saw you, you were so beautiful that he couldn't help himself."

"He said I was beautiful?" I couldn't keep the sarcastic skepticism out of my voice.

"And he says you have the most beautiful eyes he's ever seen."

I rolled my eyes. "Really?"

"He also says you should wear your hair down more often." Dimitri turned and smiled at me playfully.

"No he didn't," I said sharply.

His playful smile grew bigger. "Just because he didn't say it doesn't mean it's not true."

A strange silence filled the car. *What is this man playing at?* His actions confused me beyond measure. He had this way of making me feel better about myself, and it felt wonderful, but how much of it was an act? He was the consummate Greek playboy, after all. He'd probably just honed his skills to such an extent that he knew exactly what to say and do to make a woman feel special. But to what end?

The car finally stopped outside a small, quaint white cave house with a blue gate and white wall. I climbed out too enthusiastically, which I shouldn't have. It felt like all the alcohol had settled while we were driving, but upon jumping out of the car I seemed to have shaken it all up again. My head felt woozy and my eyes started to blur the shapes around me. It was so bad that I needed to hold on to the car door to steady myself for a moment or two.

I carefully followed Dimitri into a small, well-appointed courtyard.

In the middle stood a blue table and two chairs, flanked by two small olive trees and some bougainvillea, which I had come to understand was an absolute prerequisite in these parts. He took a key out of his pocket and slipped it into the lock.

"Where are we?"

"My house." He opened the door and started leading me inside. I stopped dead on the threshold.

"This isn't my hotel," I said, stating the obvious. I took a step backward as if the entrance to his house was the gates of hell. *Dramatic*, I know. I took another step back but miscalculated the slope. I wobbled for a second or two and was just about to fall backward when his arm shot out, grabbed me around the waist, and pulled me up. With a thud, my body slammed into his.

His arm tightened around me, and I could feel the heat of his hand on my lower back. Our faces were close now. Our noses were almost touching, and our lips were mere inches away. The sensations running through my body were enough to make me shiver. I hoped he hadn't felt that.

If I were a confident, flirty girl I might have just leaned in and kissed him, but I wasn't. I had the self-esteem of a tree stump. I was vaguely aware of his hand rising to the side of my head, and I wondered if he was going to pull another twig out of my hair. Instead, he softly pushed my hair back out of my face. My legs felt like they were going to collapse under me, and I wasn't sure if it was from the alcohol or my intoxication with Dimitri. I suddenly became very self-conscious, and the proximity to his face was just way, *way* too much for me to bear. I quickly wiggled my way out of his grasp.

"I want to go to my hotel," I said as every fiber and cell in my body shouted something completely different.

"Take me to your room and have sex with me. Sex. Room. Now. Sex!"

"I don't want to leave you there like this."

"Like what?" My eyes snapped back up to meet his.

"It looks like you've had a bad night, maybe you need a friend to talk to." He flashed me a warm, caring-looking smile that almost made me forget my name, what country I was in, perhaps even the planet I lived on. He'd put it so nicely, too. Using euphemisms like *bad night* and *need a friend*.

I was so conflicted right now. I paused and glanced at his little door. It looked so innocent. It was hard to imagine that he even lived here. He seemed more like the kind of guy who would live in a modern penthouse apartment with lots of glass and chrome and marble and phallic-looking pillars, and perhaps a secret sex room. But this place looked rustic. Charming even. Friendly. *Maybe it's his girlfriend's place?*

"I don't want to intrude on you and . . ." I pointed into the room behind him.

"It's just me." His reply was quick.

I wasn't sure if this should make me feel pleased, or scared. He was basically a stranger. But he couldn't be too dodgy; otherwise the travel company presumably wouldn't use him as a tour guide. Surely they would check someone's credentials before putting him on the payroll? *What am I thinking* . . . of course he could be dodgy. People hire sickos and weirdos and perverted kiddie flashers all the time. And they probably don't even realize it. I'm pretty sure it's not the kind of thing that comes up in job interviews, or becomes fodder around the watercooler. So *yes*, Dimitri Spiros could be as dodgy as fuck!

"I don't bite," he said with another smile that was less panty-dropping and more reassuring. "But if you really want to go to the hotel, I'll take you." He paused and looked at me expectantly.

Walk into a stranger's home at two o'clock in the morning? Intoxicated! A stranger called Dimitri who also happens to be, by some sick cosmic twist of fate, a hot, charming irresistible tour guide?

If I were myself I think the answer would have be glaringly, screamingly obvious. But since that Wednesday-morning mental breakdown, I wasn't sure about anything anymore, and I was starting to long for the reassuring confines of a padded room.

Perhaps I was having a quarter-life crisis. I'd read about them and apparently they were as real as the crisis that sees your father buying himself a sports car, setting up a Twitter profile, and dating one of your friends. I was also at least three drinks (okay, at least six) over the legal limit, and it was clearly messing with the part of my brain that usually dispensed sound, solid advice. It was messing with my brain full stop, actually. I felt mad and unrestrained and quite frankly, it worried me.

"So?" he asked again.

"Fine. But let me just say that I'm a dentist so I'm no stranger to inflicting pain on people so if you dare try anything I'll…" I slapped my hand over my mouth. What the hell had I just said?

"Sorry. I didn't mean to imply that you are some kind of hot Greek playboy who takes advantage of…*Shit!*" My hand flew up to my mouth again.

"Sorry. Sorry! Sorry! I really didn't mean to say that you were hot, either, like I'm some kind of woman with a lusty crush… *Fuck!*"

This time I slapped both my hands across over my mouth and bit my lip to stop it all from falling out. What was happening to me? Normally I had filters that stopped me from vomiting out the first thing that came into my mind. Why weren't the filters working?

He laughed. "No worries. I'm a perfect gentleman."

"You don't look like a gentleman," I screamed in my head; luckily my hands were over my mouth. He held the door open with a smile that seemed to have spread from ear to ear now. I quickly averted my gaze and looked at my ever-so-large feet as I walked into his house hoping to hell that whoever was controlling my mouth would stop soon.

"So a doctor then," he suddenly said. "I should have been calling you Dr. Jane Smith this whole time. Why didn't you tell me?"

"Why would I tell you? I mean, it's not like it's a big deal." I wobbled into the middle of his lounge and looked around.

The interior of his place was just as surprising as the outside, if not more so. I looked around the room, and nothing looked right. It was small and, much like my hotel room, looked like the inside of a cave. On a small kitchen table, a bowl of fruit looked like it had been placed perfectly as if he was waiting for *Garden and Home* magazine to pop around for a photo shoot.

I glanced to my left to see a small lounge area with a blue sofa and perfectly laid-out scatter cushions. A large bookcase jam-packed with books stood to the left of the sofa—for show? The coffee table in front of the sofa had a vase of flowers on it—flowers? The room was so neat it looked like no one had ever lived here. Everything looked clean and perfect. This place screamed *girlfriend, girlfriend, girlfriend* and I wondered where the hell she was.

There was only one disorganized-looking element in the whole place, and that was the wall opposite the sofa. It was covered entirely in a massive, old-looking map of Greece. Pins and photos and little notes had been stuck all over it. But the rest of his apartment was impeccable.

Where were the bachelor beer cans on the floor? The self-absorbed pictures of himself hanging on the wall? The hot model panties strewn across the sofa? I looked up and realized that he was watching me.

"What?" he asked, looking vaguely concerned.

"It's so, so…neat."

He walked over to the stove and turned it on. "That's what growing up with six sisters does to you." His voice had a lightness to it.

"Six?" I echoed.

"Sisters," he said again with a teasing tone to his voice. "I had to take showers at the neighbors' house. Our bathroom was always busy."

"I bet your neighbor enjoyed that." Oh fuck! I shouldn't have taken my hands off my mouth. Maybe if I deflected quickly he wouldn't notice. "Did you know that a shower uses about two gallons of water per minute?"

He smiled again. "I do now."

"I mean, obviously you would use more gallons if there were say, *two* people using the shower...like maybe you do here...?" Oh God! I couldn't believe I was trying to ask him whether he had a girlfriend. It was so embarrassingly obvious.

His smile grew bigger, "No. Only two gallons a minute is used here, unless one of my sisters crashes here after a night out."

"Oh. I wasn't really asking that, you know. I was just starting a fact about water usage and all. Since water is one of our scarcest resources."

Dimitri nodded. "Of course. I didn't think you were." He folded his big, muscly arms and looked at me. It was only now that I realized what he was wearing. A casual pair of knee-length shorts and a really worn V-neck shirt that looked like the kind of thing he slept in. It was so worn and stretched that the V hung low enough to offer a glimpse of his rather solid, tanned chest. The whole ensemble might have looked casual, but if you put a horse and an emaciated woman in a cardigan next to him, and gave him a polo stick, you'd have a full-page high-fashion spread.

"I'll go make the coffee, which I know you don't drink," he said playfully, "but I'll bring you one just in case you change your mind, even though I know you don't change your mind about things."

He moved off and I made my way to the small sofa. My legs were starting to feel like overcooked strands of spaghetti, and my head felt like someone had poured fizzy liquid into my skull. I collapsed into it with a loud thump—*so ladylike*. But the sofa was soft, the pillows rather fluffy, and it was exactly what my sore body needed. I closed my eyes for a moment and quickly realized it wasn't a good idea when the room started to spin. I opened them again and let them float around the room once more. They finally came to rest on the massive map on the wall. Something about it drew me, and I got up and walked over to it. The photos that had been pinned to the map looked old. They had tatty corners, as if someone had spent hours looking at them. There were small handwritten notes stuck to the map as well as a dried flower; a few postcards and some small souvenirs, like a key ring, hung from one of the pins.

"Here." Suddenly Dimitri was next to me and presented me with a thimble-sized cup of black liquid. I took it tentatively and peered inside. The cup looked like it was full of thick black tar. "And here." He held out his other hand and presented me with my sunglasses.

"Where did you find these?" I reached out and took them from him, slipping them onto my head for safekeeping.

"You must have dropped them on the ground when you were hiding in that bush...I nearly didn't give them back to you, though."

"Why?"

"Well, despite the fact that they protect your eyes against harmful UV rays..." He smiled. Did he remember everything I said to him? "...you wear them too much, and your eyes—"

"I know. Weird."

He shook his head. "You've got the most beautiful eyes I've ever seen."

His words slammed into me like a slab of concrete falling from the sky. We locked eyes and a strange feeling worked its way through me—not quite shivers or tingles, but something even more paralyzing. He held my gaze and I felt like I couldn't blink.

"Try the coffee." Dimitri flicked his eyes down to it. "It'll make you feel better."

I raised the coffee to my lips slowly even though I wasn't sure coffee beans would be any help to me right now. I needed something stronger. Perhaps a lobotomy. I took my first sip and the bitter liquid assaulted my mouth.

"What's all this?" I asked, indicating the map.

"My adventures," he said.

"Your adventures? But these photos look really old."

He reached out and touched one with care, as if it was something precious and breakable. "They were given to me as a boy. I used to spend hours and hours looking at them and trying to imagine these far-off magical places that I wanted to go to one day."

"Really?"

"I grew up on a tiny island. Only five hundred people actually lived there, so not much happened. For as long as I can remember, I used to stand on the beach and look out at the sea, wondering what the hell was beyond the blue horizon and when I'd be able to see it all. I wanted to leave so badly, I even built myself a raft once and packed a bag of food and a pair of binoculars. I had visions of sailing the seas and fighting pirates." He chuckled softly to himself as if remembering something amusing. "First wave the raft hit, it broke into pieces."

"You must have given your mother nightmares," I said.

"I did. I was always disappearing on these huge adventures. These photos were like puzzle pieces to some great, giant treasure map for me. I still have a box of them that aren't up on the wall yet."

"They're beautiful," I admitted. Not that I had any desire to see any more of Greece. I brought the coffee back up to my lips and sipped again. It didn't improve on second tasting, so I just glugged it down in two large gulps before placing the empty cup on the table. It started to work its magic instantly. The black liquid entered my veins and seemed to chase all the alcohol out. Suddenly I felt alert. Very.

"Whew! Strong stuff."

Dimitri nodded with a smile. "So?"

"So what?"

"Tell me about yourself. I've told you about me." He walked over to the couch and sat. "I bet you have interesting stories."

"Trust me. I don't." I sat opposite him.

"Everyone has an interesting story." He leaned forward and his eyes seemed to challenge me. "Who is Dr. Jane Smith?" His accent was so gorgeous, you almost didn't hear the words when he spoke.

"I'm just a dentist, you know. It's not as if I'm running around performing cutting-edge neurosurgery on dying children. It's not that impressive. Trust me."

"I think it's very impressive. It takes dedication and hard work to get through . . . how many years is it?"

"Seven. I've just finished."

"Impressive," he said again, sounding completely serious. He wasn't mocking me because I was a dentist and pulled people's teeth out for a living. Or telling me how much *everyone* hated dentists, or how much he hated going to the dentist—all the usual things people did when they found out what I did for a living, which did wonders for my ever-diminishing self-esteem.

"So? Who is Jane Smith?" he again.

"Mmmm...Who is Jane Smith?" I repeated his words, contemplating them as I went. I rolled them around in my mind a few times. I felt vaguely detached from myself now, as if I could look at things objectively. For starters, the Jane Smith I knew, and had known my whole life, wouldn't be here. She wouldn't ever find herself in a situation like this, sitting next to a man like Dimitri. She would be at home in her neat apartment with the laminate wood flooring, cooking herself a healthy microwave meal, feeding her pet fish, and settling down to read the latest dental periodical and ensure she was ahead of all the latest oral trends. If she was feeling wild and crazy, she might be out having a glass of wine with her friends.

"She's not the person sitting here right now, that's for sure. She doesn't do things like this."

Dimitri studied me for a moment or two, as if he was unsure of what to say next. He looked confused by my answer. "Why?"

"Never mind. You wouldn't understand. I barely understand it all myself, so it would be a totally useless exercise trying to explain to someone else when *I* don't even know what's going on at the moment." I was vaguely aware that my speech was getting faster and faster as I spoke.

"Try me?" He sat back and crossed his legs.

The coffee buzzed through my brain, making me feel more alert than I had in a few days. "You're not really interested in all this," I said quickly, remembering the guy in the bar.

"No. I am. Really." He said it so empathetically that I believed him...maybe I *wanted* to believe him. "Seriously, Jane. I couldn't be more interested in you if I tried."

"Huh?" My mouth dried up again. Maybe it was from the coffee, maybe it was from the way he'd just said that to me. The way it had oozed with charm and the way he had leaned forward and placed his elbows on his knees and was now cupping his face in his hands, as if he was a child at story time waiting for the teacher to read to him.

"Fine," I conceded. "Okay, how do I explain this to you without you thinking that I'm completely mad?"

"I don't think you're mad."

I *tsk*ed. "Well, I'm definitely not myself."

"Why not?"

"*Because I'm here!*" I slapped the sofa with my free hand. "Here, in this room, on your sofa, in Greece running around on a stupid whim. Trust me, it's soooo unlike me to do something like this! I don't run around chasing invisible ghosts on some kind of weird, barely there hunch and get drunk in bars and then throw drinks in people's faces and run and fall and trip into the night and... *Whoa* ... this coffee is really strong! Talk about sobering up in seconds. See, and I don't even drink coffee. Just more proof that I am not myself."

I stopped my rant and looked up at Dimitri, who seemed to be smiling. That was not the reaction I was expecting. I was half expecting him to look at me as if I had just mutated into some strange alien creature.

"No... no... I don't think you quite grasp the severity of the situation here, Dimitri," I continued. "Jane Smith, Dr. Jane Smith as you like to say, is logical, precise. Jane Smith doesn't say things like she's been saying all night tonight. She doesn't speak her mind and say what she wants and do what she wants, she barely knows what she wants anymore and . . ." I paused. *"Oh God*, and now I'm speaking about myself in the third person."

Dimitri laughed out loud. It was the second time I'd heard him laugh, and it did something to his features that made him even sexier and more appealing. He was mesmerizing and hypnotizing and all of a sudden I was swept away again on a bubble of lusty thoughts where I imagined that the two of us were naked and having sex on the beach, except there wasn't any sand there.

"So if you do one thing right now that you really want to, what would it be?" he asked.

"I want to sleep with you."

Chapter Fifteen

⌒

I waited for the earth to open up and for gravity to pull me down into the lava-filled pits below. I waited for a bolt of lightning to strike, a gale-force wind to sweep through his place and carry me off. I would have welcomed bandits running in and kidnapping me at this point...

I was so stunned by my own words that I was incapable of speaking, which made the whole thing about a million times worse. The deathly silence just seemed to highlight my words. I swear, I could almost hear them echoing around his cave-like room.

Speak, Jane. Open your mouth and explain that it was a mistake, a joke. You were trying to be funny, ironic in a postmodern way...

My brain swirled from one thought to the next, and my heart started pounding again. "I...I...it...I..." I stuttered like those bandits had stolen my tongue and inconveniently left the rest of my body behind. "I didn't mean to say that. I don't expect you to, you probably wouldn't want to, either. I mean, you're so, so, so hot and I really do want to sleep with you, but I don't, because you are Dimitri the tour guide."

"What's my name and profession got to do with it, Jane?"

"Everything!" I spluttered. "It has everything to do with it and why I'm here and acting like a total moron and wanting to have sex with you when I shouldn't." I shook my head. "Oh God, I don't know what I'm saying anymore. I never do these kinds of things, never. And certainly not with men that look like you because... look at me."

"I *am* looking, Jane." His words came out breathily.

"You are?" His words stopped me dead in my rambling tracks.

"I've been looking at you since I met you."

"Huh?" My legs turned to Jell-O, and despite all my better judgment I wanted to have sex with this man more than I'd ever wanted anything in my entire life. Besides, what was the harm? I'd already decided I was going to leave this stupid island tomorrow anyway. I was leaving and I'd never, ever see him again and how often does a girl get to say she's had sex with the hottest guy on the planet?

My head seemed to start nodding on its own. "Uh-huh. Okay, yes. Sure." It continued its nod as Dimitri stood up and moved toward me. Anxious panic mixed with excitement and surged through my body, putting every one of my senses on high alert. *Is this really happening?*

He shifted a little closer and suddenly I could see it, an intention in his eyes that was undeniable. A magnetic force that hadn't existed a few moments ago started pulling us together slowly until in one swift movement he was sitting next to me, cupping my face, and kissing me.

He was kissing *me.*

My body reacted in a million different ways that it had never reacted before. I was so stunned that at first I didn't kiss him back. The shock seemed to have paralyzed my mouth. But then as his kiss deepened and slowed, I was swept up in the moment and I kissed him back. *God, I haven't used my lips for kissing in so long, I hope they're doing the right thing!*

My hands took on a mind of their own and suddenly they were wrapped around the back of his head, pulling him closer. *Who is this girl that's doing these things?* He reacted by shifting even closer to me on the small sofa, until my back was pushing into the hard wooden arm. One of his hands left my face, trailed down my neck, and continued even farther until his fingertips grazed my breast through my shirt. I flinched at his touch and natural forces took over control of my body, making me squirm and tremble for more.

It was pure, unadulterated lust, and it warmed my body from the inside out until I felt like I was on fire. Our lips tangled together and his hand slipped up under my top. He caressed my breast through my bra until I was an incoherent lump of blubber in his hands.

I think I heard myself say his name in a breathy tone I didn't recognize. Then we were up on our feet—I'm not sure how. He was pushing me toward his room, kissing me the whole time. *Oh my God, he's going to have sex with me!* I was about to have sex with the hottest man on the planet. I needed a bikini wax! I needed to brush my teeth! I needed a quick crash course in how to do this!

"I, I have to warn you," I said breathily in between the kissing, "I've been told that I'm not very good at this. You know, sex."

"I doubt that." His lips trailed down my neck and he started to nibble on my earlobe. I nearly died.

"And I've only slept with two people in my entire life. I'm not very practiced in this department and I'm sure you've been with a million different models who are probably really beautiful and don't have thigh cellulite and are probably really supple because they do a lot of yoga."

Dimitri stopped kissing me, smiled at me, and then silenced me with a finger to my lips. "Shhhh."

"I'm not supple," I said through his finger, which was pressed down on my lips. "I don't think I can even touch my toes."

"I don't want supple, Jane. I want you."

Holy shit! He did not just say that to me! But it was the thing that seemed to give me the confidence to let go. To get lost . . .

I'm not sure how I mustered the courage to do it, but I started pulling his shirt off over his head. The next thing I knew my hands were frantically trying to unzip his pants as he crushed me against the wall and kissed me deeply. We stumbled into his bedroom in a desperate frenzy of hands and lips and tongues and tumbled onto his bed. He pulled me onto his lap and ground me into him, which just seemed to be my cue to completely lose it. I had officially surrendered all control of my body to the mysterious forces of nature and there was no longer anything I could do to stop it.

I pulled my top off over my head and tossed it enthusiastically across the room, where it hit the wall and landed on the floor with a soft thump. Dimitri reached up and undid my bra, tossing it against the wall as well. I let out a loud moan as my breasts tumbled free and straight into his hands and warm mouth.

"Holy...crap! I mean, is this..." I moaned again as he moved his mouth to my other breast. "Um...are we really doing this? Is this actually happening?"

"This is so fucking happening right now, Jane," Dimitri said, pulling me off him and rolling me over onto my back until he was right on top of me. The weight of his body crushed me into the bed and I opened my legs and wrapped them around him. I closed my eyes again when his lips came crashing back down on mine.

"Oh God," I moaned and arched my body toward him. The sensations were almost too overwhelming to handle. I slid my hands between us and unzipped my pants and started trying to wiggle out of them while his body was crushing into me.

"Let me help with those?" Dimitri sat up and grabbed the top of my pants. I lifted my hips off the bed to give better access and he pulled them down to where my shoes were keeping them from coming off. He grabbed my sneakers and pulled them both off simultaneously, tossing each one at the same spot on the wall. I burst out laughing, and he smiled down at me. Next my pants came off and he held them up to me for a second with a kind of questioning look. I nodded at him and the pants flew into the same wall. We both laughed as he collapsed back down onto me, but the laughter stopped in seconds and was replaced by the sounds of my moans as he ran a finger over me.

"Wait!" I stopped him. "Do you have condoms?"

Dimitri looked at me and smiled. "You do."

Shit! I hated to admit this, but my mother's little gift might actually come in handy after all.

"They're in my bag." I pointed to the living room. Dimitri

looked at the living room and then shook his head as if it were too far away. He leaned over me, opened the drawer next to his bed, and pulled out a pack. He ripped the plastic off with his teeth and then seconds later had me pinned under him.

I moaned loudly when he was finally inside me. The anticipation and buildup only made it feel even better. I couldn't believe I was doing this! I wrapped my legs around him and ground up to meet him with every thrust. Our bodies moved faster and faster together in a desperate need for each other. There was nothing polite and restrained about this. This was lust. Pure and simple and fucking amazing.

Our bodies slammed together over and over again. They were hot and sticky with sweat. Our breathing was loud and jagged and punctuated with moans and cries. I dug my fingernails into his back and closed my eyes as I felt the waves of pleasure building inside me.

Dimitri thrust harder and faster and I clung on for dear life as the orgasm tore through me. Dimitri, too, moaned loudly; his body stiffened and then totally collapsed on top of me. We lay there panting together and dripping sweat all over each other until he finally rolled off me.

I lay there on my back looking up at the ceiling in a state of shock. Could sex really be that good? I smiled happily to myself and closed my eyes and just before falling asleep a thought hit me. *Whoa . . . well, happy birthday to me.*

* * *

I shot out of bed, and my brain thumped against the inside of my skull. Agony! I looked around and had no idea where the hell I was. For a moment the confusion was so overwhelming that I didn't even remember my own name. Okay, I knew this wasn't my hotel. And I knew this wasn't my house. I was in Greece, that much I was sure of. I looked at the bedside table. Two aspirin and a glass of water with a small note that read:

Take these.

I grabbed the pills. I didn't need any convincing; without further ado I popped them into my mouth and swallowed. But who had written the note...

"Oh God no!" I hung my head as waves of unadulterated shame twisted my stomach into knots. Images from last night started ticking through my head, like an old black-and-white movie. I'd acted like a complete moron last night. Getting drunk, throwing drinks around like a lunatic, getting lost, calling Dimitri, drinking that evil coffee and making a total idiot of myself and...

"Oh no!" I moaned loudly and clutched my head, not daring to look up. I'd asked him to sleep with me and, and...

My heart jumped into my mouth and I looked down. Sure enough, I was completely naked. I'd had sex with him. I'd had sex! What the hell was wrong with me?

"Jesus, Jane," I hissed out loud. I felt disgusted. Despite vowing that I would never do it, I'd come to Greece and done the exact same thing as my mother—fallen for the charm of the Greek tour guide. I glanced around the room, looking for my clothes. I stood up quickly. The immediate head rush forced me to clutch the chair nearby. I held on until the horrific feeling passed. The nausea was so intense that I didn't know if I would be able to fight it, or whether I was about to get sick all over his room. *Classy!*

I saw that all my clothes had been folded neatly and piled on a chair; he'd brought my bag into the room and placed it on the floor next to my clothes. I went for my clothes and started putting them back on. Then I walked over to the mirror on the wall and looked at myself. I wished I hadn't. My makeup was smudged, and I had grown a massive pimple in the middle of my forehead overnight. It was probably all the toxic sludge in my veins trying to come out. It was the kind of pimple that you might as well pencil an eyebrow above and accept that you have a third eye. But worst of all, there was something very wrong with my hair. I reached up and ran my fingers through it, and that's when I realized that it looked like someone had taken a pair of scissors to it. What the hell had I done to myself?

Chunks of hair stood up straight at the top of my forehead because they were substantially shorter than the rest. Had someone cut my hair last night? A blurry image of me ripping my hair out of a tangled bougainvillea and hearing snapping sounds flashed through my mind. I looked down at my leg, which was scratched and dotted with splotches of dried blood. I think this would go down in history as the night I made the biggest fool of myself. It would probably be something they write on my tombstone:

HERE LIES JANE. SHE LED A NORMAL, BORING LIFE EXCEPT
FOR THAT ONE NIGHT SHE GOT WILD AND CRAZY AND ENDED UP
LOSING HER MIND AND HAVING A ONE-NIGHT STAND WITH A
TOTALLY HOT STRANGER!

I wondered how many women had stood here in front of this mirror looking at themselves and wondering how the hell they had ended up doing this. Dimitri had a way of making you forget yourself in the moment. I was so inexperienced in situations like this. I needed help, I needed...

I went for my bag, unzipped it, and pulled my phone out. There were various happy birthday messages on it, but I ignored them all and went straight to WhatsApp.

WHATSAPP GROUP: Jane goes to Greece

Jane: HELP! I just had sex with this guy and I'm in his room and I don't know what to do.

I typed faster than I'd ever typed before and it felt like hours before the first message came bouncing back.

Lilly: WHAT?

Annie: WTFH

Val: Who?

Jane: This guy. I got drunk last night and lost in the streets and he saved me and gave me coffee and brought me back to his place and he's just so hot and I asked him to have sex with me.

Lilly: You asked him to have sex with you???

Annie: Who is this? What have you done with our friend Jane?

Val: LMFAO! ☺ You asked him! You said, "please have sex with me?" hahaha Clearly you partied like it was your birthday.

Lilly: haha! Sipped Bacardi like it was your birthday.

Annie: Go Shawty it's your birthday LOL

Jane: Stop rapping. It's not funny. I'm in his room.

Annie: Where's he?

Jane: I don't know.

Lilly: Are you safe? Should we be worried, he's not some ax murderer or something.

Jane: No. He's not. At least I don't think so. So what should I do?

Val: This is hysterical! Hahaha

Lilly: Well, usually you might go and have a cup of coffee together or maybe breakfast or—

Jane: No, you don't get it. I don't EVER want to see him again.

Annie: Was the sex that bad? ☺

Lilly: Oh God! Awkward.

Val: He couldn't have been as bad as Mr. Klingon.

Annie: What did he do . . . and don't leave out the details.

Val: Please don't tell me he was one of those guys that just spanks your ass in the middle of it without asking?

Annie: Tell me there were no nipple clamps at least.

Val: LOL

Jane: Guys!!! Stop. It's not that, the sex was . . .

I stopped typing and stared down at the phone wondering if I could even say it to them.

Jane: OK. Best sex ever. Best sex of my life. Amazing. Mind blowing. I literally passed out at the end. You happy?

Val: LOL

Lilly: So what's the problem? Go and find him for seconds.

Jane: No. I still don't want to see him again.

Annie: Why?

Jane: It's complicated. Really, really—

Stormy: do Yuo see. A window ?

Annie: Stormy, it's about time.

Stormy: I once climb.ed out of Wimdow and dowN fire escapes !

Val: Of course you did!!

A noise coming from behind the door made me look up.

Jane: Shit. I think he's coming. Bye

I froze to the spot and waited for the door to open and for Dimitri to walk in. But he didn't. The noise continued, though, and I walked over to the door and peered out. Dimitri was standing in the doorway talking to another guy. They were both laughing at the top of their voices. Dimitri gestured in my direction, and the two men looked at each other with a smile. Oh my God, he was talking about me! He was telling this guy that he had a chick in his room that he had shagged the hell out of. I knew it would mean nothing to him, that I'd amount to nothing more than another notch on the old belt; believe me, I was under no illusions. But to have it confirmed, and in such a public manner, *no words . . .*

And then he did something that made me want to puke. He began to hit his fist into his hand, over and over again. Harder. Faster. Oh my God, he was reenacting the sex! He and the other man laughed hysterically now and talked merrily. I could only imagine what was being said about me.

Hahaha . . . yeah, I bent her over and showed her who was boss!
Oh yeah, and she took it all!

I tried to stifle a gasp as Dimitri bent imaginary me over and his hands came down in spanking gestures. I quickly closed the door. This was horrifying. I needed to get out of here, but there was no way I was doing the walk of shame through his living room and out his front door.

Then I looked at the window. It was small, but big enough to climb through. I could climb out and make a run for it, and deal with how to get back to my hotel later. Then I would pack my bags and get off this island as fast as humanly possible. I would never have to see Dimitri again, ever. I could forget this night and this stupid quest I had come on and just go home. I couldn't believe I was actually considering taking Stormy's advice. I would probably, under normal circumstances, take my mother's advice over Stormy's . . . but desperate times.

I grabbed my bag—it felt even heavier this morning, or maybe I was just weaker from all the night's activities—and started climbing through the window. Luckily it was round and smooth so there were no sharp corners to contend with. But it only took a few seconds to realize what a bad idea this had been, and by then it was too late.

The window didn't actually lead out into the street, but seemed to lead onto the retaining wall that bordered the neighbor's property. I should have known: These houses were packed together like sardines. An ear-piercing shriek rang out and I realized I was looking directly into an old woman's bedroom. I held my hand up indicating that she shouldn't panic. I was friendly, I wasn't here to rob her of her life savings, but she continued to scream. She got louder and louder. Suddenly she ran outside and turned on the hose. The water hit me with such force that it stung.

The pelting continued for what seemed like ages. Then I heard a man's voice, and another, and the steady stream of water stopped. I looked through the wet curtain of hair covering my face and to my horror Dimitri and his friend stood there. Another neighbor had come out to see what all the commotion was about, and at least eight more people had emerged from the house next door. How many people lived there?

Greek was being screamed and hand gestures were being thrown around. I stared in horror at the scene that had broken out in front of me. I tried to wiggle free from the window . . . and that's when I realized I was stuck. *How can this moment get any worse?*

Dimitri stepped forward. "What are you doing?"

I felt lost. Every little bit of self-respect I had, every iota of sense and sanity and any filter that had once existed . . . were all gone. I felt empty, and although I was now surrounded by at least ten people, I had never felt so alone in my entire life. I had nothing to lose right now. I had already lost it all. I was wet, nauseous, headachy, and way past feeling embarrassed.

I opened my mouth and the rage tumbled out. "What the hell does it look like, Dimitri?" I yelled. "I should think it would be pretty damn obvious to everyone, wouldn't it?" I looked pointedly at my audience.

The people all stepped a little closer; they were gathering in droves now. They actually looked excited, foaming at the mouth as if they were watching an episode of *Dr. Phil* where the results of the polygraph were about to be revealed. Only this was real. This was my life and it had completely fallen apart. Ripped at the seams and exploded.

"Why didn't you come through the house?" His tone was soft and gentle. God, it pissed me off.

"Why? *Why?*" I wailed at the top of my lungs, which seemed to cause more heads to pop out of windows and passersby to stop. "Maybe it's because I don't want to make the walk of shame past you and him"—I pointed an accusing finger at the man next to him—"after you so explicitly showed him how we had you-know-what last night. Which we should never, ever, never, ever, do you hear me...*ever!*"—I yelled that last word—"ever have done." There was wild mania to my voice now. I had officially crossed over into the dark side and it wasn't pretty. The look that washed over Dimitri's face was one of shock, followed by horror and maybe even pain. Then he rushed up to me.

"Jane. There's nothing wrong with making love."

I burst out laughing hysterically—think *pack of hyenas in mating season*. "Make love. Make *love?*" I wailed at the top of my voice, which had a high-pitched, shrill quality to it. "What a load of shit! What's with you Greeks and all this love and romance? Island of love this, and island of love that!"

A few more roars of laughter rose up from some of the neighbors, and amused words were thrown around in Greek. He turned to the crowd and shouted at them, which only seemed to spur more laughter from the whole peanut gallery.

"Jane, I would never tell anyone what happened between us last night."

"Then what was all this about?" I tried to mime the smacking hand movements that he had made this morning. More laughter rose up. Someone even clapped.

"And you lot can all stop laughing at me!" I shot angry dagger looks at everyone, which shut some of them up.

He looked confused for a moment or two, then, "Jane, this is the plumber, Dimitri. I was just telling him about my burst pipe last week."

At this, I screeched. My vocal cords felt like someone had just run sandpaper over them. "And that's the other thing about this place...why is everyone named Dimitri? Huh? Can't someone be named Christo, or Nic or Meze-madopolo-poulus-stuses or one of those other Greek-sounding names? But no, it has to be Dimitri so it's impossible for me to come here and find my biological father who also happens to be, surprise, big surprise, Dimitri!"

I slapped my hand on the windowsill to try to give vent to the feelings that were overwhelming me. "I hate it here. I hate Greece. I hate all your stupid dipping sauces and potted plants and your bougainvillea and I hate your coffee and I'm allergic to cats by the way! And most of all, I hate myself for coming here. How did I think I was ever going to find him? I mean, all I know is that his name is Dimitri and twenty-five years ago he was a tour guide sailing the fucking seas, or whatever else he did. That's all. That's *it*. I don't even know which island he's on! My biological 'mother,' Phoebe, who wants nothing to do with me I might add, didn't bother telling me that little piece of info and I only discovered yesterday that there are two hundred and twenty-seven inhabited islands. Let that sink in, people." I turned to the crowd, who all seemed transfixed (this had become a full-blown dramatic monologue). "I would need a lifetime to look on every island for him."

I hung my head in silence. There was a sense of anticipation buzzing in the air; everyone was hanging on my every word, and I knew they were waiting for more. Waiting to watch the train wreck crash and burn even harder, and I didn't care that I was giving them what they wanted.

"And then there's stupid me. Who comes here and does the exact same thing her biological mother did. And I vowed I would never be anything like her, *ever*. I don't want to be anything like the woman who gave me away because I meant *nothing* to her." My voice caught in my throat. "And now I'll *never* meet my father— and I'll *never* find out where I come from or where I belong. I'll never know who the hell I really fucking am and that's why I'm climbing out of your window, Dimitri!" My awareness of the crowd disappeared and an internal silence fell over me. I could hear a whisper of the most painful loss I've ever experienced in my life.

"I just want to go home. *Please*. I just want to go home and forget that any of this happened." When I looked up again, everyone's faces had changed. They were looking at me with a mixture of sympathy and shock. A few were muttering to one another in Greek and nodding.

Then the old woman stepped closer. "Perhaps," she said in very broken English, "the man you are looking for you cannot find, until you find yourself."

I gazed down at this little woman who had gone all Deepak Chopra on me. "What does that even mean?" I said to her. But deep down, I knew. There was something in that statement that cut me to my core and resonated with something deep inside.

"Jane." Dimitri spoke softly, as the audience had started to clear. "Just come down from there."

"I can't." I was defeated.

"Yes, you can!"

"No, you don't understand. I'm stuck."

He walked over and studied me. God, this couldn't get any more humiliating if I were naked.

Dimitri smiled at me, a soft, sweet smile that just made me want to cry, if I knew how to. "The strap of your bag is hooked on the window clasp. Let me help you." His hand shot up and he wiggled the bag free. He pulled it toward himself and as he did, something slipped out.

I watched in slow-motion horror as Dimitri's cardboard head gracefully flew out of the bag and wafted down to the ground, where it elegantly landed by his feet.

Chapter Sixteen

⌒

I sat in the back of the cab that Dimitri had called for me. I was still damp from the hosing I'd received but at least he'd been kind enough to not acknowledge his cardboard head. He'd helped me out of the window and ushered me inside. He'd then tried to sit me down, calm me, feed me, pacify me, and tell me to stay.

But all I wanted to do was get home and resume the life I'd created for myself. I needed to stop asking myself all these stupid existential questions about who I was and where I came from and just accept that I was Jane Smith. Twenty-five, half Greek, adopted dentist who still felt like a foreigner in her own family. People had it so much worse than me and here I was complaining. After fetching my bags from my hotel and checking out, I walked into the airport in a weird ghostly state. I soon ascertained that the only flight back home was the next day and it was full. The best they could do was put me on standby and see what happened. The reservationist was positive, though. "So many people decide not to go home. They fall in love with Greece, or a man, and they stay." She'd winked at me. Clearly she didn't know who I was.

For a split second I thought about going back out there and booking myself into a hotel, but it was clear by now that Greece and I did not agree with each other. I didn't want to be in Greece, and airports are considered neutral territory anyway—neither here nor there. At least I wasn't in Greece when I stood inside this building.

I spent the next few hours walking aimlessly up and down the international terminal. My phone beeped again with more birthday messages from my family. I ignored them all. I just wanted to forget that I had even been born. It wasn't even dark outside yet, but I was exhausted. I'd do what those people stranded in airports for days because of some freak snowstorm do—make myself a little nest on the chairs and settle in. I rolled up one of my shirts and used it for a pillow as I stretched out across three rather uncomfortable seats. I pulled my phone out.

WHATSAPP GROUP: Jane goes to Greece

Jane: I'm coming home.

Annie: What? Why?

Val: So soon?

Jane: This thing just hasn't worked out. You were right. It's impossible to find my father.

Annie: I'm so sorry.

Lilly: And what happened to the guy?

Jane: Long story.

Lilly: Let us know when you're home and we'll come over. XX

Val: I'll bring the wine.

Stormy: U musn:t comes home ! YoU nnot finished there yetr

Jane: What the hell does that even mean?

Stormy: just don;t gET on that plane . STay there

Jane: Not going to happen!!!!

I put my phone back into my bag, closed my eyes, and felt the pain wash over me. I'd wanted to find my father more than anything in the world. Finding him was the last hope I had of finding myself. Without him I was doomed to a life of never knowing. Floating nebulously from one concept of myself to another, not quite Jane, but not quite Tracy, either. Not really Greek, but not really a South African...just nobody. A nameless, faceless ghost of a person.

* * *

I felt a gentle hand on my shoulder and became aware of a soft voice. I must have fallen asleep.

"Jane?"

I opened my eyes and through the strands of hair hanging in my eyes, Dimitri's face came into focus. He gave me a small smile, and I felt his fingertips push a strand of wayward hair out of my face. He dropped down to the floor and sat cross-legged in front of me. I didn't move; instead I lay there looking at him sideways.

"What are you doing here?"

"I came to ask you to stay," he said, looking straight into my eyes. It didn't look like he was joking.

"That's not going to happen. I'm going home."

"Just hear me out. I've got a proposition for you."

This vaguely piqued my interest and I sat up in my chair, crossing my legs under me. I wondered what kind of proposition this guy could have for me after everything that had happened between us.

"I called a private investigator," he said. At those words I sat up straight. *Why the fuck didn't I think of that?*

"And?" I asked anxiously.

"He thinks he can help find your father."

Excitement bubbled in my veins and I almost shot out of my seat, but then as fast as it bubbled, it diffused. "It's too late. This was such a stupid thing to do. I need to stop looking for answers I'll never find and just get on with the life I have."

"Jane, you came here for a reason. Don't leave without trying one more time. Please."

"How does the investigator think he's going to find him anyway? I have nothing to go on other than his name and what he did."

"Well…" Dimitri paused for a moment and looked around. "He said something about looking at flight manifests from that time and seeing if he could find a South African flight with someone called Phoebe on it. Then he said something about cross-referencing that with a list of travel agencies from that time on that island…anyway, he said he thought it could be done. Not definitely, but possibly."

"Possibly?" I tried to hold them back and rein them in, but my excitement levels skyrocketed. Would I really be able to find him? I looked over at Dimitri and could see there was more. "So what are you proposing?"

"Stay for a few days while the investigator searches for him and come with me on a tour of the islands. Let me show you Greece, Jane. Let me show you how beautiful this place is and let me show you what it means to be Greek and—"

"No." I crossed my arms crossed my chest. "I'd rather sit here for a few days than go back out there...*with you.*"

Dimitri got up off the floor and sat next to me. "I'm really sorry about what happened last night. I shouldn't have let it go that far."

"You are?"

"Yes, I am. But it was just so hard to stop..." He briefly looked at me and then broke eye contact again.

"It was?" I asked.

He nodded. "I'd thought about it so many times since meeting you, and then when you asked me to and...but I shouldn't have."

"So you regret it all? I see." I couldn't hide the disappointment in my voice, which embarrassed me to no end.

"No! I don't regret what happened. Just how it happened."

I shrugged. "I suppose. I wasn't really myself last night." A long silence kicked in and we sat side by side saying nothing to each other for the longest time until eventually Dimitri broke it.

"Jane, let me show you around. Let me be your tour guide. You came here looking for something; let me help you find it. What happened last night won't happen again. I promise."

"And you really think this investigator can find my father?" I couldn't believe I was seriously considering his proposal. But I was.

"If there's one person that can, it's him."

I nodded slowly. My head was swimming with all this new information and with his proposal. I was also thinking about

Stormy's words, "*don't get on that plane.*" And a part of me didn't want to. But then again, look what had happened last time I'd listened to her.

"So what is your daily rate then?" I asked.

"My what?" This question seemed to throw him.

"If this is going to be a professional relationship, I want to know how much you cost?" I pulled my wallet out of my bag and opened it. I only had fifty euros.

He shrugged. "Leave that for now, we can talk about it later."

I shook my head. "You are providing me with a service, so I'm going to pay you."

He sighed and looked into my wallet. "Fifty euros is fine." He held his hand out reluctantly, and I placed the money in his palm. Somehow paying him made me feel better about what I was about to do. I was hiring a professional tour guide for the duration of my stay in Greece. Simple. Clean.

"Thanks," he mumbled halfheartedly as he shoved the note in his pocket. "Now come. Do you really want to spend your birthday in an airport?"

"How did you know?" I asked.

"I saw your birth date on your passport."

"Oh. That."

"Come. I want to show you something." He stood up and looked at me expectantly.

"What?"

"Trust me."

Chapter Seventeen

*W*e drove for ages in total silence. It felt awkward in the small space together, especially given that inconvenient little thing about us having sex with each other last night. I was desperately trying not to think about it, but every time his hand shot out to change a gear I wanted to either grab it and put it on my leg, or slap it away for daring to be so close to me. Dimitri finally stopped driving and pulled into a large and busy parking lot.

"This is the town of Oia, and you haven't lived until you've seen the sunset here."

We climbed out of the car and started walking, slowly. I looked around; more of those quaint little cave houses were dug into the steep slope of the town. We turned and walked down a narrow cobbled street. Oia was very much like Fira, with white cobblestones and whitewashed houses. Everything had that warm white glow but for the splash of a blue gate, or a hanging basket of bright-red flowers and bougainvillea.

We lazily wound our way up the small steps that seemed to be never-ending. We passed a large archway in one of the walls, and the sounds of cheerful chatter made me look through it. It was a small courtyard full of tables of laughing, eating people. Their happy noises harmonized with the sounds of music and the nearby water feature. They all looked so content. From there, the stairs got steeper still and the streets even narrower.

"Not far now." Dimitri turned and smiled at me.

The sun was starting to dip in the sky; the temperature was dropping, too. We had reached the top of the stairs, and his hand gently came around to my lower back as he guided me onto a small white wall. I climbed on, dangling my feet over the edge, and looked out at the world. From this little throne of stone I could see all the way across the sea and over the black cliffs as they fell steeply into the blue waters below.

Dimitri sat down next to me, shoulder touching shoulder. We sat together in silence as the sun slid lower and lower until it looked like it was bobbing up and down on the horizon. The sun began to spray bright-orange light across the sky and the sea below. The light flickered and shone off the luminous white buildings, creating a golden-orange glow throughout the whole town. It was as if a warm orange mist had descended and was winding its way through the streets and into every nook and cranny.

The thin wisps of clouds above had turned pink, and the sea rippled with an orange fire. The orange grew more intense until it was almost luminous and totally overwhelmed the blue of the sky and the sea. It was the most magical thing I'd ever seen. I turned and looked at Dimitri. He was bathed in a golden light.

"It's beautiful." My voice was an almost-inaudible whisper, and for the first time on this trip I could really see the beauty of this place.

"It only takes a moment to fall in love with Greece, Jane," Dimitri whispered in my ear. Something about his words, coupled with the view, the fact it was my birthday, *everything*: I suddenly felt overcome with so many emotions all at once. They flooded my body, one after the other, and rushed through me, shaking me to my core. The shock waves shook and rattled my internal walls, the ones I had carefully built up to keep my feelings contained. But as small hairline cracks started appearing in those walls, my feelings began to leak out, like a dripping tap at first, and then exploding out of me with a *whoosh* like a dam wall bursting.

It was only when I tasted the wet saltiness that I realized I was crying. I lifted my fingers to my face and touched it. It was wet and warm. *I was crying.* I was actually crying. I inhaled deeply, feeling a mixture of sadness and pure, unadulterated joy all at once.

"I'm…" I whimpered and the words got stuck in my throat. "I'm crying," I said and then started to laugh softly. The more I laughed, the more the tears started to stream down my face. Warm relief swept through me, leaving a calm, relaxed sensation in its wake. I felt like I could breathe more deeply than I had in ages.

"I'm crying," I whispered. "I haven't cried since I was eighteen years old." I turned and smiled at him while the tears continued to stream down my face. "I've never told anyone that before."

"Why?"

"I don't know, I guess I was ashamed. Like it wasn't normal or something. I've never told anyone this before, either, but I didn't even cry at my grandfather's funeral. I used an onion to fake the tears..." I burst out laughing and crying at the same time.

Another wave of pure, unadulterated relief felt like it was about to knock me off the wall. "Whoa! That feels good to say." I cried even harder. "This feels so good." I looked at my wet fingertips. "I'm crying."

Dimitri looked at me and smiled. I smiled back at him, tears still streaming down my face.

"I'm crying."

"Happy birthday, Jane."

* * *

But now that the floodgates had been opened, they were impossible to shut. In fact, my crying had escalated into full-on hysterical sobs. My blubbering and whimpering and borderline snot-bubble blowing was punctuated by a volcano eruption of words that shot out of my mouth at the same time. I was choking on the words as they came out, as if something had been stuck in the back of my throat this entire time, never allowing them to come out, until now. And now...everything was coming out of me. We walked back through the village to the car, and all the while it continued to spew out of my mouth.

I started telling him things, all sorts of things. And it felt good. The crying, coupled with the impromptu confessional, was some-how cathartic. My mind whirled from one thing to the next and at some stage I lost track of what I was even saying. Words spewed and tears flowed and it didn't look like they were going to be end-ing anytime soon...

"...I always felt like a disappointment to my mother..."

"...and some days I crave carbs sooooo badly..."

"...they are so fucking gorgeous and sometimes I hate them for it...how can I hate my own sisters..."

"...It's like I always felt like the ugly duckling and that people judged me by the way I looked..."

"...he screamed in Klingon when he came. I mean, Klingon!"

"...always the odd one out. Always!"

"...not that he ever gave me an earth-shattering orgasm..."

"...I just want someone to love me, *me*. The real me..."

"...and that's why I prefer the company of my pet fish..."

"...not that I know who the real me is..."

"...I just always feel like I'm not good enough..."

"...Okay, yes, I had a sex dream about you on the plane, no big deal..."

The car stopped, but my tearful rant continued.

"...but I just don't think anyone will ever love me..."

"...and I swear I put on ten pounds just from eating that bread stick..."

"...sometimes I just feel so unlovable..."

It was then that I noticed we were parked outside Dimitri's house and that he had turned in his seat and was listening to me intently. Two thoughts ran through my mind. One, what the fuck had I just told him? I'd been talking for half an hour and it was pretty blurry. And two:

"This isn't my hotel."

"You checked out of your hotel, remember?"

"So what does that mean?"

"You'll be sleeping over tonight."

And that set me off again instantly. More tears streamed. "But I don't want to stay here." I felt all the shame and embarrassment over what I had done with Dimitri last night rush back.

"I told you, that's not going to happen again," he said reassuringly.

"But what if your neighbors see me again? I don't think I could face them, after what happened with the window."

"No one cares about stuff like that, Jane. We Greeks are always having big public scenes. It's our way; if you aren't shouting dramatically, you aren't Greek. Your inner Greek is just coming out."

Truthfully, I wasn't sure I wanted my inner Greek barreling out. I sniffled as I walked back into his house for the second time in twenty-four hours. I mentally cursed myself for every step I took. I was sure that somewhere in my mind I knew this was the wrong thing to be doing, but for some reason I just wasn't able to stop.

"I'm so sorry I told you all that stuff in the car. I didn't mean to blabber and cry like that."

"Don't worry. I have six sisters, remember? I'm used to this kind of stuff." He gave me a soft, encouraging smile, and the friendly warmth in his eyes made me believe he wasn't just saying that.

"I should probably call my mom and tell her that I'm staying. I called her at the airport and told her that I was coming home early." I took my phone out of my bag, headed out the front door to the small courtyard, and dialed. She answered immediately and didn't even say hello.

"And can they get you onto the flight?" She sounded panicked. It was actually nice to hear her voice. It sounded like she was genuinely worried for me, and it felt good.

"Well…uhm…I've kind of decided to stay a little longer, Mom."

"Why?"

"The tour guide I was telling you about, he's helping me get in touch with a private investigator who thinks he can help me."

"Oh. That's great news."

"Really? You think that's great news?"

"Yes. I know how much finding him means to you, and I just want you to be happy."

"Uh…you do?" Who was this woman I was talking to? She had been acting strangely since I'd left for Greece.

"Just be careful, though. You know what Greek tour guides are like."

"Sure, Mom. I heard you the first time." And just when I was really wondering whether someone had kidnapped my mother, she returned in full force.

"And don't have an orgy."

"Mom! What are you talking about? Jesus, what the hell has that got to do with anything?"

"Well, they invented the bloody thing. It's practically all over their pottery and art. I Googled it last night."

I looked up to make sure Dimitri was out of earshot. "You Googled orgies last night?" I whispered down the phone.

"No, no," she laughed, "I Googled Greece. I realized I hardly know anything about the place you come from. We should have all gone there for a family holiday or something."

"Oh." I didn't know what to think. She'd never said anything like this before, or showed any iota of interest in where I came from, or how I felt about it.

"It looks really beautiful there, and I hope you at least try to have some fun there, too."

"I'll try." I put the phone down and looked at it for a moment or two, feeling genuinely confused by my mother.

"Is everything okay?" Dimitri asked, standing in the doorway.

"Oh yes. Fine. Fine. It's just my mom."

"Come," he said and led me up a small staircase in his kitchen that I hadn't noticed earlier. We popped out on a balcony that was just big enough for a small sofa and a table. I walked to the edge of the balcony and looked over. His house was set far back on the hill and looked out over the sea and the town below.

It was dark now; the orange light was gone but the whole town below was lit up. The sea in the distance was dark, except for the odd shards of silver that the moon sprayed on the water's surface. There were some stars out, not that many, or maybe they were just hard to see given the lights of the village. A huge cruise liner was making its way across the sea and cast yellow lights across the ocean as it traveled. Everything was just so *warm*, almost *comforting*.

I was so overcome by the beauty of everything that I tasted the familiar salty feeling. I had started crying again, thankfully softly and more dignified this time. It felt like I had seven years of tears trapped inside me and they were just now coming out.

"You okay?" Dimitri came up behind me.

I nodded slightly and we walked over to the couch and sat down. "I just feel so emotional. It's hard to explain."

"It makes perfect sense." He looked tentative for a second and then very slowly wrapped his arm around me.

"It's not strictly professional, but do you mind?" he asked.

I shrugged. "I suppose not."

He pulled me closer and I didn't object. It felt good.

"You must think I'm some sort of madwoman."

"I don't." It sounded genuine, but I wasn't totally convinced. How could he not think I was partially insane? Or at least had a mild case of hysteria.

"I told you, I'm used to this. I went through this at least once a year when one of my sisters was going through a breakup. In fact, they were far more dramatic than you. Trust me, this is a mild meltdown. You haven't seen a full Greek meltdown yet."

I laughed and then cried at the same time. "I don't know how to make it stop."

"You don't have to."

"It can't go on forever. You know a person can actually get dehydrated from crying," I whimpered.

"It'll stop when it's meant to." He didn't say another word; he only pulled me closer until my head was against his shoulder. I was aware that I was probably wetting his shirt with my tears.

I'm not sure how long I cried or when I finally succumbed to the pull of sleep; all I remember was how good the process of falling asleep on his shoulder felt. He smelled like a mixture of deodorant, saltiness, and some amazingly fragrant conditioner that I vaguely reminded myself to ask him about when I wasn't crying.

When I woke up, there my head was still on Dimitri's shoulder. I looked over to make sure I hadn't woken him. His head was back, his mouth slightly open, and he was fast asleep. To my relief I realized that I was no longer crying. Maybe I could turn it off for another seven years or so. I gazed at his profile. God, he was so beautiful, and this moment felt so weirdly surreal.

I held my breath and leaned in slowly to take a closer look at him. I might never get another chance to examine someone so good-looking up close. I almost felt like I was doing some kind of necessary scientific research. This was very important information that I was gathering for the sake of womankind.

I leaned in until I could see the pores in his skin. I could see almost every small hair making up his five-o'clock shadow, and everything looked magnified. His eyelashes were remarkably long, too. Why do men get blessed with such long eyelashes when we're always trying to find serums and things to make them longer?

He had the smallest collection of laugh lines at the edge of his eyes, and somehow that made him even sexier, as did that slight line in his forehead. Men get wrinkles and it's sexy; women get them and, like my mother, plow needles into them. And then I noticed the tiniest, most perfect little freckle just under his left eye. I think I was about an inch away from his face now, my eyes sweeping from left to right, trying to emblazon it into my mind so that I could come back and examine it further at a later stage—for scientific research obviously. I was just marveling at the wondrous shape of his nose up close when an eye opened. Then another.

Big fucking oops! I froze. My face barely an inch from his.

"Hi." His voice was sleepy and sounded like pure sex.

"Hi." Awkward. So, very very awkward. "I was just…" I stopped. There was no way out of this. He knew what I was doing; anyone who saw this would have known what I was doing. I shrugged. "I was examining you."

His smile grew. "I see that. And what did you find?"

"Well..." My face still hadn't moved. I was so busted. I might as well tell the truth. "Do you know how good-looking you are? It's almost unnatural on a genetic, perhaps even molecular level. You shouldn't be this good-looking; it's not very fair. To anyone. To women, to men. It's not right. Are you aware of that?"

His eyes lit up. "No one's ever put it quite like that."

"Well, it's true. You're so good-looking it's obscene. But I'm sure you know that, what with all the black-and-white well-lit spearfishing you do. Not to mention all that sex on the beach with those fancy wristwatches and the important thinking you do on giant chessboards and all."

I was on a roll now and felt strangely uninhibited as my confidence grew. "You must notice how women and some men look at you. They basically look as if they are one second away from tearing you apart with their teeth. You could quite literally have any woman in the world you wanted and I suspect could convert a few straight men, too."

His smile grew even more. His eyes gave off a kind of seductive air that made me swallow hard. My face was still only inches from his and not moving. *God, why am I not moving my face away from him?*

"Anything else?" he asked slowly.

"Yes, and on top of all that you don't seem to have any of the qualities that I expected someone that looks like you to have. It's all a bit confusing actually."

"Qualities?"

"You know, the types of things people might think about you when they first meet you?"

Dimitri suddenly leaned in even closer until our noses were almost touching. *Move, Jane! Move backward.* But I didn't. "And"— his eyes locked onto mine, and his voice was a mere whisper now— "what do people think when they first meet me?"

"Well, uh, that you might be…that someone who looks like you could be a bit vain and arrogant and not very nice, maybe. You know?"

"Are you saying you think I'm a nice guy?" He sounded playful.

"Maybe." I smiled.

"Anything else you want to share with me?"

"Nope. I think that about covers it all really." I started to stand up.

"Hey, where're you going?"

"I thought I should go to bed."

"But it's your turn," he said matter-of-factly.

"My turn for what?" I asked nervously.

"You can't do that to me and not expect me to do it back."

"Oh God, please don't." I wanted to die of embarrassment at the mere suggestion. I hated having people look at me.

"Come." He patted the sofa next to him and I lowered myself tentatively, waiting for him to speak. But instead, he leaned in all the way to my face, as close as I had been. I instinctively closed my eyes tightly, the closeness was so intimidating. Not just because I could feel the hotness radiating off his flawless skin. It was more because of the strange new feeling that was starting to creep in. It was easier to be nervous around the hot Greek playboy from before. But this guy on the sofa—he was downright unsettling.

"Uh-uh, open them." He wasn't asking; it sounded more like a command, and I felt absolutely compelled to obey. I snapped my eyes open and gave him the most relaxed *see how fucking cool and unperturbed I am* look I could muster. But I suspected I was failing dismally from the smile that leapt into his eyes.

"Please don't," I begged.

"Scared of what I'll say?"

I nodded and cringed all at the same terrible time. This was my worst nightmare realized.

He leaned in, brought his lips up to my ear, and spoke in a husky whisper that paralyzed me. "You're beautiful, Jane."

I gasped from the shock of it and the intimacy of this strange, surreal moment. How had this happened? I couldn't handle all these hushed, husky compliments. I pulled away from him, feeling so unbelievably uncomfortable I thought I was going to crawl out of my prickly skin.

"I'm not!" I said, backing away from him. "I'm totally tearstained and probably have red eyes and my hair is a complete mess, I'm not sure what I'm going to do with it." I ran my hand through my hair and could feel all the weird strands sticking up. He reached up and took one between his fingers and looked like he was examining it. A smile swept over his face.

"It's not funny," I said.

"It's not that bad." He let the piece go and I could feel it was sticking straight up and not flopping back like it should. I reached and tried to pat it down. And then he said it...

"I wish you could see yourself through my eyes right now."

I stopped mid–hair pat and my hand hovered above my head, unable to move. It was the single sexiest and most downright unnerving thing anyone had ever said to me. I didn't know how to handle it and my mouth opened. I could feel I wanted to spew out a fact about global warming and melting icecaps or tell him that anatidaephobia is the irrational fear that a duck is watching you. My MIA (Male Induced Awkwardness) often coincided with my UFB (Unnecessary Fact Bingeing) and I didn't know if I could stop it.

"Okay! Righty then…wow, look at the time. It's so late and totally past my bedtime and did you know that lack of sleep puts you at an increased risk of diabetes and heart disease as well as lowering your immune system?" I smiled and made a move toward the staircase. "Eight hours is actually not nearly enough, according to scientific research."

Dimitri stood up and followed me. "Really?"

I scuttled down the stairs and back into the kitchen with him hot on my heels. "So, where should I sleep?" I looked around, feeling panicked now. I really was sleeping over at his house. Again.

"You can sleep in my room," he said.

I glanced at his room. The room where that *stuff* had happened last night. That mind-blowing, earth-shattering sex stuff. "I'm not sure, I think that would be a little, you know, awkward. Besides, where will you sleep?"

"I'll take the spare room," he said.

"You have a spare room? I'll take it." I jumped.

Dimitri shook his head. "It's tiny and messy. Trust me, you don't want to take it."

"It's fine. Don't worry. Where is it?" I looked around. I hadn't seen another door.

Dimitri pointed to the stairs, and there, tucked under them, was a small door that you would have to duck to get into. I quickly moved across the room and opened it.

"Be careful of your head," he said, following me in and flicking the light switch on. I gasped when I saw what was inside.

"What the..." I looked around. The walls, floor, shelves, tables, and even bed were covered in pictures, maps, and all sorts of strange artifacts. "What is all this stuff?"

"My room of treasures," he said from behind me. I walked over to the table and picked up a black rock.

"What's this?"

Dimitri rushed over and took it from my hands excitedly. "This is a piece of volcanic rock. It's probably a couple of hundred years old."

"Wow."

"And this..." He put the rock down and went for the next thing. "This might not look like much but it's a small piece of pottery dating back to the ninth century, I found it on the island of Samos. And this..." He moved on to the next piece, a beautiful green plate. "It's not old, but I got it from Sifnos, they have a long tradition of pottery making there. And this"—he put the plate down gently and picked up an instrument that resembled a guitar in some ways—"is an oud. I bought it from a man who's been hand making them for over sixty years. Can you imagine that? Doing the same thing day in and day out for sixty years?" He said it like he sounded impressed. He then handed me the instrument excitedly and moved around the room like that for the next few minutes, showing me everything in it and giving me long explanations to where it had all come from and what its history was. At some stage I sat down on the bed and watched him, mesmerized once more by his passion. I wished I was as passionate about something as he clearly was about this.

"I try and collect something from every island I go to," he said, finally coming to a stop and standing in the middle of room.

"You really do travel a lot," I said.

He nodded. "I can never stay in one place for too long. I hardly stay here actually. There's just so much out there to see and find."

"You're very passionate about all this." I gestured around the room.

"I'm Greek, we're passionate people. Especially when it comes to our heritage. We're very proud of it…you should be, too." He looked down at me, and my heart thumped in my chest.

"Okay, well, it's getting late." I turned away from him and started adjusting the cushions on the bed, moving the maps onto the side table next to me.

"Can I get you anything?"

"No thanks, I'm fine."

"And you'll be okay in here?" he asked with a strange tone in his voice, as if he wanted me to say no, I wouldn't be okay, and then take me to his room and have *more sex with me. More sex. Now!*

"I'll be great. Thanks."

"Okay. Well, good night then." He started walking to the door and then stopped in the entrance and turned around. "Did he really speak in Klingon when he came?"

"Oh God, I can't believe I told you that," I moaned. "Good night, Dimitri."

He smiled at me. "Good night, Jane," he said but didn't move from the doorway.

"Uh, was there something else?" I asked, wondering why he wasn't leaving my room.

"You're much prettier than your sisters, by the way," he said.

"What? How do you know?"

"I went onto your Facebook page and stalked you a bit while you were on the phone with your mother. I hope you don't mind." His smile was downright devilish again.

"How can you say they're not pretty?"

"I didn't, I just said you were prettier."

"Really?" I said sarcastically. "Well, I think ninety-nine percent of the male population would disagree with you. If you had to line the three of us up together, I bet you every man would choose *Twin-tasia*."

He was laughing again. "What was that?"

"If my sisters were a porno, that's what they would be called," I said, thinking back to the time my friends and I had made that intrepid expedition to a sex shop and rented *Ocean's 11 Inches*. My brain gutter-plunged again as I started to remember how many inches Dimitri was hiding under those shorts of his.

Sex. Have sex with him again. Seven-inch sex (at least).

My filthy thoughts frightened me. "It's really time for bed now." I said it very emphatically this time. "You have tour guiding to do tomorrow," I added, trying to remind him of our professional arrangement. "And who knows, maybe the private investigator will get back to us tomorrow and I could be meeting my father."

Dimitri nodded at me and then walked out, closing the door behind him. I collapsed back onto the bed and held my head in my hands. How had I managed to end up at this man's house again? Two nights in a row; that wasn't an accident. I took my clothes off, changed into a pair of pajamas, brushed my teeth for two minutes at the small washbasin in the room, and then climbed into the bed. I closed my eyes and tried to switch my brain off, but it was racing. I looked around the room again; it really did look like it was packed with every Greek item that had ever existed. For someone who was allergic to Greece, this was like drastic exposure therapy. The artifacts all seemed to be staring at me pointedly, and I couldn't shake the feeling that they were mocking me. Smearing their Greekness in my face.

Look how Greek we are.

Aren't we so, so Greek, Jane? Just like you.

You can run from it, but you can't hide...

I pulled the pillow over my head and was attempting to shut them up when I heard a message buzz on my phone. I stuck my hand into my bag and pulled it out; it was from Dimitri.

Dimitri: Hi.

I couldn't help but smile.

Jane: Hi.

Dimitri: What you doing?

Jane: Trying to sleep. But someone keeps interrupting me.

Dimitri: Do you want me to have a word with him?

Jane: Yes.

Dimitri: OK.

There was a pause.

Dimitri: He apologizes. He just finds you so intriguing that he couldn't help himself.

My face flushed red. Was he flirting with me? Over texts? I felt like a giddy teenager. I shouldn't be getting so flustered over this—we'd already had sex!

Jane: I'm totally boring.

Dimitri: He says he doubts that.

Jane: Well, then he clearly doesn't know me.

Dimitri: He says he'd like to get to know you.

I typed What does he want to know and then paused. I'm sure my mother once told me to add dot, dot, dots to conversations because they made them flirty. Left them open-ended and full of connotations. *Oh well, what the hell.*

Jane: What does he want to know...

There was a longish pause and I wondered if my dot, dot, dot approach had tanked like a lead balloon.

Dimitri: Are you flirting with me again, Jane?

A stab in my stomach.

Jane: Again? What do you mean again?

Dimitri: You were pretty flirty last night.

Jane: I was not!

Dimitri: Jane, why do you carry my cardboard head around with you?

"Oh my God!" I screeched, threw myself off the bed, and ran back into the living room and straight into his bedroom. "It's not what you think, by the way," I said, standing in front of his bed, which he was lying in.

"How do you know what I think?" His smile was so devilish and delicious right now that I wanted to throw myself at him.

"You probably think that I'm some kind of perverted fan girl or something. That I carry your picture with me and take it to bed and fantasize about you."

"Do you?" He raised himself up onto his elbow, revealing a totally bare chest.

"I . . . I," I stammered. "I am not going to answer that!" I finally said indignantly, putting my hands on my hips.

"Fine." He smiled at me.

"Fine," I repeated.

We stopped talking and stared at each other. I was trying really hard to hold his gaze in a cool, indignant manner. "Fine," I echoed in silent panic. "Bedtime!"

"Good night again, Jane."

"Good night again, Dimitri." I turned and walked out. I crossed the living room and was just about to go into my room when he said something that stopped me dead in my tracks.

"I could get used to you sleeping over at my place."

CHAPTER EIGHTEEN

*W*hen I woke up I had that same feeling as if I'd overslept again. I glanced at my watch. I had: It was already eleven in the morning. Half the day was gone. I leapt out of bed with a panicky feeling. I hated oversleeping. I hated being late. I went into the living room and Dimitri was there.

"Sorry, sorry, I totally overslept."

He glanced up at the clock on the wall. "No you didn't, it's only eleven. Nothing in Greece opens before eleven anyway."

"Really?"

"We like to enjoy life. There's no such thing as running late here."

I nodded, although I had no idea what the hell he was talking about. This concept was so foreign that it might as well have been said to me in Latin.

"Have you heard from the investigator?" I asked.

Dimitri quickly shook his head. "No, not yet. But he did say that he would call the second he knew something. So let's go and have some fun in the meantime. I've got a whole plan worked out for the day." Dimitri smiled and pushed a list over to me. I took it and started reading. "I want to show you as much of Santorini as I can today, before we leave tomorrow."

"Leave?"

"Yes, I have a boat I use for tours." His tone was casual. "And you agreed to let me take you on a tour."

"I meant show me some ancient rock on a hill, or a souvenir shop, or something. Not boats and island-hopping."

"Jane..." Dimitri walked over to me. "You said I could show you Greece."

I glanced back down at the list. "Beach, swim, sunbathe? You put *that* on the list."

"That's what people come to Greece for? The sun, the sea..."

"But what do you do on the beach?"

"Nothing."

"Nothing?" I repeated.

"You lie in the sun, you tan, you—"

"I don't tan."

His face broke into a smile. "You're Greek. You'll tan."

"But—" I was trying to think of a legitimate excuse other than *"My thighs have cellulite and you have the chiseled body of the statue of David."*

"I don't have a bathing suit," I quickly said.

He grinned at me. "Yes you do. What about the pink one?"

"I can't wear that!"

"We could go to a nude beach then?" He had a naughty twinkle in his eye that made my heart stop.

"*No!* No! The pink thing will be fine."

"Good." He clapped his hands together happily.

"Are you sure we should be going to the beach just after midday? That's when the sun is at its hottest. Lots of UV rays."

Dimitri laughed. "Jane. Stop trying to control everything. In Greece we have a saying, 'Go with the flow.'"

"I think they have that saying everywhere," I interrupted.

"So then it must be true."

"Just because everyone says it doesn't mean it's right!"

He reached out and put his hands on my shoulders. "Just go with it."

I felt my shoulders tense up at the mere thought of relaxing.

"I dare you to relax," he said with a challenging tone.

"I can totally relax and go with it," I said defensively.

"Really?" He lifted his brows in a mocking way.

"You don't believe me! I can go all the way with it. I am great at going all the way actually!"

He burst out laughing. "So glad you said that."

"I didn't mean it like that, by the way. In case that's what you were thinking." I put my hand on a hip and tried to sound like I was scolding him.

This made him laugh even more. "Oh Jane. Jane, Jane, Jane."

"Yes, Dimitri, Dimitri, Dimitri?"

"Nothing. Just Jane."

Just Jane. What the hell does that even mean?

"You're in Greece. Have some fun."

Fun. I could do fun. I glanced back down at the list. "What's the last one? Family dinner?"

"It's my sister's birthday tonight, so you're coming along."

"Oh no! That's okay. You don't have to take me to be polite, I'll be fine on my own. Besides, I hardly think your family wants me to intrude."

"In Greece, everyone is invited to dinner. If the neighbors suddenly came around it would be okay. Come, get ready for the beach."

"Ready for the beach?" I echoed. It sounded terrifying and I felt wildly uncomfortable with this beach idea. But there was no way of wiggling out of it now. "Fine," I said and walked back into my room. I rummaged through my bag and found the pink thing, slipped it on, then put a dress over it.

"Red or black?" Dimitri asked as I stepped out back into the living room.

"Sorry?"

"Red or black beach?" he qualified.

Without thinking I answered, "I guess black, since we've already been to the red one?"

Dimitri paused and looked at me. "When did we go to the red beach?"

"Don't you remember?" I asked flippantly as I did a final check of my handbag to make sure I had enough sunscreen, a hat and my glasses, another pair of sandals in case something happened with these, and some extra hair bands.

"No," he replied.

"I was lying on the beach and you were climbing out of the water holding that—" I froze. Oh God, what a Freudian slip. That had happened in my dream. I flushed a bright shade of red that actually made my cheeks sting.

"Your face has gone the color of the beach," Dimitri stated.

"It has?" I touched my face, pretending to act shocked. "Must be the heat."

He eyed me suspiciously. "When exactly did we go to the beach?"

I started to stutter, which just made the whole thing far more suspicious. "It was when…actually, I'm mistaken. I thought that we went, or something…"

"You had a dream about me, didn't you?" He suddenly looked somewhat amused.

"I had no such thing!" I snapped defensively.

He continued to eye me suspiciously. "You had another sex dream about me."

"I did not. Why would you even think that?"

"You told me, remember?" He raised an eyebrow playfully.

"I did not—" I stopped myself halfway through the sentence as the realization came crashing into me. *Yep*, I had told him. In my dazed and confused crazed confessional state yesterday, I had admitted to having a sex dream about him. Not that that was worse than sleeping with the guy. "I did. Okay. And what's wrong with that? I am a young virile woman who shouldn't be ashamed of my perfectly natural human desires. It's biological. An evolutionary imperative actually. Who am I to fight my innate human nature, I ask you?"

"I agree, you shouldn't fight it if you don't want to, Jane." Dimitri moved in closer. His eyes crinkled into a smile. "Black beach it is then." He turned away from me and called over his shoulder, "But first, I'm about to take you on the wildest ride of your life!"

Mmm, I kind of think you've already done that!

CHAPTER NINETEEN

⌒

"Aaahhhh!" I screeched. "Aaahhhh!" I screeched again. But in my defense I wasn't the only one screeching. There were many people screeching. In fact, everywhere I gazed people looked like they were about to either cry or scream.

"Oh come on, it's not that bad," Dimitri said from behind me.

"Dimitri! I'm riding on the back of a donkey while it zigzags down the narrowest path I've ever seen. There is a sheer cliff face that plummets hundreds of feet into the sea, no one is leading this donkey, and this donkey keeps losing his footing." At that the donkey slipped again and I came dangerously close to the edge of the cliff once more. My heart jumped into my mouth and stayed there. Why would anyone choose to ride a donkey anywhere, let alone down the deadliest path in the world?

"Does this thing have a death wish?" For a second I looked down over the cliff. It was a sheer drop. You know how in movies when someone tumbles down a cliff face, there is always that one tiny little twig or bush sticking out that they grab onto before they plummet to their deaths? There was nothing of the sort here. It was all straight down.

"Relax, people have been riding donkeys up and down this path for thousands of years."

"That doesn't make it right." Suddenly my donkey lurched toward another one and snapped at it. The other one snapped back and then started chasing mine. "He's going too fast! He's going too fast." The ride had just gotten a million times more bumpy and horrific and awful. I held on to the reins so tightly that my shoulders tensed into a ball.

"It's only ten minutes," he shouted as my donkey slipped and slid its way down the 596 steep stairs to the port.

"I'm going to die, I'm going to die. I am going to die."

"Think of it as a roller coaster."

"I don't ride roller coasters," I yelled.

The descent became even steeper, and the only reprieve I got was when my donkey stopped to eat some plants sticking out of the wall. We finally made it to the bottom and I disembarked as quickly as humanly possible. I felt such a rush of exhilaration at being alive. The adrenaline whooshed around in my veins and I wanted to scream and hug people. In fact I did, another woman nearby who looked like she was also feeling lucky to be alive.

"I'm alive!" I screeched with a kind of joyful exuberance that I hadn't felt, maybe ever.

"And doesn't it feel great to be alive?"

My heart was still pumping. It did actually feel great.

"And you get to say you rode a donkey on Santorini. It's a rite of passage. It's the ancient Greek way."

"So what's down here? It better be good," I said, glancing around the port that I'd actually already been to.

"Nothing," he said casually.

"Nothing?"

"Nope." He shook his head.

"So you made me ride that donkey, endanger my life, almost plummet to my death down a cliff for nothing?"

"But will you ever forget it?"

"No. Not for as long as I live. On my deathbed I'll remember that bloody ride. That was the single most awful and memorable thing I've ever done."

"Exactly." Dimitri walked off. "We'll take the cable car back up and then go to the beach."

"There is a cable car? That goes up, and *down*?"

"And it's got a great view." He smiled like he was having the best time of his life. Like a child at Christmas ripping open his presents and stuffing his face with candy.

"Why are you enjoying this so much?" I ran after him.

"Oh, Jane." Dimitri turned and faced me. "The fun has just begun."

* * *

The view from the cable car was good, though. It was great, in fact. The port and the blue waters below stretched for miles and miles in all directions. The mountains rose up out of the water, climbing steeply to a summit dotted with the bright-white houses of Fira. But the view inside the cable car was far more interesting, and downright awkward. The snug little car was designed to fit exactly four people, with two seats on either side. Dimitri and I sat shoulder-to-shoulder, trying not to stare at the couple sitting across from us.

I've never been a big fan of public displays of affection. And it was almost worse that these two were so nauseatingly sweet. He was whispering sweet little nothings in her ear. All *"ti amo"* and *"bella, bella."* I assumed they were Italian.

Their hands were tightly intertwined and they were sitting so close they may as well have been glued at the hip. It was as if they wanted to have as much physical contact with each other as possible. Even their feet were playfully touching, and the looks they were exchanging dripped with love and lust. And then it got a little bit more awkward as they started to kiss.

I could feel the flush slowly crawl up my neck. I felt ridiculously uncomfortable, but I just couldn't take my eyes off them. I must have voiced a mildly audible sigh, because the woman suddenly pulled away and gave a slightly embarrassed giggle.

"Scusa. We just got married yesterday." She held up her hand and showed off her ring.

"Congratulations," Dimitri quickly said. The couple beamed at him and then each other and then went back to the lip-locking.

I squirmed in my seat, caught somewhere between embarrassment and, well, an overwhelming urge to be doing the same with Dimitri. I tried not to look in his direction, tried not to acknowledge his very presence. But my heartbeat became so loud that I was sure everyone in the tiny cable car could hear it. I crossed my legs as Dimitri sat back, his shoulder now pressing harder into mine than before. It felt very deliberate. There was no need for such sitting back in the chair. There was also no need for him to shift his leg just that tiny bit to the left, either, which meant that it came into contact with mine. Nay, none of these things were necessary, and what was *very* unnecessary was when he shifted nearer to me. I felt the flush creep up my neck and warm the tips of my ears as the lovers momentarily disconnected their lips.

The cable car finally came to a stop and I leapt out of the thing, followed closely by Dimitri. The other two were in no rush to leave and stayed there, probably moving on to the next base.

"Why the rush?" Dimitri came up behind me and put a hand on my shoulder. I turned and must have had some weird look in my eye that cued him to my thoughts.

"Sweet, wasn't it?" he said with a small smile.

"What was?"

"They're so in love they can't keep their hands off each other."

"It wasn't sweet, it was inappropriate. People should control themselves in public."

"But haven't you ever felt that way? So in love you feel you might die if you're not touching him all the time."

I gulped and shook my head. "No."

"You cannot go another day, minute, or second without hearing his voice, or being close to him?"

I shook my head again. Speechless. Absolutely dumbfounded and at a loss as what to say next.

Dimitri moved closer to me. "That's a pity. Everyone should be in love like that at least once in their life."

No thoughts penetrated my conscious mind. There was nothing. A dark, empty room of nothingness. The world around me started to shrink and narrow until it was just Dimitri and me staring at each other while the tourists and the donkeys and everything else passed us by.

"So?" The playfulness in his eyes was gone now, replaced by something that unsettled me. He scanned me intently, as if he was trying to read my innermost thoughts and feelings. I felt a stab of longing in my chest. A longing to reach out and touch him and...

"Have sex with me again! Sex. Now..."

His eyes suddenly widened and then a strange smile etched its way across his face. I was getting a strange feeling. Very strange. A terrible, *bad*, very bad feeling...

"Oh. God. Did I just say that? *Out loud?*" I didn't need a body language expert to tell me that the way he dropped his head in a slightly coy manner, then lifted it again and looked straight into my eyes while biting down ever so slightly on his bottom lip, meant that I had...

"Shit! I didn't mean to say that, I only meant to think it. Not to imply that I was thinking about it, by the way, just in case you thought that I was thinking that thought."

"But you *were* thinking about it."

"Technically, yes, but on another level...no." I attempted a look that implied indifference, coolness, and aloofness. It failed. Totally. Especially when I tried to put my hand on my hip and cock my head to the side like a hip-hop diva. My neck cricked. Dismal failure. Why was I so bad at acting cool?

"Oh Jane, you're so lovely."

The word echoed like someone had just thrown a stone into an empty well. *Lovely?* What did that even mean? *Lovely?* A day could be lovely. That knitted scarf your grandmother gave you would be called lovely in that placating way.

I climbed back into the car in a state of shocked silence. The air between us had somehow changed. The playful smiles we'd exchanged earlier were gone, replaced by something completely different, something I was unfamiliar with. It frightened me more than the physical feelings I was having for this man. Dimitri turned in his seat and looked at me and then opened his mouth. He quickly closed it again. What the hell was going on in that pretty little head of his? More important, what was going on in my heart right now and why was it ignoring everything my head was telling me?

And then his mouth opened again. He paused. I looked at him with such anticipation. "I'm not sure what it is about you. But from the moment I saw you in the airport..." He stopped, and it looked like he was considering his next words very carefully. Then he shrugged. "You're not like any woman I've ever met before. In a good way."

I had no idea what to say to that and I wondered if my father had said something similar to my mother. Had they also ridden donkeys together and watched a beautiful sunset? Had they also driven together in a car, struggling with conflicting feelings for each other and trying to fight them?

Dimitri finally slowed the car and pulled onto a gravel road. "This is Kamari Village," he said as he parked the car and climbed out. I looked around: There wasn't really that much to see other than a hill, a deserted parking lot, and gravel beneath our feet.

"So where are we going?" I asked.

"Back to the very beginning," he said with a loaded smile. I followed him as he started walking up a small footpath. It was steep, and the stones beneath my feet were loose.

"I'm taking you to see the ruins of a village that was built in the ninth century BC," he said. It was hard to comprehend anything being that old, or what life would have been like back then. When we finally reached the top of the long and windy path, I gasped. I was standing on the top of the world, and it felt like I could see all the way to the ends of the earth.

"This is the highest point of the island," Dimitri said. "And this is where we all came from. It's the start of it all." He had a sense of childlike wonder in his voice. "Did you know the Greeks invented theater, democracy, the Olympics, geometry, math, and philosophy? We even invented alarm clocks and plumbing, coin money, and those showers that only use two gallons of water a minute."

I stared in awe at everything around me. I felt like I was peeping behind a curtain and looking back in time. Looking at the entire history of a place and its people...*my history*. I inhaled. The air smelled sweet, as if there were blossoming trees somewhere. Something about this place was very soothing. It was broken but beautiful, and walking through the fragmented pillars and piles of rocks I could almost imagine the people going about their daily lives here. Children running through the streets playing ancient games, mothers making olive oil and cooking, men plowing fields and harvesting.

"You should be proud of your Greek heritage, Jane. You shouldn't run away from it." He turned and looked at me meaningfully.

I knew what he was trying to do. He was trying to wake that part of me that was Greek—to show me the beauty in a part of myself that I had never known, or liked. But his statement also felt offensive. "Is that what you think I'm doing?"

"You won't even eat Greek food. It's time to let out your inner Greek, Jane."

"I don't have an inner Greek."

"Yes you do. I can see her, and she's dying to come out."

I looked at him for a few moments, trying to figure out how someone even let their inner Greek out.

"Come, let's go to the beach!" He was already scuttling down the slippery path as if he'd walked it a million times. "Your inner Greek is going to love it."

* * *

I stood on the edge of the sand. I'd never seen black sand before, and it was beautiful. I bent down and grabbed a handful of it to admire more closely. It wasn't exactly soft and it wasn't exactly sand. It was a combination of pebbles, black shale, and something that looked like black glitter sparkling in the sun. I glanced up; the pebbles close to the shore, where the waves were lapping, were even darker than the ones I was holding. A single white pebble caught my eye, and I walked over and picked it up. I turned it over in my hand; it was a perfect circle, smooth and shiny and almost soft to the touch.

"Makes sense that you would pick up the odd one out." Dimitri was standing next to me now.

"I guess," I said faintly, knowing exactly what he meant. I lifted my eyes and met his. My stomach tensed into a knot. Only this time it wasn't the same kind of *trying too hard to relax* feeling; it wasn't a *worrying about being late* feeling. It was like I could feel the knot forming and loosening in my stomach as excitement and happiness clashed.

"So the beach, hey?" I said, breaking the moment, although I don't know why. Every part of me wanted the moment to continue, except for this one little part, the voice that had me asking, *Is this real?* Could a guy like this really be paying me this kind of attention? Sure, we'd had sex, but that was nothing like what was going on now. That had been primal and manic and hungry and probably would have just been some meaningless one-night stand for him if I'd left. But this—this was odd. Too odd. I needed some advice.

"Would you excuse me for a second or two, there's something I need to do." I scuttled off and stood under the shade of a nearby tree. I turned my back to him and pulled out my phone.

WHATSAPP GROUP: Jane goes to Greece

Jane: Hi.

Lilly: That was quick, are you back in SA already?

Jane: No.

Lilly: Where are you?

Jane: Well that's kind of a funny story.

Annie: Does it have something to do with that guy?

Jane: Sort of . . . he's offered to help me find my biological father. He contacted a PI.

Annie: Why would he do that?

I looked back over my shoulder at Dimitri, who was standing on the edge of the beach watching me. He smiled and I reciprocated.

Jane: I guess he's a nice guy.

Lilly: Is this the same guy you never wanted to see again?

Jane: I know, it doesn't make sense.

Val: Hi! I'm here.

Jane: Hey.

Val: Who is he exactly?

Jane: Well, that's kind of the funny part . . .

I stopped typing and stared at my phone imagining what their reactions would be if I told them. But if I couldn't tell my best friends in the world, who could I tell?

Jane: His name is Dimitri and he's a tour guide.

Annie: What!!!!

Val: WTH . . .

Jane: I know. I know how it sounds.

Annie: Really? Do you?

Jane: Yes, it's like history repeating itself.

Annie: Have you had sex with him again?

Jane: No. God no!

Annie: So, what, you guys just pretending it didn't happen?

Jane: Something like that.

Val: Impossible to pretend you never had sex.

Annie: And you better believe he's probably wanting to have it again.

Jane: No. This is a strictly professional thing. I'm hiring him as a tour guide. Plain and simple.

Val: Once you sleep with someone it's no longer simple, Jane. Not for the chick anyway.

Lilly: Are you falling for him or something?

Annie: Please don't tell me you're falling for his Greek charms?

Jane: He's not like that. Well, I think he's not. I don't know. I'm confused, OK?

Annie: Jane, whatever you think you're feeling for him, it's probably not real. You're looking for your dad who is also Dimitri, it must be very emotional and your feelings must be all over the place. You've probably mixed them all up and now think you're feeling something you're not.

Lilly: Annie is probably right. It's totally understandable that you feel a connection with a tour guide named Dimitri.

Jane: I never said I was feeling things for him, guys!

Annie: It's what you didn't say.

Val: True. The Jane we know would have scolded us and shot us down for even suggesting she was falling for him.

Lilly: Why don't you just come home?

Jane: And never meet my father?

Val: Do you really think a PI can find him after all this time?

Jane: I don't know. But if there is a slight chance, shouldn't I at least try?

Stormy: YES ! it isyour dEStiny too find him ./

Annie: Stormy, you give the worst advice!

Jane: You guys are all freaking me out. I'm going.

Lilly: Wait. Should one of us come out there?

Val: ?

I didn't respond. Instead I put my phone on silent and slipped it back into my bag. I turned and looked back at the beach. Dimitri was still standing there waiting for me. He extended his hand, beckoning me toward him. And I went.

The beach was full of lounge chairs and umbrellas. Dimitri walked up to one and put our bags down. I stood there under the umbrella and looked around.

"Now what?" I asked.

"Now you lie in the sun. You tan, you listen to the sea, you stare up at the sky, you relax."

"Why?"

"Because it's the Greek way."

"It's the Greek way to expose your skin to deadly UV rays?" I stuck my hand into my bag and started pulling out my tube of sunscreen, but as I did Dimitri snatched it away from me.

"Tan. Live a little."

"What? That is the most ridiculous thing I've ever heard, equating 'living' with having a tan, that's ab…ab…ab…" Dimitri started taking his shirt off and I started stuttering stupidly. "*Abs.*" My voice sounded dreamy and strange and then I quickly realized what I'd said. "Ab*surd*. That is completely *absurd*," I said, trying to correct and cover, but truthfully all I could see and think about were his ridiculously perfect, glistening-in-the-Mediterranean-sun abs that my eyes were now boring into. What was absurd? What had we been talking about?

I glanced around at the other females on the beach. There was the usual jaw dropping and eye popping, as well as the odd bit of loose drool tumbling from lips. But he just carried right on. Slowly. Seductively. As if he knew what he was doing to people and he didn't care. Now my eyes moved away from his abs and rolled.

"Really? Are you doing that on purpose?" I challenged.

"Doing what?" He tossed his shirt down onto the lounger.

"Taking your shirt off like you're trying to attract the attention of every female in a five-mile radius. Can't you just take it off normally? Like a normal person would. Or do you want everyone on the beach to stare at you?"

He shot me a smile. "I did take it off normally."

"No you didn't." I pointed an accusatory finger at him. "Put your shirt back on and then take it off again."

Dimitri's eyes glinted. "Are asking me to take my clothes off?"

"No. I'm asking you to put them back on and then take them off in a manner that is more normal instead of this whole *Oooh I'm a hot Greek model oozing sex on the beach* thing you're doing that is driving all the woman mad and making them stare at you."

Dimitri smiled at me mischievously and then put his shirt back on. "You know, there's another way to show me how to take my shirt off." A strange inflection hung in his voice. "You could always take it off for me."

"I'm not doing that!" I said quickly, trying to act defiant rather than shocked and mildly excited by his statement.

"But don't you want to teach me the correct way to take off my shirt?" He was teasing me now. Egging me on.

I shook my head quickly. "I'm not taking your clothes off."

"Come on, Jane, take my shirt off." His voice was playful and teasing and just so damn sexy, it was futile to resist.

"Fine. Fine," I said, walking toward him. "But don't think I'll enjoy it or anything. I'm just doing it to prove a point and show you how a normal person would take a shirt off. Think of it as a kind of scientific endeavor."

"Purely scientific," he repeated, sounding amused.

"Exactly. An experiment of sorts."

I was trying to look calm and unfazed, but inside I was freaking out. *You can do this, Jane! You can remove the clothes of the hottest man on the planet, in public, and look totally cool and calm while doing it. Think of it as giving someone a routine filling. It's simple; you've done it a million times before* . . .

Dimitri eyed me as I crept closer. When I was close enough, I stuck out my thumb and forefinger like two little crab pincers and tried to delicately take the hem of his shirt between them.

He burst out laughing. "I'm not going to bite you."

"I know that," I snapped back at him. "I'm just deciding on the best approach. The most effective manner of proceeding." I gazed at the hem of his shirt. I'd managed to lift it a little—enough that I could see the start of those rock-hard abs that a sledgehammer probably wouldn't shatter.

"Run your hands over my abs and have sex with me. Have sex with me now. Abs. Sex. Beach. Now!"

I reached out slowly again and started tugging at the shirt. With each tug, he was looking more and more naked. Despite my previous decision to remain as indifferent as I possibly could, I let my fingertips linger and trail ever so slowly up his stomach. I felt him quiver under my touch and I was suddenly overcome with the same unfamiliar feeling from before.

I felt like I was an actress on stage, playing the role of a woman who pulled Dimitri's shirt off with an expertise I never knew I had. This woman was also not subtle about letting her fingers linger on his body and trail up and over his chest. I finally tugged it off and threw it down on the sand aggressively, as if to say, "*Ta-da!*"

"There," I said, feeling rather pleased with myself. "The correct way to remove a shirt in public. Note how it was done at a much quicker speed, instead of looking like you were actually doing it in slow motion for the benefit of an audience."

He seemed amused by my statement. "So, do you need help taking yours off?" he asked, sounding innocent.

"No thanks. Believe it or not, I have been undressing myself since the age of four. I am quite adept at taking my own clothes off, but thanks for asking."

"You sure?"

"I'm sure. I think I'll manage."

"Really, it's no bother." He moved a little closer to me.

I shook my head firmly.

"That is completely unfair. You can't go around undressing me and not expect me to do the same for you."

I very dramatically rolled my eyes and started saying, "It's just not going to..." Suddenly I felt his hands slip under the hem of my shirt and start pulling on it. "...to happen*nnnnn*..."

The last word came out very breathily.

Shirt. Sex, beach. Now...beach shirt. Sex...beach shirt? Even my inner monologue was scrambled.

I gasped and shivered as he let his fingers graze my skin in exactly the same way the actress version of myself had. He did it for a lot longer than I had, though. He stepped closer to me and slipped another hand under my shirt. His fingertips trailed all the way up my body as he pulled it off. The shirt finally slipped off my head with a final tug—and that's when I saw the dancing pink dots of light playing on his chest, and the erotic little bubble I was in burst.

"Oh God." I slapped my hands over my breasts. "I forgot about the sequins. What is wrong with my mother, honestly? Sequins?"

"I think your mother has great taste," Dimitri said as he sat down.

"Don't ever tell her that! She'll start dressing you, and it's so subtle in the beginning you won't even notice what she's doing until it's too late and she's replaced your entire wardrobe."

And then he laughed again. What was going on? I wasn't funny. I was told once to never try to make jokes. *"Jane, joking is not your strong point,"* they would say. *"Please don't try to make a joke,"* they would urge.

"Why do you find me so funny?" I asked.

"Are you kidding?" Dimitri turned to me and propped himself up against his elbow. My heart came skidding to another full stop. "You're not just funny, Jane, you're also fun to be around."

"But I'm not. I'm not fun, or funny. I'm boring and lack social skills. I'm a dentist for God's sake. No one likes people who make children and grown men cry, which by the way I do on a daily basis. I don't have a spontaneous bone in my body, and I can guarantee you that not one person would describe me as fun."

But he was still laughing. "You're fun. Trust me."

"Really?" I asked, absolutely dumbfounded by his response. I was just about to ask him more when a large shadow fell over us.

"Dimitri, *kalimera*," a sweet-sounding female voice said in a flirty singsong manner. I shielded my eyes from the sun so I could better examine the source of the voice. Standing in front of us was a little troupe of three gorgeous, topless, stunning, did I mention *topless* girls. I was shocked. I hadn't expected to see so many mammaries so close to me, and on a beach no less. Dimitri sprang to his feet, looking very pleased by this sudden female interference. In fact, he went over and kissed each one on both cheeks. Why were they topless?

I glanced around quickly and suddenly realized that almost everyone was topless. What the hell kind of a beach was this? Boobs everywhere, regardless of the shape or size or age of the things. They were all just hanging out (some hanging more than others).

I stared in horror as Dimitri talked, and joked, and ran his hands through his hair with these three topless Greek seductresses who were all so obviously pouting and twinkling their sparkling little eyes at him. I stared and I could almost feel the daggers shooting out of my eyes. I'd never experienced such a pang of deadly jealousy before. The thought I'd had earlier—the one I hadn't been able to quite grasp—started rising to the surface.

The thought bobbed for a moment or two in the same place it

had been, that weird limbo between conscious and unconscious. But this time it broke into my consciousness.

I...I...

Impossible, it cannot be.

I...I...

Nope, there it is again, the thought is there and it's starting to form itself in my head.

I...I...was really starting to *like* this guy.

I like this guy. I *like* Dimitri Spiros?

The realization made me sit up straight in my chair, and my sudden movement caught Dimitri's attention. He turned to me and almost did a double take when he saw the look of shock on my face. Then his eyes settled onto mine. He looked like he was trying to communicate telepathically with me, and then he smiled.

He smiled like he'd never smiled at me before, as if he knew exactly what I was thinking.

CHAPTER TWENTY

Despite the warm and thrilling smiles from Dimitri in the wake of my own confusing discoveries about him, I hated the beach. It was hot. It was sandy. The sun was beating down on me and pulling every last drop of moisture out of my skin. I was sweating. And every now and again the wind would pick up and slap me in the face with a handful of sand.

I'd tried. I'd tried to do the whole Greek thing and lie in the sun as if there were no tomorrow. I'd tried looking out over the sea and contemplating its blue magnificence. Contemplating the warm, glorious sun and beauty of nature . . . but I couldn't.

"Okay. I've tried," I said. "I've tried everything, but I just can't get into it."

"Mmmmm," Dimitri moaned. His eyes were closed and he looked like a snake on a warm rock soaking up the rays.

"I hate the beach. I always have. I especially hate sand, it gets in all sorts of places, and did you know that the bacteria content in sand is actually very high? I've also never seen the point of lying down and doing nothing. And I don't like not wearing sunscreen, either, okay?"

Dimitri sat up and pulled his glasses down. "Okay. We can go."

"Just like that? We can go?"

"Sure." He stood up and started collecting our things.

"You're not going to give a lecture about letting go and getting my inner Greek on?"

"No. If you aren't enjoying the beach, we'll go."

"Okay." I was slightly stunned. "So what's next on the list again?"

"One of the highlights of your trip," he said.

We walked along the beach for about twenty minutes in total silence. The black sand was beautiful and the water was so warm that I waded in ankle-deep and kicked it up with my feet.

"So will you tell me where we are going yet?"

"Over there." He pointed in the direction of a few brightly colored boats that were moored on the sand. Behind them stood an old-looking building. Long tables stretched out lazily under shady trees. There were a few people sitting at the tables drinking glasses of wine and laughing. The sign on the door read WINERY.

"Wine tasting in Santorini is a must." Dimitri smiled, took me by the hand, and led me to a table right there on the beach under a tree. A woman rushed over to us and greeted Dimitri like she knew him, and naturally—like every woman that seemed to know him—she was gorgeous. There was more smiling and hugging being thrown around again. *Pang of jealousy*

"Do you know every woman on the island?" It had been my

intention to hide the sarcasm in my tone, but it hadn't worked very well.

"Why, are you jealous?" He smiled, looking very pleased with himself. Too pleased.

"No!"

"It kind of sounded like it," he teased.

"No, it's just an observation." I tried to brush it off but couldn't. "And," I continued, "they're all so beautiful and they flip their hair a lot and they fawn and they look at you all flirtatiously and do things like this—"

I pouted my lips and tried to give myself a pair of cute Bambi eyes. "Oooh, Dimitri. How are you? Hair flip, hair flip," I said while flipping my newly cut hair and giving it a good shake.

First his eyes slowly crinkled into a smile, and then his whole face joined in. "Do that again, please."

"Why?"

"I'm trying to work out if that was the cutest or the hottest thing I've ever seen."

I froze. My mouth opened and I thought I could feel my eyes widen unnaturally. He must have thought I looked like an idiot. I closed my mouth—I might as well have taken my hand and pushed it shut—and focused very hard on relaxing my neck and shoulders in an air of indifference. I felt like a contortionist. Why was he still watching me? I smiled and placed my hand under my chin, leaning my head on it not-so-nonchalantly.

"Nice place," I finally said, deflecting.

"Nice place," he echoed, still holding eye contact. "They are famous for their nice wine."

"Nice," I said. God, this was such a useless conversation, and the word *nice* was being way too overused. I was happy when the waitress suddenly arrived with our glasses of wine. After some explanations and discussions about them (I heard something about oak and citrus and pairing with lamb), we began tasting. Each wine was more amazing and delicious than the previous one. I'd never been one to consider the flavors of wine before, but today, sitting here with him, under the trees, on one of the most amazing beaches I had ever been on, everything tasted better. Everything looked more beautiful, like I was seeing it all in crisp high-definition detail. Perhaps it was the gentle buzz of the sixth sip, but a feeling of courage started to bubble up in me.

"Can I ask you something?"

"Anything." His face was flushed from the sun. His hair was slightly messy and tussled by the wind. His eyes were that gut-stabbing, hypnotizing green color. He was perfect.

"Are you..." I cleared my throat as the next half of the sentence got stuck there. I couldn't believe I was about to ask such a question. I'd never asked anyone this before. "Are you..."

I coughed a tad. My words were still stuck and I reached for my glass of wine, holding up my finger to him, indicating for him to wait.

"Take your time." He watched me closely.

I swallowed and the liquid somewhat soothed my dry throat. I tried again. "Are you flirting with me?" I finally managed.

A slow, languid, and downright filthy-sexy smile lit up Dimitri's face. "What do you think?"

"Well..." I gathered my thoughts logically. "Many of our conversations have seemed to err on the side of s-e-x. Understandable in a way since we did h-a-v-e i-t." I didn't know why I was spelling out all the words like a parent swearing in front of a toddler. "But we did agree to keep things professional—I even paid you—yet it just doesn't feel that professional."

"What's not professional about it?" he said, leaning across the table.

"Well, there's that leaning you're doing right now. You did take my clothes off earlier on the beach, and there is all that looking and husky-toned talking. So if I add all those things together, they are fairly congruent with the hypothesis that you are in fact flirty."

I finished and looked at Dimitri expectantly, but he said absolutely nothing. He simply stared and continued his table lean. Silence. More silence. Oh God, maybe I had crossed a line here and had totally misinterpreted the situation between us. Maybe he was trying to think of a way to say no without embarrassing me.

"What?" I asked nervously. A movement caught my eye and I watched as his hands stole their way across the table. They stopped inches away from mine. We both gazed down at them expecting them to do something, like they were somehow not connected to us. A solitary finger reached out and twirled itself around one of mine.

"Have you only noticed now?" he asked, looking up at me. "I'm flirting with you, Jane." His words came out firmly, and he couldn't have sounded sexier if he tried.

"I see." I nodded, taking in the information and trying to process it in a logical, reasonable manner and not one in the vein of a . . .

"Push the glasses of wine off the table and have sex with me. Now. Sex. Now."

"So what do you think?" he asked.

"I don't know," I admitted. "I've never been in a situation like this before, and for the first time ever I regret not reading all those articles my mother sent me about flirting and sex and…" I stopped midsentence. This was so bizarre; honestly I had no idea what to do. Only one way to find out. I might as well ask him.

"You tell me what usually happens next," I asked tentatively.

"That's up to the woman. I've made my intentions clear, and you can decide what you want to do with that." His smile was gone now; instead he stared at me with a look that made my blood reach boiling point, only to completely freeze over immediately after.

His intentions were clear. He wanted to sleep with me again. Just like Val had said. And it terrified me. A part of me wanted that so badly, but this time it was different. It would be different from the other night when I'd considered it a one-night stand with a man I would never see again. This time, *I liked him*. And that was a dangerous place to be.

Chapter Twenty-One

*I*t was already well into the afternoon, and the evening was creeping fast. We'd left the winery and were walking back down the beach. Our intense conversation had been interrupted by the waitress, and after that I'd tried to pretend it hadn't happened. The beach was totally quiet now—in fact, there was no one in sight.

"You want to swim?" Dimitri stopped walking and turned to me. The sun was behind him so his body looked silhouetted against the background, and at that exact moment a gentle breeze picked up and tugged at his shirt. Chest flash.

Oh come on! Really? It was as if he had control over the elements, too, and could bend them to his will whenever the occasion required. *Cue dramatic storm so his white shirt gets soaked and clings to his firm chest.*

"So?" he asked innocently, clearly unaware that in my mind the strong winds had just ripped his shirt from his body and carried it away over the sea.

"Sorry, what?" I said absentmindedly.

"A swim?"

"Oh that!" I glanced over at the water. True, it looked inviting. Blue, calm, refreshing. But another not-so-inviting image flashed through my mind. It wasn't exactly flattering.

Me, in my glittery, trashy as hell, borderline *something a stripper would wear when sliding up and down a pole* pink bikini.

"You can't come to Greece and not swim in the sea! It's basically against the law."

"But, you know..." I gestured to him and then indicated my general bikini top area and back to him. "...This hideous sparkling bikini thing...and you, you know!" (For someone who went to mcd school, I was becoming more and more inarticulate by the day.)

"Take it off then," Dimitri said as he started pulling his shirt off over his head.

"What? My bikini top?"

"Sure. It's how most people swim anyway." He sounded casual.

"I kind of noticed that. What the hell is up with that anyway?"

"What do you mean?"

"The nudity. Breasts everywhere. Don't you think it's a bit indecent?"

"It's very European to swim like that. Here, women are less embarrassed about their bodies. We're very open about that kind of thing. The body is nothing to be ashamed of, it should be celebrated, whatever shape it comes in."

"You really believe that?"

"Of course. A lot of people go nude, too."

I cringed at the image.

"Here! Nothing to be ashamed of." And with that, in one swift horrifying movement, he pulled his pants down. Just pulled those little suckers down and let them fall to the sand. I turned and flung my hands over my eyes, but not before I had caught the slightest glimpse of his...*yes*, I had seen it. And it was now flashing through my mind like a neon sign.

"Are you crazy?" I still had my back to him.

"It's liberating. You should try it."

"Never. No. Nope and no."

"You haven't lived until you have skinny-dipped in the Aegean Sea." I heard a small chuckle escape his lips and then heard the crunch of pebbles under his feet. I peeped through the gap in my fingers and that's when I saw it. Not the penis. Another thing.

He had the best ass I'd ever seen in my entire life. I hadn't gotten a glimpse of it the other night. My mouth opened and my hands fell away from my eyes and I felt myself gape. At that exact moment, Dimitri turned his head and looked at me and beckoned with his hand. Did he really expect me to follow, especially considering the fact that he was completely fucking naked? He had no clothes on, for heaven's sake.

He waded in all the way to his waist and then turned to face me. Oh God, this was just like that advert I'd seen of him in the plane—minus spear...*Well*...

"Come on," he shouted.

"No," I shouted back. "I am not coming in there naked." I looked around to see if anyone had heard that. No one in sight.

This was the perfect time and place for nudity, I guess. Just not mine.

"You don't have to. Just come and swim, though."

This was too much. This was so far out of my comfort zone that the uncomfortable zone wasn't even on this planet—that didn't even make sense. My brain wasn't making sense right now. It was too busy fighting a war with my body, which was screaming bad things...

"Sex. Now. In sea. Jane, come (in more ways than one)."

I looked around again. Still no one. *It's just a swim, Jane. And you will be fully clothed.* Although I knew that all I would be able to think about the second I got into the water was the naked penis that would be bobbing up and down in it. I would keep a safe distance from him, ten yards, at least. Preferably more.

It was with great trepidation, anxiety, nerves, and horny surging hormones that I eventually managed to slip my clothes off and reveal my bikini. I tried not to act self-conscious. I tried not to show how terrified I was as I walked into the sea, my eyes focused on the sand below my feet. I waded in. I started walking off in a different direction, away from Dimitri, as I crept farther and farther into the calm, warm water.

"Where are you going?" Dimitri called out and started wading toward me.

I stuck a finger out. "Stay back. Stay back."

He burst out laughing.

"It's not funny, I'm not comfortable with a naked penis coming toward me."

He laughed louder than I had ever heard him laugh before. "That sounds so clinical."

"I'm a doctor!" I snapped back. "It's my job to be clinical."

"You weren't that worried about my naked penis coming toward you the other night, if I remember correctly."

"What?" I screeched loudly. "There were...I had...it was... besides, if I remember correctly we both agreed that I wasn't really my normal self so with that in mind, and all, it was...and...so..." Fuck my noncompliant mouth and its inability to form proper sentences!

Dimitri just smiled at me. It was the kind of smile that turned your stomach inside out and stole your beating heart right out of your chest.

"Now that, Jane...*that* was flirting. Just in case you were in any doubt." He was so close now. The ripples of water he was creating as he walked started gently splashing my body until he was right in front of me. Bare chested, water just covering his general groin area.

"Did it work?" he asked with a slow smile.

"Uh, did what work, exactly?"

"The flirting?"

I nodded. "Yes. It was sufficient."

"Just sufficient?" he asked.

"Well, how does one measure the success of it?" I was mesmerized by this strange moment. It was a moment that a few days ago, I never could have imagined happening to me.

"It's measured by the way it made you feel." Dimitri came a little closer now. "Now it's your turn to say something." He was right in front of me.

"Like what?"

"Well, you might say something playful like, '*I didn't see you complaining, either.*' Or you could choose something more direct, like"—he leaned in and whispered in my ear—"*'Actually, I don't really remember all the details. Why don't you bring it over here and remind me.'*"

I think I fainted. Or passed out. Or maybe it was a blackout or something like that, because suddenly everything was blank and silent. I just stood there and gaped at him. Dimitri pulled away slowly. His green eyes were boring holes in me. The tip of his tongue came out and touched his lip. His eyes narrowed and his pupils darkened. Then he suddenly turned me around, hard. The movement caught me off guard. I felt a hard tug on my bikini top and it started to loosen.

"What are you doing?" I clasped my arms across my chest as my bikini started to fall.

"I told you, you haven't lived until you have skinny-dipped in the Aegean Sea."

I inhaled sharply as he pulled my straps down and, eventually, pulled the top fully off. My back was still to him, but it felt like I was standing in front of him completely naked and he could see everything. He passed me my bikini top and I clutched it.

And then his finger trailed all the way down my back and I felt it tug gently at my bikini bottom. "Don't make me take these off for you."

"Oh my God." I dove into the water. I wasn't sure if this was the most pervy thing that had ever happened to me, or the hottest. I made sure to keep myself completely submerged while I looked over at him. And I'm not sure what the hell came over me, either. Maybe it was the intoxicating surroundings, the cool water, the black beach that was now sparkling like glitter in the evening light. Maybe it was the way he was looking at me. I have no idea.

But I did it. I slipped them off and held them in my hand. I was totally naked now. I swam underwater and he was right, it did feel good. To be completely naked swimming in the sea felt like one of the most liberating and freeing things I had ever done. The water washed over me and caressed my body and I felt everything start washing away. It was as if the water was pulling any negative thoughts or feelings I'd ever had out of me.

I emerged from the sea, not even aware or concerned where Dimitri was. This wasn't about him, this was about me. I stood up and let the breeze blow against my wet skin as I stared out toward the blue ocean in front of me. I breathed in deeply; the air felt crisp and smelled like flowers and salt and the evening. As I stood there all on my own, I realized that for the first time in a very long time, I was content. I was happy. Truly happy.

I turned around, not even caring that my naked chest was on show. Dimitri was far away from me now; he'd climbed out of the water and was sitting back on the beach. He looked at me and smiled and gave the tiniest wave. I smiled and waved back before diving back into the water.

CHAPTER TWENTY-TWO

I felt alive. All of my senses were alert and prickled. I was filled with a sense of wonder and adventure and a desire for new experiences. Something in me felt like it had been woken, and it felt great.

Dimitri had walked out of the sea and was sitting on the beach watching me. Even though he was far away, the sexual tension that was building between us was still very much there. I slipped my bikini back on under the water and walked out. He passed me a towel and I flopped down on the sand next to him. We both sat in silence for a while looking out over the sea. The view was incredible. This place was magical; I had never been anywhere or seen anything so beautiful before.

"Can I ask you a question?" I turned to face Dimitri.

"Anything."

"Why are you a tour guide if you're a model? And a successful-looking one at that?"

"You've asked the wrong question. You should have asked why do I model when I am a tour guide?"

"What's the difference?" I asked.

"This is my passion. This is what I really love doing."

"So then why model?"

He shrugged and then winked. "Because I'm hot."

"You did not just say that?"

Dimitri smiled at me and nudged me playfully with his shoulder. "I just do it for money."

"Really?"

He stopped smiling and turned to look at me. "I come from this big, crazy, loud Greek family...I loved growing up with so many siblings. But when I was sixteen my dad got sick. Cancer. He knew he was dying and he made me promise that when he was gone, I would step up and become the man of the house. That I would take care of everyone."

"But you were so young," I said, putting a hand on his shoulder without even thinking about it.

"And I had no skills and no way of earning enough to support seven women." He forced a small smile. "So I used my looks. It was the only thing I had at the time. I'll stop soon, I just have two more sisters to get through college and then that's it."

"You've put all your sisters through college? All six of them?"

"Most of them. My youngest sister, the birthday girl, is doing fine art, and my other sister is finishing off a business diploma. I would have loved to study something, but there was just no time... Maybe when I stop this modeling crap I'll be able to go back and do something. Truthfully, I hate it."

"Modeling? Please! What could you hate about dressing up and posing half naked with hot women on the beach?"

Dimitri reached for my hand that I had accidentally left on his shoulder. He took it in his and looked at it. "It's not real. Not like this. This moment here, with you, this is real."

His fingers traced the back of my hand, and all I could think about was taking his hand and putting it on my body. I wanted to be wrapped up in his arms right now. His eyes locked onto mine and I felt myself transported to somewhere else. *Oh God, I am in trouble.*

"Besides, you of all people know what it's like to only be judged on your looks. Sometimes people don't bother looking past that stuff."

His words echoed through me, ringing true in every way possible. There was such a strangeness between us now. The crazy sexual heat of earlier was gone, replaced by something warm and calm.

"So why is this your passion?" I asked.

"I love showing people around and watching them fall in love with this place. The people that come here all leave with a little bit of Greece in their hearts. Like you will. And…" Suddenly a strange smile swept over his face.

"What?" I leaned in, intrigued.

"You know all those photos I have in my house?"

"How could I not?"

"So, when I was young, there was a woman who lived in our village. One day, her son left and he took to the seas and started sailing them. There were so many stories about why. Some said he had his heart broken so badly that he couldn't take it; others thought he was looking for a treasure, or running from the law."

I laughed. "You Greeks are such storytellers."

"And we gossip. Everyone talked about it. Anyway, once a week he would write to his mother and send her photographs of all the places he'd been…"

"Those are the photos?" I asked.

He nodded. "I used to get so excited to run up to her house and see them. She would always pour me something to drink, and we would sit outside under the trees and she would make up these amazing stories about him and the places he was visiting. I think she missed him and the stories she told me were a way of keeping his memory alive when he wasn't there."

"That's so sad."

"It was. But her stories about her son totally changed my life. He was my idol. Even though I'd never met him, I wanted to be exactly like him. I used to imagine he was this great pirate searching for a buried treasure and I wanted to go on the same adventures that he was going on and see the same places he had seen. She used to give me one of the photos every week and I kept them all and vowed I would visit all the same places one day."

"And have you?"

"Almost." I gazed at Dimitri's face now: It had a totally adorable childlike quality to it. He lay back on the sand, making himself more comfortable, and I did the same. "Of course when I got older I realized that there was no pirate treasure." Another small chuckle escaped his lips. "But I still wanted my adventure." He turned to me. "You know how you're looking for something? Well, I feel like

I'm looking for something, too, I just don't know what it is. But until I've found it, I feel like I can't stop exploring."

"I'm not looking for *something*," I quickly qualified. "I'm looking for my father."

Dimitri turned back to me and shook his head. "I think we both know you're looking for much more than just him." His words were so pointed and so steeped in truth that they unsettled me.

"What would happen if you didn't find him, Jane?" he asked, sounding serious again.

"Why, has the investigator said something?" I sat up straight.

"No. Nothing like that." Dimitri was very quick with his response. "I was just talking hypothetically." He turned away and looked back at the sea. "Come, it's getting late." He stood up and pulled me to my feet, too. "We still have to go back home and get ready before dinner."

I had forgotten about agreeing to go to his birthday dinner. I stood up and once again pulled my heavy bag onto my shoulder. The pain of the strap cutting into me was getting too much to bear, and the bag fell from my shoulder and splattered into the sand. I gazed down at the stupid, heavy, oversized thing and a realization slammed into me with such enormous force. It overwhelmed me and shook me to my very core.

"I can't do this anymore. I just can't fucking do this." This bag that I had been lugging around with me wasn't *just* a bag. All the lipsticks and straighteners, the brushes and combs—all the paraphernalia that was physically weighing me down—was mentally weighing me down, too. Every time I tried to find the perfect shade, make my hair into something it was not, I was trying to change and push away that unchangeable part of me. This bag contained all my dashed and trampled hopes. It contained all my perceived failures and all the pain I'd been carrying around with me my entire life. *This was not a bag at all.*

"I've had it. I've just…I can't." There was an edge of desperation to my voice.

"Fuck this!" I bent down and pulled the rest of the contents out of the bag. "I hate this thing!" I held a hair straightener in the air. "Do you know how much I hate it?" I must have looked a little wild as I waved the thing in the air in front of Dimitri's face.

He smiled back at me. "So what are you going to do about it?"

What was I going to do about it? I hadn't thought that far ahead, actually. All I knew was that I wanted all this crap out of my bag. I wanted it out of my life. I wanted to stop feeling like I was lugging the weight of the world around with me and it was slowing me down.

I looked around. "This! I am going to do this." I ran as fast as I could to the edge of the sea and tossed the hair straightener in as hard as I could. It was so dramatic. In my mind I imagined hurling it across the ocean, where it would finally land with an almighty gigantic splash that would shake the very world. It didn't. It plopped into the water a few feet away—but it sure felt good.

I turned and looked at Dimitri, who was now laughing. "God, that felt good." I ran back to my handbag and pulled out my oversized makeup bag. I unzipped it, and the lipsticks bulged out. I picked one up, held it in my hands, and read the bottom.

"*Midnight Angel.*" I looked at him and then out to sea and tossed the lipstick as hard as I could.

I took the next one out. *"Dissolved in Dreams.* Who names these bloody things, by the way?" I tossed this one into the water, too, and it felt great.

"Cheeky Girl." *Toss*

"Rampant Red Raspberry." *Toss*

"Love Me Nude, D Is for Danger, Pink Me Up, Meltdown ... at least the last one makes some sense." I laughed as I tossed them all into the sea.

I went back to my bag. "And do I really need all this sunscreen?" It was a rhetorical question, because before he could answer, I was tossing. "And why do I carry a brush and a comb around with me all the time, too?" I tossed again, and again, and again. Until I had tossed almost everything out of my bag and into the sea. I was laughing like I hadn't laughed in ages, and with each throw I felt lighter and happier.

I turned and looked at Dimitri, and then without thinking about it I ran up and hugged him. I threw myself at him so hard that he almost toppled over, but instead he managed to lift me off my feet and swing me around. I let go of him and tears started streaming down my face, this time tears of happiness.

"I can't tell you how good that felt," I said.

"I'm glad." He reached out and wiped some of the tears from my face. "Only thing, we don't want the turtles to choke."

"What?" I gasped. "You're kidding?"

He shook his head. "Nope."

"Oh crap, I don't want to be a murderer of sea creatures." I turned and ran back to the sea and straight into the shallow waters. Dimitri came running up behind me.

"Luckily it's shallow and pretty see-through," he said, bending down and pulling a lipstick from the seabed. He burst out laughing. "That was quite something, though."

For the next few minutes the two of us ran around in the water splashing each other and collecting my stuff from the sea. We laughed the entire time, and I couldn't remember when I'd last had so much fun. We finally emerged after managing to retrieve about 90 percent of the stuff; the rest was unfortunately lost. We both walked back onto the beach with bulging arms.

"There's a trash can over there," Dimitri said.

I looked, and sure enough there it was. "Why didn't you tell me that earlier?" I asked.

Dimitri smiled. "It was just too much fun to watch."

* * *

We arrived back at Dimitri's house about an hour later and both scrambled to get ready for dinner. I'd only brought one decent dress; it was smart and expensive. I'd imagined wearing it when my father and I went out to dinner at a restaurant where we'd sit up all night talking. Or I'd wear it when he introduced me to his family. I started to slip the dress on over my head and then heard a knock on the door.

"Are you ready?"

"Almost," I called.

I grabbed a towel and dried my hair. It was curly and bushy and for the first time in almost forever, I didn't really care. I'd seen so many women with hair like mine here that I didn't feel such a need to tame it into submission. I stood back and looked at myself, barely recognizing my reflection. Everything about me looked different, and it wasn't just the dress and the hair. It was something else. Something intangible.

My phone beeped and I pulled it out of my now much, much lighter bag.

WHATSAPP GROUP: Jane goes to Greece

Annie: Are you there? Sorry if I was a bit harsh with you earlier. I actually have no idea what you are going through at the moment. None of us do. I shouldn't have tried to tell you what you were feeling.

My fingers hovered over the screen and I was about to type a response, but didn't.

Annie: Jane?

Lilly: Me too ☺ Sorry.

Annie: You there????

Lilly: Chat later then. XX keep us posted. Please.

Annie: X we love ya

I locked my screen and slipped it into my bag again. I didn't have time to chat with them about this right now, but it was good to know—and not surprising—that they supported me in whatever the hell you'd call this journey I was on. I stepped out of the room, and Dimitri rose from the couch. Then his mouth dropped open and he stared at me. "Wow. You look incredible." He walked toward me and I was sure my cheeks were an embarrassing Rampant Red Raspberry shade.

"Thanks." I felt so coy, like a schoolgirl being asked to prom by the hottest guy in her class. (Not that that had ever happened to me.)

He looked hot, as always; shorts, a loose-fitting top, and … hang on, he looked almost exactly like he'd looked today, and yesterday. He looked completely casual. Suddenly I felt like a total moron for dressing up.

"I didn't realize that this was such a casual thing," I quickly said. "I'll go and change into something more appropriate." I turned and started walking back through the door, but he grabbed me by the wrist to stop me.

"Don't you dare change," he said, his eyes looking directly at my lips in a way that made them feel like they were tingling.

"But you look so casual and I feel way overdressed."

"I'll sort that out." Dimitri suddenly disappeared into his room and closed the door behind him.

I sat on the small sofa, picked up a newspaper, and started flipping through it. It was all in Greek and the pictures weren't very interesting. I heard the door open and looked up …

I looked straight into *GQ* magazine's Hottest Men photo shoot.

Holy fuck! That was about the most sensible thing my brain could manage. There he was, casually leaning against the doorframe. Dark, broody eyes and a slightly clenched jaw accentuated his chiseled face. But that wasn't what took my breath away.

It was the fact that he was dressed in a full black tuxedo. His hair was swept back, and aftershave wafted into the room. He was dripping far more sex appeal than bare-chested, spear-wielding Dimitri had. It was the first time I had seen him in noncardboard form with so many clothes on, and he'd never looked more gorgeous. He had deliberately posed like a model and I could see he was struggling to keep a soft playful smile from tugging at his lips.

A small breathy sound escaped my lips as I tried to regain control over my senses. "Are you doing that on purpose?"

"What?" he asked as if butter couldn't melt in his mouth.

"You're doing some deliberate modelly thing." I pointed a finger at him.

Dimitri laughed. "I am," he admitted. "What did you think?"

He struck another kind of pose with an even more clenched jaw.

"It's very 'Blue Steel.'" I smiled back at him, amused. I'd never imagined that someone like him might actually see the funny side in it. You sort of imagine male models as the kind of people that take themselves seriously, but he didn't. He was poking fun at himself—and that made him even sexier and more desirable.

"Okay. Watch this," he said with a chuckle in his voice and a kind of twinkle in his eye. "This is a *very* important look. As a model you have to master it... Right." He straightened himself and looked like he was doing something that resembled warming up, the way an athlete would.

I burst out laughing at the ridiculousness of the situation as he gave his neck a stretch and winked at me.

"Okay, are you watching carefully? This is the flirting face."

I nodded in a state of perpetual giggles.

"I'm going to look down at my watch," he said as he started fiddling with the imaginary wristwatch on his arm. "Now see what happens when I hear a sexy female voice and realize my date for the evening has arrived."

My giggling escalated into full-blown laughter as I listened to Dimitri describe the imaginary scene.

"I glance up at her from my watch, slowly, with only my eyes, and..."

He looked straight up at me and my giggling stopped immediately. "Holy crap!" The words escaped my mouth as my whole body reacted to the look and stiffened. His eyes bored right through me in a way that would make it impossible for any woman, anywhere in the world, to resist him.

"Do you want to buy the watch, Jane?" he asked in a husky seductive voice that was a mixture of danger and sex and dripped with unspoken promises of orgasms aplenty.

"Yes," I said faintly.

He smiled and looked back up in a more normal manner now. "Good. My job here is done."

He walked to the sofa and then extended his hand for me to take. "Shall we?"

I looked at his hand and, as if on autopilot, stood up and placed my hand in his. I could see he was totally aware of the effect he was having on me. He was fully aware that he had reduced me to a puddle of simpering hormones.

"You look...you look..." I heard myself stutter, although I wasn't even aware that my mouth had ever opened.

"Not as good as you look," he said before leaning in and kissing me on the cheek. This time it was different. He let his lips linger and when he pulled away, he let them trail gently down my check, coming ever so close to the corner of my mouth. I wanted to turn and kiss him so badly. So I did.

I could see it took him by surprise at first. But he soon tangled his hands in my hair and pulled me closer. I lifted my hands and placed them on his face; it was soft and rough all at the same time. I pulled my lips away but didn't move my face; instead I leaned my forehead against his, and he held me in place there. When I opened my eyes, I was so close to his face that his features were blurry. He touched his nose against mine, and I could feel and taste his breath against my lips. It was in that moment that I decided to forget all the supposed mistakes that my mother had made with a man named Dimitri once upon a time. I would not let her and the choices she had made govern my life any longer. I'd already spent twenty-five years living under her influence, and she wasn't even there. It was time to cast it off. Time to break free from this invisible pull she had on me. I'd make my own decisions and make my own mistakes, and if this was one, *which it probably was*, then so be it.

I finally pulled away and we walked to the car in total silence, a silence that drifted into the car with us, too. Dimitri looked totally relaxed, but the more we drove the more nervous I started to feel about meeting his family. Suddenly it was very important that they liked me. Halfway through the drive, he reached across and took my hand in his.

"Don't be nervous," he said, giving my hand a firm, reassuring squeeze. He continued to hold my hand and soon he was running his thumb over the top of it. I ran my fingertips up and down his fingers. Our fingers played and intertwined and engaged in a kind of perfect dance. I traced the outlines of his hand softly with the tip of my finger. This was doing a very good job of making me forget to be nervous about meeting his family—but it was causing an entirely different kind of nervous feeling.

We finally pulled up outside a house that looked like a typical Fira home, built into the hill, whitewashed and multileveled. But there was something very different about this house. The noise coming from it was overwhelming, music and what sounded like a million voices.

"Dimitri, Dimitri!" Shouts rang out and I glanced up. About ten faces were staring down at us from the balcony.

Oh God!

Dimitri led me to the front door. "You'll be fine. They're going to love you!"

The inside of the house was even more overwhelming. Every single corner and seat and space you could fit a human being into was full. Children ran around the house, almost knocking things over as they went. One almost knocked me off my feet the second I walked in.

"Kalimera! Kalimera! Kalimera! Kalimera!"

More shouts rang out, and everyone turned to look at us. Dimitri put his arm around my shoulders and said something to everyone in Greek, which seemed to set something in motion. Suddenly everyone descended on me and I was pulled into a frenzy of greetings and cheek kissing until I felt dizzy, like a spinning top being whirled around.

"I'm Dimitri's sister, I'm Dimitri's cousin, cousin, sister, brother-in-law, cousin, second cousin three times removed, sister, uncle, aunt..."

"What did you say to them?" I managed to ask Dimitri as I was being passed around from person to person.

"I just told them you were my date, Jane."

"Date?" My heart jumped into my throat and I was just about to ask him what he meant when I felt a pinch on my bum and jumped. An old man, looking well over eighty, was glancing up at me.

"Come. Uncle Nico!" One of Dimitri's sisters threw me an apologetic amused look and rushed the old man away. I stood in shock for a moment. I felt overwhelmed by the size of his family and the noise and the attention I was getting. Everyone in the room seemed to immediately accept me and want to know me. It was as if I was part of their family. It made me want to cry all over again. I didn't know these people at all, and yet they had made me feel more welcome in their home than I ever remembered feeling in my own family's home.

I turned around when I heard a noise and came face-to-face with an older woman. She looked at me for a second and then launched into a sudden and very scary mixture of shouting and spitting on me. What the hell was going on? I backed up straight into Dimitri.

"Don't worry, she's just warding off evil spirits and trying to protect you."

"Really?"

"Come, I want you to meet my favorite sister, don't tell any of the others I said that!" Dimitri led me out the room and onto the terrace, then rushed me down a small flight of stairs and onto another small terrace. I was so relieved to be away from the noise of it all. "Where's your favorite sister?" I asked, looking around.

"Don't be crazy, I don't have a favorite. I have six. Just thought you needed a break from the noise."

Truthfully I did. "This is not like my family dinners. That's for sure."

"What are your family dinners like?"

"Smaller. Quieter."

"There's no such thing as a small, quiet dinner in Greece." He sat on one of the loungers and I followed suit. "Greeks like to celebrate everything. 'Count each day as a separate life,' as one of our philosophers once said."

"Really?"

"We eat, drink, make love, and enjoy every day as if it were our last." He said that last part in a strange tone, as if trying to convey something I wasn't aware of yet. "What would you do if you knew this was your last day on earth?"

I shrugged. "I have no idea. Who even knows that kind of stuff?"

"I do." He stood up and walked over to my lounger.

"And what would that be?" I asked, looking up at him.

"This..." Dimitri pushed me back until I was lying flat and then climbed on top of me and started kissing me. "This and so much more..." he whispered against my lips before biting the bottom one gently between his teeth. Unlike my kiss earlier, this one was not soft and gentle. This kiss seemed to open the floodgates of need and want.

But it was short-lived. When I heard claps and whoops rise in the air, I pulled away and looked up. At least three smiling people stared down at us. I covered my face with my hands, wanting to die of embarrassment, but Dimitri seemed to take it in his stride. He climbed off me, straightened his clothes, and smiled up at everyone. Some loud Greek and laughter was exchanged, and then one of his sisters rushed down and started to whisk me away forcefully. I had no choice in this.

"To kitchen." Her English was broken, not nearly as good as Dimitri's. "The women go to the kitchen!" she said enthusiastically. My inner feminist wanted to stop her and explain that bras had been burned so that women did *not* need to be in the kitchen, but Dimitri shouted after me.

"Just go with it, Jane! You're Greek!"

His sister held me by the hand and ushered me through the house and the crowds, but stopped halfway. "It's so nice to meet you." She was still holding my hand in hers and then she gave it a little squeeze.

"You too."

"So you and Dimitri?" she said with a wink and a smile in her voice.

I blushed, unable to hide it.

"He's never brought anyone to meet us before." She smiled at me with a knowing kind of look.

"Really?" For some reason this shocked me.

"Yes, he's hardly here. He's always running off and on this island and that one. And he never is meeting any nice girls. We all want him to get married, but he never seems to find anyone. He'll make very good husband. He's the best brother, and Yaya want to see him get married before she dies. And she's very old, you know."

All this talk of marriage was making me seriously uncomfortable. I finally found myself sitting in the busy kitchen. It was buzzing with activity—practically bursting at the seams. I stood feeling completely unsure of myself and watched all the women cook in what looked like an organized frenzy. I didn't cook, which seemed to garner many surprised looks from the older crowd; in fact, they seemed downright horrified. But my lack of experience didn't stop them from ushering me off toward a large board of ingredients and shouting instructions at me.

"Just put in blender and turn on. Make smooth... delicious!" Those were my instructions. I stood and looked at the ingredients. They looked suspiciously like stuff that would make hummus. I cringed internally. Oh, the irony. Hating Greek food and being expected to make it. How hard could it be, though? Put in blender. Turn on. Voilà. I found myself staring at the ingredients for ages. They terrified me. It was irrational.

"Hurry! Food ready!" Shouting broke out around me and suddenly bowls and plates and utensils were being rushed out of the kitchen. "Hurry."

Mild panic gripped me. I know how ridiculous it seemed, but I didn't cook and now I was under a time constraint...

"Quickly." Someone rushed past me with the biggest tray of meat I'd ever seen and gave me a pat on the back. *Shit!* Okay. I started to scoop handfuls into the blender and then I just... *fucked up so completely and royally that this family would probably talk about the incident for years to come.*

Yes, you guessed it. I forgot to put the lid on the blender and it all flew out. Thankfully, I was the only one in the line of fire. But oh how it fired. Within seconds I was covered in oil, whole chick-peas clung to my hair, and gooey paste covered my dress. I wiped some stuff off my face, only to almost blind myself in painful agony as I smeared lemon juice into my eyes.

The commotion that had been constant in the kitchen since I'd walked in stopped. A deathly silence fell on the room, and every-one stared at me. There was a universal pause, a collective inhale followed by a sigh and then, chaos.

People ushered me away from the machine. Others gathered more ingredients to remake the hummus, and someone rushed me off to a bathroom and closed the door behind me. I turned toward the mirror, absolutely terrified of what I might see. And I was right to be terrified. I was covered. My attempt at hummus clung to my cheeks and hair, and worst of all, my dress looked like a Jackson Pollock. I shook my head in absolute despair. A knock on the door made me turn.

"Jane?" It was Dimitri. "I heard what happened." He was laughing. *He was laughing.* The bastard!

"It's not funny, okay?" I hissed back through the door.

"Can I come in?"

"Sure. Why not." I opened the door quickly, pulled him inside, and closed it again. The fewer people who saw me, the better. He took one look at me and his eyes widened, and then he started laughing again.

"Stop it." I smacked him on the arm.

"You're right. Sorry." I could see he was attempting to wipe the smile off his face, but it wasn't going anywhere.

"What the hell am I going to do? I can't go out like this."

Dimitri looked me up and down like he was formulating a plan of action. He walked over to the sink, wet a washcloth, and started wiping my face. And although he was essentially wiping gooey food off me, it felt wildly erotic, and hot and heavenly and...especially when he ran the cloth over my lips.

I don't actually recall there being anything there at all.

He washed the cloth out and then started cleaning my hair. I stared at his face: He was cleaning me off with such focus and concentration, it was as if he was performing the most important job in the world.

"Thanks," I said when it was all over.

"Pleasure."

Then we stood and stared at each other again. Both our faces broke out into massive grins and I forgot I was in a bathroom, because it felt like I was floating on a cloud, rather than having my feet on the ground.

"You still look amazing, though," he said before his eyes trailed down to my dress. "But I'm not sure what we're going to do about that?"

I looked down at my dress. The front was completely covered in a crisscross, splotchy pattern of creamy goo. Dimitri reached for some toilet paper and started scooping the thick clumps off. "I don't want to wet it. That would be uncomfortable." He wiped the dress until the worst of it was off, leaving behind giant cream-colored smudges.

"I can't let people see me like this." I said.

"I think you're going to have to turn it inside out then," he said, as if he had weighed every option and concluded that this was the only solution. I studied my dress in the mirror, and he was right: It was the only thing to do under the circumstances.

"Okay." I turned back to him and nodded, expecting him to leave the bathroom. He didn't. "So, you can go now. Thanks." I looked at the door and back to him, but he simply stepped forward with a smile and a look in his eye that was making me feel very hot under my nonexistent collar. It was the kind of look that made my toes curl and my fingertips tingle.

He reached out and took the hem of my dress between his fingers. He smiled and slowly started lifting it, his fingers trailing up my thighs as he went. My skin responded with a million goose bumps and a shiver that traveled all the way from my thighs to the top of my head. Even my scalp tingled. He lifted the dress farther and farther until I felt the cool air rushing between my legs. His eyes traveled straight down there, and I felt completely naked under his gaze.

"Have I told you yet that you wear the most amazing underwear?"

"Really?" I said excitedly. Finally someone, other than my fish, was actually seeing them. I suddenly felt justified in all that money I'd spent over the years on the sexy lacy things. Dimitri tugged the dress up until my stomach was exposed. His hands moved to my waist, and he squeezed. I threw my head back and closed my eyes. He brought his lips down to my neck as his hands traveled higher up my stomach. A knock on the door stopped us dead in our tracks once more.

"My family's timing is terrible," he moaned into my neck before letting me go and sticking his head through the door. I took the opportunity to quickly whip my dress off and turn it inside out myself.

When he turned back around I was patting my dress into place. He shook his head. "And we were just getting to the good part." He smiled at me and took me by the hand "Come. Everyone is waiting for us."

And they were: The entire table was full. I was just about to sit down when the older woman who had been spitting on me earlier jumped up and started shouting. She gestured at my dress and then kissed me on both cheeks. Everyone was smiling, and some even started clapping. The whole room erupted and I had no idea why.

"What's going on?" I asked him.

Now Dimitri was blushing, too, and I couldn't quite believe my eyes. I'd never seen him look so coy and flushed. "We have a superstition here that if you wear your clothes inside out, you're going to be getting married soon. I'd forgotten about that." He quickly averted his eyes from me and sat.

"Oh. I see." For some reason, wild butterflies started flapping through my stomach. My brain then quickly skidded off to a very bad place as I imagined what Dimitri would look like standing at the head of the aisle.

Stop! the sensible part of my brain mentally screeched to that other part. I shot Dimitri a quick glance and that stupid, giddy smile seemed to be mirrored back to me.

CHAPTER TWENTY-THREE

*I*t was as if I had never eaten food in my entire life. As if my taste buds had never experienced a single sensation. They had been dead for all these years, and now they were alive. I'd started reluctantly, under the threat that it was totally impolite, downright rude, and wildly offensive not to eat the food you were served. This was the greatest insult one could make to a woman, apparently.

Dimitri had cast me a sideways glance as if to say *"you have to,"* followed by a kind of supportive smile as I picked the first thing up. Spana-something. I didn't even know what it was. It lurked somewhere between a quiche and a pie, I had no idea, but I could feel everyone looking at me expectantly. So I raised the thing to my mouth tentatively. I assumed I was going to have to chew and swallow with great difficulty, and then plaster a fake smile across my face and exclaim how delicious it was, even though I felt nauseous.

But it wasn't like that. At all. The second it touched my lips, the second I started chewing, it was the most amazing thing I had ever tasted in my entire life…and I was *famished*. Starving. I plowed my way through a plate, and then without my asking, another one was put in front of me and it felt as if everyone was watching me with glee and egging me on. Then the wine and even more food flowed and I felt quite swept up in it all. My taste buds were basically screaming for more and more and more…

I was so caught up in this feeding frenzy that I only looked up when I heard a ting.

Dimitri was standing up tapping a glass with his spoon. He turned his attention to his sister, the birthday girl who I'd hardly had a chance to speak to yet. Everyone had put their knives and forks down and looked at him. I tried to chew and swallow my mouthful of food as quickly as possible.

"Anthea," Dimitri said, beaming at his gorgeous green-eyed sister. "I just wanted to say happy, happy birthday and even though you steal my shirts and wear them to college and get paint all over them and ruin them, I still love you." Everyone clapped again and someone even made a whistling sound.

"And she also stole your cologne and gave it to her boyfriend for his birthday," one of his other sisters yelled out, which caused more laugher.

"Hey, I'm a poor student," Anthea retorted. "And you get given so many."

"It must have smelled bad, since he broke up with you a week later," another sister yelled across the table. This was nothing like my family dinners. I was surrounded by laughter, fun, a sense of love, and something I wasn't sure I'd ever felt before... *family*. In the real sense of the word. Inclusive and nonjudgmental. Everyone looked like they had a place here and fit in. I wanted that. But it also made me more aware of the fact I had no idea where I really belonged.

"I looked everywhere for that thing." Dimitri laughed and shook his head. "Anthea, we all love you just the way you are, even if you are a kleptomaniac." He raised his glass in the air, and a lump started forming in my throat as I felt the tears welling up inside me again. *Please no, please no!* I screamed inside, hoping that it would keep them at bay.

Dimitri continued, "But seriously, you are such a talented artist and we are all so, so proud of you and I know that if Dad was here, he would be very happy with the beautiful young woman sitting in front of us today."

I burst out crying! That was me. Gone. The tears and loud wails just flew out and the whole table looked at me. "I'm so sorry," I whimpered, my chest rising and falling quickly as I tried to get air into my lungs. "It's just... that was so sweet and they all love you so much and he doesn't mind if you steal his things and they love you just the way you *aaaarrrreeeee*..." I wailed the last word and then pushed the plate out of my way and slumped onto the table. It was so embarrassing and dramatic, but I just couldn't stop it. It felt like a million hands started rubbing my back all at once, and I heard people telling me it was all going to be okay. The old lady who'd been spitting on me earlier and was now probably secretly planning my wedding had stuck her head right up to mine and was making soothing *shush*ing noises in my ear. She was talking in Greek and kissing the top of my head, which just made me cry even more.

And when I didn't stop, she pulled my hand toward her forcefully and I felt something being tied around my wrist. I lifted my head and looked down at my arm, where a big blue eye stared up at me from a bracelet around my wrist.

"It's a Mati bracelet. She wants you to have it. Every Greek should have one," Dimitri said, sitting next to me and slipping an arm around me. The old woman promptly smiled, kissed me again, spat on me some more, and then got up and walked away.

"It's a symbol of good luck here. The eye protects you, but it has to be given to you by someone else," he said, rubbing my arm as the tears started to finally dry up. I looked up and everyone was still looking at me.

"I'm sorry, I didn't mean to ruin your birthday speech."

"Don't worry." Dimitri nudged me. "Now you're officially Greek, Jane!"

* * *

We finally stumbled out of the party at around two o'clock that morning. After my crying was over I'd managed to eat another plate of food and consume far too many of those tasty licorice-flavored drinks.

We drove back to Dimitri's house and I didn't feel like going inside. I didn't want this day to end. I'd had more fun than I'd had in ages, and I was scared that if I closed my eyes and opened them in the morning, it would all be over. I was worried that all the realizations I'd had today about my life would disappear as I slept. They'd be out of my reach once more, and I wanted to hold onto them this time.

"Can we go for a walk?" I asked. I just wanted to enjoy this strange warm feeling that was buzzing in my veins.

"I was hoping you'd say that." Dimitri walked around the car and opened the door for me. He hooked his arm through mine and we started walking through the narrow streets of his town. Fira was still very much alive at this hour; many of the shops were still open, and the whole place was buzzing. People operated on different clocks here.

We walked in silence for a while along the small and winding streets. "So what can you tell me about this place?" I asked.

"Well." He nudged me with his body as we walked. "Did you know that Santorini is unique in the world? It is the only caldera that is inhabited. So we are all living on a volcanic cauldron," he said with a smile in his voice.

"Why? Why would any sane human live on a volcano that could blow at any given moment?" I looked over at Dimitri.

He shrugged. "Like I said, we live for today."

"Oh please." I laughed. "You say that now, but wait until it explodes."

Dimitri laughed. "At least we would have gotten to live in the most beautiful place in the world. Eaten the best food and drunk the finest wine. Laughed and loved with friends and family and..."

The laughter in his voice was gone now. "…and at least I got to meet you."

His words made me giddy and my heart started to shudder. I liked him. Oh God, I *liked* him.

"Kiss me." The words just came out of my mouth before I knew what I was saying.

Dimitri smiled and started to lean in and then stopped. "Wait. Not here, we're in the street." He took me by the hand and started rushing me along. When we came to the end of the street, he turned and led me up a small alley. It was very narrow and filled with low arches; we had to duck down just to get through them.

We finally arrived at the end. It was mainly dark, except for the soft light of the faraway buildings. The stones were rough and looked old, as if the alley had been built hundreds of years ago. We were both panting from the running and it took a while for us to catch our breath again. I looked around. This place felt like the most secret, remote place on the planet. We were totally alone, and there was no sign of life.

Dimitri walked me backward until my back pressed into the wall and his body pressed into mine. I stared up into his eyes.

"You're so beautiful, Jane." He took my hands, interlaced his fingers into mine, raised them both over my head, and pressed them into the wall. Hard. He pressed his body into mine even more. Then he released my hands and let his fingertips run all the way down my arms. Small jagged breaths escaped my mouth as his lips came down to meet mine and his fingers finished their trail down my arms.

"Did you know…" he whispered against my lips. "That when archaeologists excavated this island…" He stopped talking and went in for another kiss. "They found human remains from the late Neolithic period right in this very wall."

"Huh?" I pulled away and looked at him curiously. He flashed me a smile.

"Just trying to make this scientific for you, that's all." He went in and kissed me again and I chuckled against his mouth. I parted my lips ever so slightly. He kissed my bottom lip, sucking on it gently at first, and then a little harder before he let it go. This kiss hadn't even started properly, and yet it was the hottest one I had ever experienced. He took my face between his hands and pulled me toward him. His mouth opened, and I opened mine to meet him. He slipped his tongue deep into my mouth and it was warm and wet and tasted of licorice and honey and something that was unique to him. I ran my tongue over his and a thousand, million tiny needles felt like they pricked me all the way up my spine. His scent was also unique, and if I could have bottled it and kept it I would have.

I felt overwhelmed and intoxicated from all the tastes and smells and sensations running through me. I let go. I moved my arms and wrapped them around the back of his head and pulled him in closer. Our mouths opened even more and the kiss deepened and it was fast and messy and there was nothing controlled about it. I could lose myself in this moment.

Dimitri moaned in my mouth as his hands left my face and trailed down my neck.

"Jane…" His voice came out breathily in between the deep kisses. "You're amazing." He went down to my shoulders and I felt the strap of my dress starting to slip down.

"Wait. What are you doing?" I pulled my strap back up and looked around the alley.

He stopped, raised his head, and looked me straight in the eyes. "It's just the two of us." A slow, small smile broke out across his face as his fingers again moved to my dress straps and he started to pull them off my shoulders. And then I felt him loop a finger around one of my bra straps and start slipping that down.

This was by far the kinkiest thing I had ever done in my life. I gasped when I felt the cool breeze on my body as my bra came down and my breast was totally exposed. "I never do stuff like this," I whispered as his lips started trailing down from my collarbone.

"I know. You say that a lot." His lips moved down even farther and he planted kisses across my chest. I gasped as his warm lips grazed my nipple. A moan involuntarily escaped my mouth as his tongue came out and he took me in his mouth.

I squirmed under his touch and ran my hands through his hair and the back of his head and pulled him in even closer. I grabbed his shoulders, digging my nails into him, and held on to him tightly as he lowered his head and licked the space between my breasts.

"Dimitri." I heard myself say his name as he squeezed my nipples between his fingers and ran his thumb over them. And then… he stopped, abruptly. He kissed me all the way up from my breasts to my neck and then chin and then planted one last kiss on my lips and locked eyes with me. I was gasping for breath, and my body was still wriggling under him.

"I'm about to reach that stage of no return, Jane. So tell me to stop or…"

I looked around the alley once more, still empty. I'd only ever had sex in a bed, maybe a sofa at the most. All my friends had kinky stories about backseats and public beaches at night and airplanes. Now I wanted one of those stories, too! It was time Plain Jane Smith fully let her hair down.

"Don't stop."

Chapter Twenty-Four

I woke up the next morning tangled up in Dimitri's arms. I gazed over at him, still fast asleep. God, he was gorgeous when he slept. I watched him for a while before turning my attention to the ceiling with a smile. I think I must have smiled in my sleep. In fact, I hadn't stopped smiling since he'd sexually stunned me into a post-orgasmic alleyway stupor. Wait until I told my friends that I'd had dirty, kinky back-alley sex! Mind you, they hadn't exactly been that thrilled with the idea of another Dimitri. Not that I blamed them.

My thoughts then turned to my birth mother again. I wondered how much of what she had said was true. *"A youthful holiday fling."* Perhaps it had been more than a meaningless fling? It was certainly more for me at this stage.

"Good morning," a soft, sexy, sleepy voice said. I turned and Dimitri was yawning and stretching in the bed next to me.

"Morning." I turned to face him.

He propped himself up on his elbow. "How did you sleep?"

"Better than I've slept in a long time." I smiled at him and he returned it. The moment was broken by the sound of Dimitri's phone ringing, and my heart thumped.

"Is that the investigator?" I called after him as he went into the living room to retrieve his phone. I jumped up, wrapped the sheet around me, and walked into the living room to watch him talk on the phone in Greek. He finally hung up and turned back to me, naked. But not even his nudity was enough to distract me.

"So was it the investigator? Does he have any info?" I pressed.

"Huh?" Dimitri looked at me blankly for a second, as if he was still struggling to wake up. "Uh, yes. It was him. Nothing yet, he says, still waiting on some things."

"What things?" I asked, feeling the excitement bubble up again.

"Sorry, I didn't ask."

"Did he say he was close, though?" I stepped forward.

"He didn't really say." Dimitri turned his back on me and walked over to the kitchen. "Breakfast?" he called out over his shoulder.

I sighed. "Please can I talk to him next time?" I was frustrated by the lack of any new information pertaining to my father.

"Sure. His English is not great, but sure. Have you packed yet?" he asked, changing the subject.

"For what?" I followed him back into the bedroom, where he started pulling on some clothes. There should be a law against this man wearing clothes.

"Did you forget that I'm taking you island-hopping? We'll only be away for a few days, so instead of bringing your whole suitcase, you should just grab a few things."

"Okay." I nodded.

"Great. Then get ready, eat breakfast, and pack. I'm going to go get some supplies for the boat. I'll be back to fetch you soon." He kissed me on the forehead before walking out.

WHATSAPP GROUP: Jane goes to Greece

Jane: Hi guys. I'm going to be leaving on a tour of the islands now, not sure what reception will be like at sea, so thought I would just let you all know.

Annie: Are you cross with us? ☹

Jane: No.

Annie: Promise?

Jane: Cross my ♥

Annie: Good! ☺ Are you going with Dimitri?

Jane: Yes.

Lilly: What is his full name? Just tell us in case we need to send a search and rescue party.

Jane: Dimitri Spiros. He runs a company called Dimitri's Island Tours out of Santorini. Happy?

There was a slight pause in the conversation and then...

Annie: OMG!!!! He is so fucking hot!!!!

Lilly: Where?

Annie: Google him.

Val: Holy shit! You had sex with that ☺

Lilly: H O T

Val: Bravo

Lilly: But he can't look like that in real life?

Annie: Wait! Is he also a model? Because there's a guy with the same name that looks like him, only his face is not on a website for a tour company, it's plastered on a billboard!!?

Jane: ☺

Val: You're having sex with a Greek tour guide model. LOL!!

Lilly: hahaha. Take a photo of him and send it to us!

Jane: I'll try

Stormy: no hesis not my t.ype

Lilly: OMG Storm, did you just google something? Did you really just use the evil World Wide Web?

Annie: Well of course he's not your type. He doesn't breathe fire and have a ring through his dick ☺

Val: LOL Stormy you are never going to live that one down.

I laughed out loud. Stormy had recently slept with a man who had a ring through his penis and she'd had no idea what to do with the thing.

Annie: Any news on your dad?

Jane: Not yet. ☹

Val: We're crossing fingers for you.

Jane: Thanks. I want to meet him so badly. I haven't wanted anything this badly in a long time.

* * *

The boat was a good size and had the words DIMITRI'S TOURS etched into the side. I climbed onto a small outdoor deck that had built-in seats running its length with a small wooden table attached to them.

There was a covered cockpit—probably not the right word for a boat—that had a few small chairs in it. Another sofa ran the length of the room, and a small kitchen was built into one of the sideboards. A row of windows gave the room an amazing view of the blue water outside. A tiny staircase at the far end led down into a small room with a double bed. A tiny toilet and shower were closed off in a little cubicle.

I'd never been on a boat like this, one you could actually sleep in, but . . .

One room? Double bed? Used for tours? I stood in the small windowless room and started to wonder how many women Dimitri had shared this bed with. I felt nauseated.

"I usually use the boat for day cruises only, island-hopping. I never stay over in it with other people," Dimitri said, walking into the room as if he had been reading my thoughts.

"Oh!" I swung around and looked at him, feeling ever-so-slightly vulnerable and exposed at the idea that he had just figured out what I was thinking.

"In case you think I bring all the girls here, or something."

"Don't you?" I asked.

"No. Just you." He moved in closer to me and wrapped his arms around me as if we were a real couple. In fact, everything today was feeling very couple-y, from the waking up together in bed to kisses good-bye and now this. On the one hand it felt so right, but on the other I knew it was finite. This had an end. It ended when I found my father and then went back to South Africa. But it wasn't over yet, and while I was here I wanted to enjoy every moment of it. *How Greek of me!*

"So where are you taking me?" I asked.

"I want to show you something incredible." He smiled and started walking away but then stopped. "By the way, I bought you some things, they're in the cupboard." He gestured before disappearing up the steps.

I opened the cupboard and couldn't quite believe my eyes. Hanging inside was a plain black, nonsequined bikini, sans push-up bust padding. This was one of the nicest things anyone had ever done for me. It might not seem like a lot—it didn't come with bells and whistles and bright blowup balloons. Rather, it was one of those tiny, subtle gestures that only someone very close to you would know to give you.

Dimitri was officially the most thoughtful person I had ever met. How was it possible, though? Was he perfect? There had to be a catch. No one could be this perfect, surely.

CHAPTER TWENTY-FIVE

In one of the brochures I'd read on the plane, a quote had caught my eye. At the time I'd dismissed it, but now I was marveling at how accurate it was.

"Happy is the man who has the good fortune of sailing the Aegean Sea."

The island of Santorini was starting to disappear over the horizon, enveloped in the calm bright-blue waters. A breeze was rushing past me and I stretched out across the sofa on the deck, watching the waves smack against the side of the boat as it sped through the water. The sky was equally blue and totally cloudless; it dipped down to meet the sea in a great expanse of blueness that stretched out in every direction imaginable. A gust of wind sprayed water on me and for the second time in the last few days, I felt totally and utterly alive. Awake.

I'd always felt like I only had one foot in the world. Not fully knowing who you are makes it difficult to commit to the life you've created for yourself. I felt neither here nor there. Sometimes I felt like I stood on the sidelines, just outside my life, looking in and not participating fully in what was going on around me. You could say that I wasn't really living.

But right now I felt fully alive.

We raced across the water for a while before land came into view. Red-and-brown rocky-looking hills rose up out of the water. The color of the water near the shore was quite different from the blue I'd been used to. This time it was a bright-green color punctuated by patches of dark navy.

As we drew closer and closer, I saw something jutting straight out of the water. Eventually I realized that it was a massive rusted ship propped up in the green water and lying at an angle as if it had been there forever. Some of it had disintegrated into the sea, but the rest—despite the rust—looked intact.

The sea was quiet, apart from the odd small swell knocking against the sides of the shipwreck. I had never seen anything like it. A kind of ghostly aura hung over this mysterious-looking thing. There was something so haunting and beautiful about this carcass of a ship, washed up on the shore.

"Some say it was simply an accident, the captain underestimated the weather; some say he was chased by pirates." Dimitri came up and put a pair of goggles and a snorkel in my hands. "I prefer the pirate story." He smiled at me, took his shirt off, and positioned himself at the edge of the boat as if he was about to jump into the water. "Come." He held his hand out for me and I walked toward him.

We jumped into the water together; it was cool and clear and magical. We swam up to the rusty ship, which now towered above us like a haunted castle. I'd never snorkeled near a shipwreck before and I dipped my head underwater only to be met by an eerie rib cage of rusted metal bones. It was like an underwater grave-yard. We swam around the ship for a while and I was struck by how something so broken, derelict, and ugly could be so incredibly beautiful at the same time.

When we'd finished we walked out of the sea and onto the land. The rocks were sharp under my feet, and I immediately squealed as one pressed into my heel. And then, without any kind of warn-ing, Dimitri came up behind me and lifted me. I screamed in fright as he swung me into his arms.

"Sorry, I forget how rocky it is," he said, holding me like I was nothing more than a measly bag of feathers.

"You're just trying to show off," I teased him, squeezing a bulg-ing biceps and laughing.

"You're right. I am trying to show off. You see, I'm trying to get this girl to agree to go on a date with me."

"A date?"

"Yes, I'd like to turn the clock back a bit and take her out on a *real* date."

"And what would you do on this date?"

"The usual. Dinner, champagne, candlelight, some dancing, and then walk her home and if I'm lucky, I get a kiss at the end."

"Just a kiss?" I asked.

Dimitri nodded. "Yes. You see this girl I want to ask out, we've kind of gotten to know each other in the wrong order. And I'd like to fix that and go back to the beginning with her. I'd like to date her properly, like I should have done."

My heart started pounding in my chest. "I see." I played along.

"So do you think she'll go with me?" he asked.

"Possibly."

"I hope so." Dimitri paused and looked at me closely. "Because I really, really like her. A lot."

"Uh-huh?" I was rendered speechless. No words came to mind at all as I stared into and got stupidly lost in the swirling green of his eyes. I wanted to say it back, that I liked him, too. More than a lot at this stage.

"So it would be great if she agreed to go on a date with me tonight, so I could spend some time showing her how much I like her. What do you say?"

"All right. I'll chat with her and see what she says."

Dimitri laughed. "And what do you think she'll say?"

"I'm sure she'll think about it and weigh up the pros and cons and all the various factors."

"Shouldn't she just listen to her heart?"

"Isn't that a Bon Jovi song?" I said sarcastically. "Or someone equally cheesy?"

"Just because Jon Bon Jovi said it, doesn't mean it's not true."

We smiled at each other. It was different this time. It felt stupid and giddy and childish—in the best way possible.

"So what do you say, Jane? A date?"

I shrugged, trying to act casual. "Sure. Why not? Pick me up at seven?" Dimitri and I both burst out laughing and I wrapped my arms around him and hugged him.

* * *

We spent the rest of the day boating around the islands. There was so much to see. The waters constantly changed color, from dark blues to greens; in some parts they were completely translucent. And then there were all the different islands. We traveled from the sandy beaches of one to the rocky coastline of another. You could never get tired of these views. I could almost imagine the Greek gods roaming these islands in the millennia of old.

I was very actively trying out the good old Greek philosophy: "Do nothing and relax. Contemplate the sea and sunshine and contemplate contemplating, but without expending too much energy on contemplating your abilities to contemplate."

It was early evening by the time Dimitri finally pulled into a port and moored the boat. I glanced down at my phone; it was six p.m. already, one hour until this date of ours, and quite frankly I felt so nervous I could puke. The fact that this had been labeled "a date" felt like it changed everything between us. More so than having sex with someone, *twice*. Sex was one thing, but candles and romance . . . that was something completely different.

I went downstairs to get ready. My options for outfits were limited. The best I could do was a summery navy dress. Not particularly sexy and date-y, it hung to my knees and had little capped sleeves. I didn't even have lipstick to put on. Not that a smattering of red lipstick is the magic wand for your Cinderella moment.

As I walked back up the small flight of stairs, I could feel the prickle of nerves even in my toenails. And of course when I reached the top, my date was sitting there waiting for me. His face lit up the second he saw me, and when he extended his arm for me to take I felt a surge of emotion. If happiness could kill you, I was terminally ecstatic.

We walked arm in arm off the boat and onto the small beach. I could see a restaurant in the distance and presumed that was where our date was happening. The restaurant was right on the beach; intimate little blue tables and chairs were placed on the sand, and the water lapped a foot from the chair legs. The water was almost completely still that night, the moon only a small sliver in the sky, and the stars had not yet appeared. The whole place had a mystical quality to it, like it was frozen in time somehow. Greece was filled with such a sense of history, a subject I didn't have much experience with, until now. I hadn't known anything about my own heritage, but this was where I came from.

Dimitri pulled the chair out for me and I sat down and immediately fidgeted with the napkin on the table nervously. Dimitri sat opposite me and rested his elbows on the table, putting his face between his hands and staring at me. I tried to hold his look, but his gaze was so intense that I felt like I was on the receiving end of a massive wave that threatened to knock me off my feet. There was something so different happening between us tonight. It was tangible and palpable and lit up the space between us. The air felt electric and it made trying to relax almost impossible. I looked back at him, determined to hold his eye contact this time. I locked eyes with him and allowed all the feelings that I was having to rush over me and ebb and flow through my veins, making my face flush a bright red again.

"That color suits you," Dimitri said. "Everything suits you."

"That's not true. I could name a million things that don't suit me. Skinny jeans, for example."

Dimitri leaned across the table, pushed the candle away, and laced his fingers through mine. His thumb trailed across the back of my hand, and my whole body responded to his touch. "You're beautiful, Jane."

I blushed even more and shook my head. "But I'm not."

"Who told you that?"

"Lots of people, like bullies from school," I said as one particularly painful memory came flooding back.

"What?" Dimitri squeezed my hand.

"It's stupid and embarrassing," I said, trying to push the memory right back down again to where it came from.

"Tell me."

I looked up at Dimitri and he smiled gently, as if urging me on. "Okay, when I was in second grade, the girls and boys were playing a game of kissing catchers. I still remember the exhilaration I felt at the prospect of being caught and kissed, it was so intense. The game started and we all fanned out, running and screaming and giggling across the playground. I ran with such a sense of anticipation and excitement that I was already rather far when I turned and realized that not one of the boys was chasing me. Not one."

I felt a little lump rise in my throat at the pain and embarrassment that I experienced so acutely in that moment. I remember how my small, young heart had plummeted into my stomach as if it had been turned to concrete.

"I would have chased you." Dimitri finally spoke.

"Well, you weren't there," I said softly and looked out over the sea, trying to avoid eye contact with him because I felt like I was on the verge of tears again.

"I'm here now. And in case you hadn't noticed, I'm chasing you." He pulled my hands toward him and I felt him place a kiss on one of them. "And these days, who tells you that you're not beautiful?" he asked.

"Huh?" His question made me turn and look at him. "What do you mean?"

Dimitri didn't answer me. Instead he raised his brow in a questioning fashion.

"I guess..." An uneasy feeling started creeping over me. "I guess I do," I said softly.

Dimitri nodded as if he had been expecting this answer. "And I bet it's that same person who tells you all those other things you believe about yourself, too?"

"What things?"

"That you're undeserving. A disappointment. You walk around believing that you don't deserve all the good things that life has to offer, don't you? Maybe you've even been blocking them."

"I...I..." His statement and the loaded implications in it sent a shock wave through me and I had no idea what to say to that. Had I really been engaged in self-fulfilling prophecies? Refusing to believe I deserved happiness or anything good, so blocking these things at every turn? And then for once in my entire life, my mother's timing was actually perfect: My phone beeped and it gave me a great excuse to break the moment. I read her message and sighed.

"Who's it from?" Dimitri asked.

"Just my mother." I rolled my eyes and showed him the text:

I looked at the weather channel. It's postapocalyptically hot there. Remember to put sunscreen on. You know what your skin is like and you don't want to go all blotchy like scary Aunt Meg, which leads to skin cancer by the way. XX

I slipped my phone back into my bag and turned back to Dimitri.

"That sounds like something one of my sisters or my mother would say."

"I doubt that. I doubt your sisters and mother interfere as much as mine does and offers you as much 'constructive criticism.' She's always telling me what I should be doing, what I should not be doing, what I should be wearing, what my apartment should look like, who I should be dating, and how and—"

"And how disappointed she is in you?" Dimitri said that with a very strange tone in his voice.

"What?"

"Has she ever told you she feels that way?" he asked.

"No, but she's always trying to change something about me, or fix something that's broken or not up to her standards."

"Have you ever thought that maybe she just really loves you and doesn't know how else to show you?"

My eyes lifted and met his. I let him look at me in a way that felt like he was trying to look inside me, like an X-ray machine. I was stunned and couldn't help but wonder if what he'd said about my mother was true. What about all the other beliefs I held about myself; were those also untrue? Were they really my own creations, born out of my own insecurities and faulty self-worth? Had I projected my own feelings of inadequacy onto every single aspect of my life, as a result seeing my world only through those filters?

"What are you thinking about?" Dimitri asked, interrupting my thoughts.

A small tear formed in my eye. "That when you're given up for adoption, you believe there's something wrong with you. That you must be bad and therefore unlovable. That's surely the only reason you were given away, right? Because mothers aren't supposed to give their babies away."

"There's nothing wrong with you, Jane. You're perfect. Just the way you are."

I squeezed Dimitri's hands in mine. The dinner had taken a very serious turn, one I hadn't really been prepared for, but I liked it.

"How did you get so perceptive? You don't miss a thing, even the things that aren't said," I asked and then quickly answered, "Oh, that's right, you have six sisters."

"No, I wasn't going to say that at all."

"Really?"

He shook his head. "When my dad died of cancer, I was the one that mainly cared for him in those last few months. Toward the end he was in so much pain he couldn't speak or move or communicate in any normal way. I had to pay extra attention to everything he did, or in his case didn't do. I learned to read every tiny movement of his, every small expression, from the crinkle of his eyes when he was frightened and wanted me to hold his hand, to the way the corners of his mouth twitched when he was thirsty, or the way he just raised his finger off the bed because he wanted his pillows adjusted."

"Oh God, that's awful." I reached out and took Dimitri's hands this time.

"He lived a great life!" Dimitri forced a smile. "He lived every moment to the fullest. He wasn't a rich man, but his life was so full of riches. He was a great father and husband, and he would have really liked you." Dimitri's smile grew.

"I'm sure I would have liked him, too... if he was anything like you are."

"Are you saying you like me, Jane?"

"Yes. A lot," I said. I'd never felt closer to another human being. I don't think I'd ever felt so understood, either. He had seen all the way through me and into me, in the best way possible. And he thought I was perfect. Just the way I was. He didn't want me prettier, or blonder, or shorter, or with matching eyes or smaller feet or more personality, funnier, more popular, cooler... he thought I was perfect, *just the way I was.*

When dinner was over we walked through the streets of the small town. This place was far less touristy and seemed like an authentic Greek village; there were no souvenir shops and no tourists spilling out onto the streets. I was still enjoying the fact that I couldn't hear the noisy drone of tourists when we suddenly heard loud music coming from behind us. We both turned and were faced with an image I couldn't have predicted. I almost started laughing as a troupe of singing, fiddle-playing men came dancing toward us. And more than that, it looked like the entire village had joined in, too.

"What's that?"

"It's a wedding procession," Dimitri said, and he pulled me off the street as we watched it go past. People were dancing and singing and clapping with happy abandon. I glanced at the bride and groom: They were laughing together and looked so young and in love, you couldn't help but get swept up in the exuberance of the moment. I found myself clapping and swaying to the music until I was completely lost in it all. I danced like no one was watching and even sang along, although I had no idea what was being said. In the midst of the procession, a woman ran over to me and put a sweet in my hand.

"What's this for?" I asked, but she had already run back and was quickly swallowed up by the happy crowd.

Dimitri smiled at me. That strange twinkle in his eyes was back. "They hand them out at weddings. They say if you sleep with it under your pillow, you'll dream about your future husband."

Despite my best effort to control my eyes, they jumped straight up and met his. I wanted to say something, but not even the tiniest little words could find their way into my mouth. All this talk of marriage...first with the inside-out dress, now with the sweet. *Is the universe conspiring to tell me something?* Not that I believed in things like that. But Stormy did, and according to her I was getting married next year. Despite myself, I slipped the sweet into my bag...just in case.

We finally reached the boat, and he silently helped me up. I realized just how tired I was after the action-packed day we'd had together.

"That was a nice first date." Dimitri took up a position directly in front of me.

"Yes." I smiled at him. It wasn't the kind of smile that you consciously put on your face. It was one of those that just naturally arrived on your face before you even realized it was there.

"So what kind of first-date kiss would you like, Jane?" His eyes locked onto my lips, which tingled in response.

"I didn't say you were going to get a first-date kiss."

"You didn't have to say it out loud." He leaned in, and I closed my eyes. He ran his thumb over my bottom lip while kissing it softly and slowly. Then he ran his fingers through my hair as he tilted my head back and planted a soft kiss on my jawline. His mouth trailed up over my chin, and his lips grazed mine. He teased them gently, rubbing his lips over mine but never kissing them.

"Open your eyes," he whispered.

I opened them and he was so close that all his features were blurry. His lips still lingered on mine and I could feel and taste his breath. He didn't need to move his lips. It felt like we were kissing with our eyes. My whole body shivered when the tip of his tongue came out and traced my lips. I stared into his eyes feeling frozen, my lips unable to reciprocate and my body feeling unable to move. I was under his spell and I felt a bubble form around us to preserve this magical moment.

Finally, slowly, he pulled away and looked at me. He seemed as mesmerized by this spell as I was.

"So, good night, Jane."

"Where're you going?"

A small smile flickered across his lips. "I'll take the sofa tonight."

I glanced down at the sofa. It wasn't really a sofa so much as it was a long cushion-covered chair. It didn't look comfortable, and I wondered how he was planning to squeeze onto it.

"But we've already—"

He cut me off. "I meant it when I said I wanted to do things properly with you. Turn the clock back and start from the beginning. Where we should have started."

"Well, good night then." I smiled at Dimitri and my stomach filled with butterflies. There was something so sexy and exciting about the idea of just dating him. I gave him a small wave and started walking toward the bedroom.

"That doesn't mean that all the other stuff isn't going to happen again. But maybe that's more of a second-date thing," he called after me.

I turned and looked back at him.

"So you want to go on another date tomorrow night?" he asked.

"Sure." I gave him one last smile and scuttled down the staircase. I collapsed onto the bed and let out a massive breath that I think I'd been holding the entire duration of the kiss. I climbed into bed, and he was all that I could think of. And then...

No... that would be so totally stupid.

Jane, get a grip, that is ridiculous and childish and...

But... oh well, what the hell.

I reached into my handbag, pulled out the sweet, slipped it under my pillow, and curled up to go to sleep.

CHAPTER TWENTY-SIX

I felt something pushing and pulling at me. The sheet started to slip down and I tried to pull it back up in my sleepy state. The bed made a loud noise and I felt it move next to me.

"Shit!" I flicked my eyes open in fright, then realized someone was kneeling on the bed next to me. I shot up and switched the light on.

"It's just me. Dimitri."

My eyes adjusted to the bright light and sure enough, there was Dimitri kneeling next to me on my side of the bed. Suddenly a massive smile broke out across his face. "Nice top."

"What..." And then I remembered. I was wearing an oversized T-shirt that I'd gotten at a conference that read DENTISTS GET FILL-INGS TOO. I tried to cover it with my hands.

"Well, you're not supposed to be in my bed seeing it."

He pulled my hands away. "I think it's sexy."

"What are you doing here?" I asked, folding my arms in front of the stupid picture of a happy tooth running through a meadow holding a toothbrush.

"That thing I said earlier about wanting to turn the clock back—well, I didn't really mean it."

"Oh?"

"I meant it at the time, but then I got to thinking about how it feels when you fall asleep on my chest and how good it feels waking up with you in the morning. And so I was wondering if I could just come and sleep here with you?"

"Well, in that case." I pulled the sheet open for Dimitri and moved to the other side of the bed to let him in. He climbed in and immediately pulled me into the crook of his arm. I put my head down on his chest and breathed him in.

"Oh my God," Dimitri suddenly said. "What's that?" Suddenly he was holding the wedding sweet between his fingers. I felt myself melt from the fiery heat of embarrassment. He dangled it above my head, displaying it like a trophy.

"Uh...it was just, I was...um..."

"I can't believe you did that."

I sat up and tried to grab the sweet from him but he pulled it away playfully.

"You were hoping to dream about your future husband. Admit it." He was laughing now and teasing me with the sweet.

"I was just going with it. I'm in Greece, I'm trying to embrace the culture here and learn about it and participate and all that. Didn't you say I should? You keep telling me I need to let my inner Greek out."

He continued to laugh and I continued to try to wrangle the

sweet away from him. But in one of my overzealous attempts, I shot up too fast and accidentally fell on him. I was just about to get up when he wrapped his arms around me and held me in place. I was officially lying on top of him, our faces almost touching.

"So did you?" he asked.

"Did I what?"

"Dream about me?" He laughed and then pulled me into a sitting position. Holy fucking crap, I was now officially straddling a half-naked Dimitri. He lay back, put his arms behind his head casually, and gazed up at me with a kind of smug, totally self-satisfied look plastered across his face—I wasn't sure whether I wanted to slap it or kiss it, or both. It was the kind of look that told me he had me exactly where he wanted me.

"No," I said firmly. "I did not dream about you, and even if I had, we would not be getting married now based on some old superstition thing. I don't believe in stuff like that."

"Why not?"

"Huh?" His words slammed into me and I froze. *"Why not get married?* Because it's crazy. Insane. I don't know you, we've just met. You're basically a stranger, other than the sex part. There is no way I could ever consider marrying you. You're like this hot model or something, and I'm just Jane. And it's the most ludicrous thing I've ever heard. Ever. It would be too weird and too illogical and spontaneous and it would never work with someone like you. Never. It's crazy. Not you. Ever."

Dimitri's casual, playful look faded. "I actually meant, why not believe in a bit of magic from time to time?"

"Oh," I said flatly, feeling slightly embarrassed about the rant I had just gone off on.

Dimitri sat up, bringing his face all the way to mine. "But now that you've mentioned all that, I can't help feeling offended. Am I not the kind of guy a girl could marry?"

"What? No, no...I didn't mean it like that. I didn't mean there was anything wrong with you, per se. I meant that it would be crazy if *we* got married. It's nothing against you, it's more of a *we* thing, that's what I meant, you know...et cetera, and so forth."

"A *we* thing. You make it sound like there's something wrong with us. That we're not compatible."

"Well, we don't know if we're compatible really."

Dimitri's lips traveled to my ear and he whispered, his voice oozing lust and sex and danger, "But we *are* compatible, Jane." And then he slipped his hands down my back, cupped my ass, and ground me into him.

"Oh God," I gasped slash breathless-whimpered at the feeling that had just shot through my body. He locked eyes with me and did it again. And then he pulled my legs and wrapped them around him. I guess that whole "turn the clock back" thing hadn't lasted long at all. Not that I cared.

"Don't worry, I'm not going to have sex with you."

"You're not?" I sounded disappointed, and I was.

"No." He shook his head. "Not yet."

I wasn't sure how I felt about that. A massive part of me was widely disappointed—that is until he slipped his hand between us and tucked his finger through the top of my panties. I gasped loudly again as his hand slipped farther down into them and he touched me. The sensation of moving over him while he touched me was the kind of sensation that might cause a person to black out from sheer pleasure. His movements got faster as my breathing got shorter, sharper, and more erratic.

I threw my head back and closed my eyes. "Dimitri," I barely managed to whisper as my whole body stiffened on top of him.

I stayed there for ages trying to catch my breath and waiting for my heart rate to return to normal. My eyes were still closed and there were actual white sparks flashing under my eyelids. Oh yes, *this*, I could write home about—in fact, I could write anywhere the hell I damn liked about this. This *deserved* to be written about. Although I doubt any human words could do it justice—*a time for Klingon, perchance?*

My breathing and heart rate finally returned to normal, and I opened my eyes. I was suddenly very aware that I was still straddling him. I mean I knew I was, but somewhere in the moment I had gotten so lost that I had forgotten he was even there.

I tilted my head forward and looked down at him. I couldn't help the stupid and, I suspect, dopey-looking grin plastered across my face. He was lying on his back looking up at me with that self-satisfied smile again, but this time I wanted to kiss it. So I did. And then without saying a word, he pulled me under the sheets and planted my head on his chest. I lay there in my postorgasmic daze and listened to the steady thump of his heartbeat.

"Jane, Jane, Jane," Dimitri suddenly said, lifting my face to his lips.

"What?"

"Where the hell have you been all my life?"

Chapter Twenty-Seven

I woke up the next morning still tangled in Dimitri's arms and quickly became aware of the sound of flipping pages. I turned around and he was wide awake and reading.

"Hey?" I sat up and wiped my sleepy eyes.

"Morning." He lowered the book and looked at me with a smile. "I was wondering if you were ever going to wake up."

"What d'you mean? Have you been awake this whole time?" I glanced at the book; it was the cheesy romance novel that my mother had so graciously bestowed upon me. "Have you been reading *that*?"

"I didn't want to wake you. Do you know how beautiful you look when you're sleeping?" My heart tugged in my chest. "I got this out of your bag to pass the time." He opened it again. "It's not that bad really..." He cleared his throat and started reading:

She sat in the chair looking at him. He looked different this morning, as if somehow she knew him better. She longed for him. She longed to touch him, and make love to him, and tell him that she would be his forever. She was ready to commit herself to him in the most primal and intimate of ways. She wanted to know what it would be like to be loved by a man like him, what it would feel like to have him inside her.

"What!" I sat up. "You're making that up." I snatched the book away and started reading: "'She wanted to know what it would be like to be loved by a man like him, what it would feel like to have him inside her. Would she scream his name? Would he moan hers as they became one...' Oh, I see. It does say that." I cleared my throat and felt my temperature rise. All this talk of sex first thing in the morning was making me rather flustered.

"So what do you think? Will they get their happily ever after?" Dimitri grabbed me around the waist and pulled me onto him. It felt so normal, as if we were a couple waking up in bed together.

"I don't know, we could always flip to the end of the book to find out," I said teasingly.

"And you?" He stroked the hair from my face. "Are you going to get your happily ever after?"

"I hope so. I hope the private investigator can find my dad. Then I guess I would."

A frown played on Dimitri's forehead. "Is that the only way you'd be happy?" He looked at me with such intensity. "Isn't there anything else?" His hands moved to my face and he cradled my cheeks gently, bringing me closer to him.

"Yes. I guess there is." My heart began to pound again as I stared into his eyes. Something uncontrollable was happening inside me.

Words floated around in my head and then worked their way onto the tip of my tongue. I wanted to open my mouth and tell him how I felt, that I ...

The realization hit me all at once. This had crossed over from "like" a while ago. I'm not sure at what point it had happened, or what the exact moment was, but I think I had fallen in love with this man ...

* * *

We finally got out of bed and started the day—just like any other normal day. Except that it wasn't. How could it be when the nature of our relationship had changed so dramatically overnight? For me anyway. Although it seemed like it had for Dimitri, too, because any chance he got, he was either touching me, wrapping his arms around me, or kissing me, as if I was his girlfriend. *Am I?* The thought made me smile, and I found myself in the strange, unfamiliar position of feeling happier than I'd felt in forever. I felt free and uninhibited here. I felt more at home here and more like myself with Dimitri than I ever had been.

When he'd asked me a few days ago whether I'd ever experienced an attraction so strong that I couldn't bear being away from that person—I hadn't. But now I had. If it were possible to drink him in or inhale him, at this stage I would have.

"Where are you taking me now?" I asked as the boat started moving again.

"There are so many places I want to show you. And if you stayed here with me for a year, I still wouldn't be able to show you everything." He smiled at me in a way that said,

"Stay with me for a year and have sex with me. January, February, September, whenever sex."

"But right now, I'm taking you to the moon."

And he wasn't lying. It did look like the surface of the moon. Soon I came face-to-face with an alien, otherworldly place that was hard to imagine even existed on this planet. The landscape was white as snow. The sea in front of us was the bluest I had seen so far, and massive white cliffs rose up out of the water. The smooth white rocks spread out before us in strange, curvy shapes. Spires and arches and pillars of white rock punctuated the eerie white panorama.

"It's amazing," I said in absolute awe as we approached in the boat. Dimitri cut the engines and dropped the anchor and the boat came to a soft, smooth rest, where it floated on the brilliant blue waters.

"Grab a change of clothes," Dimitri said as he started filling a bag up with dry towels and a pair of his shoes. I went downstairs and returned with another dress, a shirt, and an extra pair of shorts. He put them in the bag and then tossed it overboard.

"Hey," I shouted after it.

"It's waterproof," he said with a smile before pulling his shirt off and then throwing himself overboard, doing a somersault as he went. He landed with a massive splash.

I pulled my dress off to reveal my bathing suit and jumped into the water. It was so warm and crystal clear that I could see every detail of my hands if I held them in front of me underwater.

Dimitri and I swam to the beach and climbed out. I thought we were going to join the other sunbathers on the beach, but Dimitri grabbed me by the hand. "Not here," he said, leading me away from the beach. "I know you hate the sand." We strolled hand in hand over an ever-changing white landscape. We walked across the hot surface, rounded a corner, walked under a white rocky overhang, and emerged at a small, natural pool in the rocks.

"Our own private pool." Dimitri climbed in.

He sat down on the bottom and the water just covered his shoulders. I followed him in. It was like a Jacuzzi for two, only it was on top of a strange white landscape with no one in sight and a never-ending view across the blue sea. It was magical. We were so alone it felt like we might be the only two people on earth. If that were the case, there was no one other than Dimitri I would want to spend an eternity with on a deserted planet. As soon as I had submerged myself in the water he pulled me onto his lap.

"You know what I love most about this day?" Dimitri said, running his hands up and down my back.

I shook my head, mesmerized by the feelings rushing through me once more.

"I get to touch you whenever I want." He paused and looked at me with pure lust. His eyes traveled down to my lips. "And I get to touch you however I like, too."

His hands came around to the front of me and moved up my body and onto my breasts. He brought his mouth down onto one and bit it gently through the bikini top.

"Wait, I want to ask you something." I pushed his head away quickly. "This feels like...this thing between us feels like a relationship, like we're boyfriend and girlfriend or something..."

"Aren't we?"

"Uh, I don't know."

"Jane, you like logical arguments, so here goes. Two young, single people meet, they spend time together, they get to know each other, and they..." He slipped his hand into my bikini bottom. "They do things like this. What else would you call them?"

"Wait, wait, wait!" I took his hand out and held it tightly. "But this is so unexpected and..." His hand broke free of my grip and began its wandering again. I let it. It traveled down until it was right back where it had started.

"Oh God." I winced. It wasn't from pain. "I didn't mean for any of this to happen and..." He moved his hand back and forth a little. "Ah, mmm, and..." I could barely think straight. "I was just coming here to find my father. I never meant to come here and meet someone like yyy-oo-uuuu..." His hand moved a little faster and I almost forgot how to speak.

"Wait!" I pulled his hand away again. "This is serious. I live in South Africa. You live in Greece and you love it here."

"You also love it here." His hand started to slip back down, and my body began to crumble all over again. "You know, there are only two dentists on the whole of Santorini. I Googled it."

"What?" I pushed his hand away once more and stared at him. His green eyes met my gaze with such intensity that they made my breath catch in my throat. "You're being serious?"

He smiled and then nodded.

"But how would that work? I mean, I'm meant to be taking over my father's business at the end of the year. Besides, I bet I would have to get a new practicing license all over again, it's probably not even legal for a South African dentist to practice here, and how would one even establish a practice. Everyone hates the dentist, and they would probably all go to the one that they've been going to for years and not try some new girl."

"I'd go to you." He smiled. "And my sisters."

"But do you have any idea how much money it would cost to even set that up. An X-ray machine alone probably costs twenty thousand dollars, not to mention all the lab equipment, and chairs and air compressors and drills and, and, and—" I felt quite panicked all of a sudden.

"Stop thinking for once in your life." His hand slipped back down. It was a determined little hand. And who was I to tell it not to go there.

"Buuu...ttt—" I started to object again, but the things the hand was doing silenced me into a stupor.

"Stop thinking and listen to your heart. What's it telling you?"

"But I never listen to my heart," I somehow managed to say, despite growing waves of uncontainable pleasure.

"That's not true. You're in Greece with me, aren't you?"

I couldn't argue with that. My heart had been the organ that had governed this decision; my brain had no say in it whatsoever.

"You know what my heart is telling me?" he asked.

"No."

"My heart is telling me that I've met an amazing woman. I really like her, I like spending time with her and kissing her and..." He leaned in and whispered in my ear, "and if she'll let me, making love to her?"

"Uuuhhhh..." My throat dried up instantly. "It sounds, *yes*, it sounds like a pleasant idea."

Dimitri burst out laughing. "See, that's what I love about you. You say the funniest things."

Oh my God, did he just say that he loved me? Suddenly the words bubbled up in my throat and I didn't think I could hold them in, at all. They felt like they were swimming around in my mouth now and if I opened it, they would dive out uncontrollably. I bit my lip in an attempt to keep my mouth shut and the words trapped. But I was failing dismally. They were on the tip of my tongue again and they were about to force their way through my sealed lips, whether I wanted them to or not. There was no stopping them now...

"I think I might be sort of falling in love with you, too." They flew out. I couldn't stop them, and it was only when I heard them that I fully realized what I had just said.

Dimitri didn't say anything. He just looked at me and I thought I saw a flash of disappointment in his eyes. This was not how I had imagined this going. Sudden panic gripped me: Maybe I had spoken too soon, maybe he didn't feel the same way...

"Come." Dimitri climbed out of the water and pulled me with him. "I have a surprise for you."

He proceeded to lead me away from our private little paradise and before I knew it, we were in a taxi winding our way through the town. I was going through the journey in a kind of a giddy haze, vaguely aware of us stopping in front of a hotel and checking in. But when we walked into the room, my senses turned back on. My eyes flitted from the emperor-sized bed to a bottle of champagne, a huge basket of fresh fruit, a box of truffles, not to mention scented candles and roses strewn on the bed; the room practically screamed *"romance"* and I couldn't believe what I was seeing. I stared at it openmouthed.

"What is this?" I asked.

"I planned a whole romantic evening for us. I think they went a bit overboard with the petals, though," he said.

I gave him small, coy smile. "Planned? What kind of plan did you have in mind?"

"It goes something like this..." He walked over to the champagne and opened it. It exploded with a loud pop and he poured two glasses and handed one to me.

"I thought it might start with champagne. Then I thought we could do this..." He took me by the hand and led me onto the balcony. We were high up, but you could still see the sparkling sea below. The veranda had a small plunge pool and a large hammock that stretched across its entire length. It was spectacular.

"Then what?" I asked, sipping on the champagne. He turned and smiled in a way that almost made my fingers loosen around the glass and drop it to the floor. He walked up to me and took the champagne flute from my hands. He put his glass down, too, and then pulled his shirt off, tossing it aside exuberantly. He reached out and pulled my dress over my head and dropped it on the floor. Then he started tugging on his shorts and boxers until both had fallen to the floor. I glanced down for a moment and saw him in his full nakedness. Then he did the same to me: pulled all my clothes off until I was standing completely naked in front of him.

"And now what?" I asked. I couldn't hide the feelings in my voice. The whisperiness was a dead giveaway.

We stood opposite each other and just stared. Our eyes roving up and down each other's bodies. Awe. That was the only word I could think of at this stage.

"And now…" he said, looking at me intensely, "now I am going to do this…" He pulled me toward him and walked us backward to the hammock and then laid me down on it. He slowly lowered his body onto mine and the hammock swayed. I felt weightless underneath him.

"And now this is the moment that I was going to tell you, that even though I only met you seven days ago, I think I've developed really strong feelings for you. I also think I'm falling in love with you, Jane. And then I was planning on doing this."

I gasped as he parted my legs and slipped inside me. So, so slowly. The hammock swung gently back and forth as I wrapped my legs around him. I pushed my hips up toward him and heard him exhale sharply. And then he kissed me gently on the lips and it felt like an act of pure love.

"Is it crazy to have fallen for someone in seven days?" he whispered loudly before going back in and kissing me again. It was slow, sensual, and deep.

"I don't know," I whispered back. "This whole thing has been crazy." The feel of his hot tongue, his wet lips, his warm breath on me as it escaped from his mouth in tiny groans. His tongue explored, his hips started moving, slowly, fluidly, thrusting and receding. His mouth moved to my neck, where he nuzzled me softly and sensually.

A moan escaped my lips as he got into a rhythm on top of me, the hammock swinging gently below us. I wrapped my arms around him and let our bodies rock as one together. I had never felt closer or more connected to another person than in that moment.

Dimitri's movements started speeding up. I clawed at his back as I felt myself speeding toward my release. He grabbed my face between his hands and attempted to kiss me in between the gagged, sharp breaths coming out of his mouth and then the start of a low moan.

We both moved faster together until his body stiffened on top of me at exactly the same time as mine did. We finished together, and held on to each other for ages. I could feel his heart pounding against my sweaty chest, and mine got into a rhythm with it. He finally climbed off me and lay beside me on the hammock. He wrapped his arm around me and pulled me into the crook of his arm. There was a gentle evening breeze rushing past us, and we just lay together swinging and looking up at the sky.

I felt at peace, truly at peace for the first time in a long time, possibly ever. The tight ball that had taken up permanent residence in my stomach was gone, and I felt completely comfortable with the silence and closeness. In that moment, looking up at the evening sky, I realized how different I felt. I was a totally different person. Greece *had* changed me. Just like Dimitri had said it would.

I was no longer Plain Jane Smith, the girl that didn't do spontaneous and wild. I was the girl who followed her heart and went with the flow. I was the kind of girl that ended up in Greece, who had wild sex in an alleyway and skinny-dipped and was now lying naked in a hammock with the most amazing man.

I wondered how many times my father had stared up at the exact same sky. I wondered if I had also walked in his shoes and seen and done the things he had. Maybe he was even looking up right now? Had he ever looked at the sky and wondered if I was looking up at it, too? Of course, I still had a little nagging doubt—I had no way of knowing whether he even knew of my existence. My father's name was never put down on the birth certificate. Back then the law didn't even require him to know that Phoebe was pregnant with me.

But there was just something inside me that somehow made me sure. I felt some strange connection to this person I had never met. And the more time I'd spent here, the stronger it had become— and in turn, the stronger my connection to myself had become.

I snuggled up even closer to Dimitri as I watched the night grow even darker. Coming here had changed me. Dimitri had helped change me. Somewhere along the way—and I couldn't pinpoint when it had happened—I'd fallen for this man.

I had discovered my own deep connection to this place, which I guess had always been somewhere inside me. It was probably the tiny piece I had gotten from my father. In some way, coming here had made me feel more whole and complete than I ever had. This was the cheesy ending to my novel: *I'd come to Greece looking for my father, but had also found love and myself along the way.*

"You know, in this really weird way, I feel closer to my father than I've ever felt before. I feel like I've gotten to know him by seeing and doing all the things we have. It sounds silly . . . I know."

"It doesn't sound silly." He turned and looked at me and a massive smile broke out across his face, and then he sighed. It sounded like a sigh of relief. What was he so relieved about? "I hoped that would happen. I really, *really* hoped you would tell me that."

I rolled onto my side and propped my head up on my elbow. "I just can't wait to really meet him, though. I feel like meeting him will be the final piece of the puzzle that comes together."

"Jane, can I ask you something?"

I nodded.

"What if he doesn't believe you? What if the private investigator can't find him and you never get to meet him? What if he doesn't want to…" He stopped. I could hear that he was choosing his words very carefully.

"I'm not naive. I know it's a possibility, but I also know that I have to try. And if he doesn't, or I can't find him, at least I've gotten to know him in a way that six days ago I didn't."

"You really believe that?" he asked.

"Yes." I nodded and inhaled deeply. I breathed it all in. I breathed in all of life's possibilities. Its beauty and its joys. I held on to Dimitri and closed my eyes. He smelled good and felt warm and I'd never felt so loved and wanted before.

He kissed my forehead, "Jane, I need to say something to you…"

"I know," I whispered, on the verge of giving myself over to sleep, "I think I'm in love with you, too."

CHAPTER TWENTY-EIGHT

I woke up the next morning to a soft light flooding the room and a very vague recollection of Dimitri carrying me to the bedroom at some point. But the bed next to me was empty and for a moment I wondered if last night had been real. Had Dimitri and I really made love and confessed love to each other? I saw a distinctly blondish brown hair on the pillow next to me and smiled. It had been real. I glanced around the room for him, but he wasn't there.

I got up, totally naked, wrapped the sheet around me, and strolled out to the veranda. The sun was barely out. The light was soft and hazy, and in the distance the sea looked quiet with the slightest bit of mist hanging over it. And there he was, sitting on the wall looking at the sea. He looked unreal.

"Dimitri?" I called out. He turned around and smiled at me and my heart swelled. He walked over and kissed me on the forehead.

"Ready for your last stop on this adventure?" he asked with a small smile. It seemed slightly sad, and I wondered if he was also wondering about what was going to happen to us when this adventure came to an end.

* * *

We were speeding across the sea again. It looked even more spectacular than it had yesterday. Although I was mainly staring at Dimitri, not the view. It wasn't long before we came to a small dock on yet another beautiful-looking island. Its only occupants were a few old-looking fishing boats tied to the pier. But before docking, Dimitri slowed the boat and came and sat next to me. He didn't look at me for the longest time, and a feeling rose in my stomach. This time it wasn't giddy butterflies, but a sense of dread and foreboding.

He turned slowly, and when I saw the look emblazoned across his face, I froze. The light in his eyes looked like it had been switched off and a cloud of something serious and dark hung over him. It made me shiver. Overwhelming nerves chewed and gnawed at me. This could only mean one thing.

"Just say it." My voice quivered. In my heart, I knew exactly what he was going to say.

Dimitri continued to look at me. He seemed dumbstruck.

"I'll say it then." I took a big breath and steadied myself. "The private investigator phoned and he says there's no way of getting hold of my father? That's what you were trying to warn me about last night." I felt the sting of salty tears forming in my eyes. "I'll never meet him."

A cold, scratchy feeling clawed its way through my body. I knew

I had said that it didn't really matter—that I'd gotten to know him already. But meeting him would have been the cherry on top to this trip. It was, after all, the reason I was here.

"Dimitri?" I asked again. He wasn't speaking, and the silence and absence of words was making the whole thing even worse. "Talk to me," I begged with a slight hysteria in my voice.

"Jane…" I'd never heard him say my name with such sadness. I didn't like it. "There was no investigator."

"What do you mean?"

"No one was looking for your father."

"What?" I shrieked as my skin prickled. "But he's been messaging you, you spoke to him…"

He shook his head. "No. I never spoke to one."

"But you did. You were on the phone the other morning and you were talking to him. I heard you."

"I lied. I'm sorry, it wasn't him."

My mind was swimming and spinning and the thoughts were all so messy that I didn't understand what he was saying. "I don't get this, at all. At the airport, you said you spoke to an investigator, you told him everything, and he said he could find my father and that's why I stayed. He was going to look for him while I was here… I don't understand."

He paused for the longest time. It felt like the pause went on forever and that there was never going to be an end to this torturous moment. It felt like every last bit of breath was being sucked out of my body, and my legs began to feel weak underneath me. Luckily I was sitting.

Dimitri pulled something out of his pocket and handed it over.

It was a few of those old photos that had been hanging on his wall. "Turn one over," he said.

I turned one over and looked. Some Greek had been scribbled on the back. A name maybe? "I can't read this. What is this?" I demanded. My voice was shrill and high and bordering on a yell. I looked at the back of the other ones.

"Xexos Dimitri Constantinides." He paused. "This is the Dimitri you came looking for."

"What?" I turned the picture back around and gazed at it. The photo was of the pool in the rocks that we had just been in yesterday. "I don't…this makes no sense…I…?" I looked at the next photo: the sunset over Oia. The next was of the open blue seas and the shipwreck we had visited. I kept flipping and more and more familiar images come into focus: winery, ruins, small streets covered in bougainvillea…I had been to all these places. "What is going on?" I was almost in tears now.

"Your father brought us together."

I shook my head. "Stop speaking in Greek fucking philosophical crap. Tell me what is going on. Facts. Explanations. What?"

"The old woman in our village, the woman that used to tell me all the amazing stories that made me want to travel? She is your grandmother. The stories she told me were about your father."

My mouth fell open. I turned one of the pictures over in my hands again and ran my fingertips over his name; it had been written so long ago. "Are you sure? I mean, how can you know. He might not be…it's too much of a coincidence, it's—"

"Fate. Not a coincidence. Fate." He tried to reach out and touch me but I pulled away. "That day when you were at my house and you told me you were looking for your father, that he was sailing the seas and you told me your mother's name, I...I wasn't certain at first. I remember the old woman telling me he had these different-colored eyes. I was young, I thought that he was a pirate, maybe he wore an eye patch, I didn't really understand properly. And then I went to the photos and turned them over and saw his middle name. And then I saw this..."

He handed me another photo, and my heart crashed against my chest. Adrenaline surged in my veins, making me feel drunk. A bright-red boat was docked in the water, and my mother's name was written across it. PHOEBE. The dock looked strangely like this one. I looked up. Our boat had floated closer now and I could make out more details. And then I saw it.

And when I did, an electric charge shot through my body. For a moment it buzzed and screamed in my ears and burned my skin and evaporated all the moisture in my mouth. I couldn't breathe. I gasped a few times, trying to get air into my lungs. Through the loud internal buzz I vaguely heard Dimitri say, "Wait. I have to tell you something." But I didn't wait. I just flung myself off the boat without even thinking about it.

"Jane, wait. I need to tell you..." His voice faded out completely as I swam as fast as I could for the shore and the boat. Eventually the water got shallower and I half ran, half swam there. The force of the water felt like nothing and I moved through it as if I was running in a vacuum. I climbed onto the pier and ran for the boat, and when I go to it, I came to a complete halt and stared.

PHOEBE.

There it was in orange cursive on the side of the red boat. I felt slightly woozy from the frenzied swim, but I had no control over myself anymore. I was acting on complete instinct again and my mind was simply floating along, observing everything that was happening.

"Whose boat is this?" I heard myself scream at the top of my lungs. "Whose boat is this?" The scream grew louder and more hysterical until someone rushed up to me. An old fisherman appeared out of nowhere. He brought his face close to mine and as he looked at me, he gasped as if he had seen a ghost. Without saying a word he grabbed me by the arm and started dragging me across the pier.

"Wait! Jane!" Dimitri yelled and I heard a splash, as he must have dived into the water, too.

I wasn't going to wait. I couldn't. Instead I went with this man who was now dragging me up some stairs. They wound their way up and onto the small paved streets of a village. He pulled me down a small street of tightly packed houses and finally came to stop at a small blue door.

He knocked frantically and called out in Greek. The door finally swung open and I looked straight into a mirror. A young girl stared right back at me with eyes identical to my own. There was a small moment, a pause when the two of us just looked at each other, and then without warning she threw her arms around me and pulled me into a hug.

She held on to me tightly, and it was only after a few seconds that I realized she was crying. Her body was heaving and shaking in my arms and the strangest feeling came over me. I rubbed her back in a comforting manner and she held on to me even tighter. I knew this girl. Somewhere inside I knew her. Her smell and touch and the sound of her cries were all so familiar to me and I felt an instant connection to her. A deep one that swelled up inside me and made me hug her even tighter. She finally pulled away and looked right at me.

"I'm so sorry, I'm so sorry…I'm so, so sorry…" She continued to repeat the words as if she were a record, stuck in a perpetual loop.

She called out in Greek and suddenly another, older woman was at the door. Her mother, I presumed. She looked at me and the color drained from her face. She held my gaze and then the tears started streaming down her face, too. This wasn't exactly the welcome I had expected; I had expected it to be emotional, but this seemed over the top. I turned and looked at the fisherman who'd brought me here; the look on his face was also one of devastation. He looked up at me and shook his head, something flashing in his eyes that I did not recognize.

My eyes drifted back to the two women in the doorway. They had been joined by more people now. Each of them looked consumed by sadness.

"Come in," the older woman finally said in a thick accent. This whole moment was so surreal. As I stepped inside the house I heard Dimitri's voice and looked back at him. He looked up at me and mouthed something; it looked like "sorry" but I couldn't be sure. I turned back around and disappeared into the house.

The older woman guided me toward the couch. Everyone else had left the room, as if they had been told to. The woman lowered herself on the couch next to me, and I could see that her hands were shaking.

"What is your name?" she asked.

"Jane," I whispered. Our words tumbled out into the eerie silence that was now filling the room.

"I have imagined this moment so many times before," she said softly. "He has been waiting for you to return for so many years now. He always knew that you would find him one day."

My heart skipped a beat. "Dimitri?"

The woman nodded slowly and looked me straight in my eyes. "You have his eyes." She smiled up at me. It was the saddest smile I had ever seen, and I wondered what was behind it.

"Where is he now?" I asked.

As I said those words, her eyes began to tear up and...

I just knew. I knew.

It was written in the solemn tearstained lines of her face. I could feel it in the heaviness that had descended on the room and the pain that was searing my chest.

"He's dead?" I asked.

"I'm so sorry."

Chapter Twenty-Nine

I looked around the room. The girl with the same eyes as mine was peering at me through a doorway. Her face was ashen and her breath quick. I continued to scan the room, and there, on a mantel, was a picture of him.

I recognized him immediately. It wasn't just the eyes, it was everything. I knew it was him like I knew that I lived and breathed. The photo was set in a beautiful gold frame, surrounded by flowers and a solitary burning candle. I stood up and walked over to it. My feet did not touch the floor.

I touched the photo and ran my hands over the flowers. They were fresh and I could still smell their scent. I gazed at his photo and let my father's eyes look directly into me for the first time in my entire life.

"When…When…" My legs wobbled beneath me as I looked from the woman to the girl with the eyes.

"Nine days ago," she said.

I'm not really sure what happened next, but within seconds the world around me lost focus; it shook and it buzzed and suddenly I could see all the atoms that made everything around me; then they pulled apart and the world got fuzzier still until nothing around me existed anymore. And then everything went black.

* * *

It felt like hours had passed. But it was only seconds. The blackness had lasted for a tiny moment as my legs collapsed and my body went limp. I felt two hands come up and catch me under my arms and more hands help me onto the couch. Someone gently placed my head between my knees and someone else stroked my back in large, comforting circles.

The girl with my eyes came over and gave me a glass of Coke. I took it and looked up at her. She was so beautiful. Her eyes gave her a quality of otherworldliness; her thick dark hair accentuated it even more, and her unusual features blended into one of the most exotically stunning faces I had ever seen. She smiled at me.

"What's your name?" I managed.

"Alexandra." She was soft spoken and couldn't have been more than fifteen years old.

"That's a beautiful name."

I looked over at the woman, clearly her mother, who was sitting next to me again.

"Kalli," she said softly.

Alexandra came and sat on the couch opposite me and the three of us stayed like that in absolute silence. We all looked at one another, each taking turns. It was as if some kind of invisible strings bound us together in some way. I took small sips of the Coke, and with each sip the strange swirling in my head dissipated.

"How, how..." I finally asked.

"Heart attack," Kalli said quietly, wringing her hands together. Her grief was palpable. It was a fresh open wound that hadn't even been given the chance to start healing yet. There were bags under her eyes, and she looked a little gaunt, as if she had not been eating or sleeping.

"It was very sudden. He didn't suffer," she qualified, as if she had been holding on to that tiny piece of information like a security blanket that somehow made her feel better.

The shock was so great that I wasn't ready to process the injustice of it. The sheer cosmic injustice that was this moment. Nine days ago. If I had been here nine days ago I would have had the chance...

I ran through the days in my head. Nine days ago had been that Wednesday morning when I'd woken up and everything around me had been wrong and felt different. That Wednesday morning was what had led me to this point. But how was that even possible? Was it possible that my father and I had had some strange, intangible connection that I hadn't even realized?

"And his mother, uh...my grandmother?" I asked.

Kalli just shook her head. "Would you like to see his grave?" she asked. Alexandra stood up with her and she held her hand out, inviting me as if I was one of the family. There were so many questions that I wanted to ask them, but this was not the time.

I gave a faint nod and took her hand. We linked arms and she gave me the faintest of smiles as we exited the house. As we walked up the street, people stuck their heads out of the windows and many of them came out to speak to us. One woman rushed over to me and gave me a single rose. I stopped and looked around. It was as if this whole place knew who I was. How?

"He always told the story of the daughter he never knew who would one day find him. In a way, everyone here has been waiting for you, Jane." The tears began to well up in my eyes again as I glanced across at everyone's faces.

We walked all the way up a hill and into a small cemetery at the end of the road. It was located high up and looked down over the sea below. It was easy to see which gravestone was his: The fresh flowers had overtaken it. I walked up to the grave and stared down at it.

Was this real? Was this even happening? But when a hard gust of wind rushed past me and pulled at my hair and clothes, I knew it was real.

A sense of finality made me want to cry out loudly and scream in anger and rage. I had reached the end of my journey and there had been no big, shiny pot of gold. Instead there was just this one small, gray headstone. Tears rolled down my cheeks.

A pain in my hand made me flinch: I had pricked my thumb on the rose I was holding. The blood pooled on the surface of my finger and I wiped it away. I bent down and laid the single rose across his grave. I wanted to open my mouth and say something, but there were no words to adequately describe this moment.

I trailed my fingers across the cold stone as I set the rose on it, then I stood up again and started walking away. I didn't know where I was walking to. I had nowhere left to go; there were no more roads and paths to walk to find the answers I was looking for. Instead they had all come to a dead end right here in a tiny cemetery on a hill.

I was aware of the footsteps walking behind me. I walked back through the streets, past the houses I had seen. Some of the people were still outside waiting and watching as if this was some kind of a tragic show. It felt like a tragic comedy, that's for sure. I continued to walk in silence; the only noises were the trees swaying in the wind, the birds chirping, and our footsteps on the paving. I was walking in a kind of ghostly, zombielike trance.

I felt a gentle arm come out and take my elbow as I was about to walk past the house.

"There is a letter for you," Kalli said softly.

"A letter?"

"He wrote you one in case he never got to meet you." She tried to give me the softest, most encouraging-looking smile and my heart felt like it was going to break into a million tiny pieces.

* * *

I held the envelope in my shaking hands and closed the door behind me. I was alone on the small balcony looking out over the port. I could see Dimitri's boat still there swaying gently in the small swells. My fingers tightened on the envelope as the anger surged through my veins. He'd known about my father this whole time and kept it from me. He had kept from me the one thing that I had wanted to know more than anything else. The thing I had been searching for my entire life. I tried to push the feelings aside and return to the moment I was in. The moment just before I was about to meet my father for the first time—well, sort of.

I opened the envelope carefully, savoring the idea that my father had sealed this envelope. His DNA was laced on this paper and I was running my fingertips over it. I almost wanted to raise it to my nose to see if it still contained his scent.

My fingers were trembling as I pulled the letter out of the envelope. I opened the folded pieces of paper, and a small dried flower fell to my feet. I picked it up and twirled it between my fingers before putting it back in the envelope.

I took a deep breath, ignored the stabbing pain in my chest... and read it.

To my daughter,

I am writing this letter in case my dream of meeting you one day never comes true. I hope that I can find the right words to say all the things I have always wanted to say to you and I hope this letter can answer some of the questions I'm sure you've had.

Your mother and I met on the island of Santorini in a warm and beautiful summer. We were both so young, eighteen years old, and filled with a childlike excitement for life. She was on vacation with her family and I had just started working for a man who ran a tour guiding company. From the moment I saw her I was in love. She was the most beautiful woman I had ever seen and I knew that I had to be with her. It only took a few days before we fell in love. This all happened out of the sight of her parents, who we knew would never have approved.

She was a young girl from an upper-class family, still at school, and I was a poor Greek boy from a small island village with nothing to offer her, other than my heart. On the last night she was in Greece, we made love. That night I asked her to stay with me. I could see my whole life with her. I wanted it all, a family, children, and grandchildren. But we knew her parents would never allow it and when they found out the next day her father and I got into a fight and they took her back home. We promised to call each other when we could, and one day soon she would come back to Greece and we would be together. That was the plan.

I tried to call the number that she had left, but it had been disconnected. I tried to write to her, and for a whole year I never heard back. Then one day, I remember it so well, it was raining and cold when I was called to the phone. I knew immediately it was her. She was sobbing and I could feel her pain all the way across the ocean. Only then did I learn of you. She had been pregnant and her parents had forced her into giving you up for adoption. I wanted to scream at her, and ask her why she hadn't contacted me, but the pain in her voice made me realize how scared she had been. A young girl, alone and pregnant by a poor boy living all the way across the world with no way to be with him.

She told me all about you. How you had the same eyes as me, how she had been allowed to hold you in the hospital, and how in that moment, she wanted to keep you with every cell in her body. She told me that she whispered in your ear over and over again how much she loved you, and how much she wished you a life filled with love and joy and happiness. She had to give you up that day, and neither of us would ever know who you were given to, or where you were. You were gone. That was the last time I ever spoke to your

*mother. I believe she was in too much pain to ever speak to me again.
I was left here alone knowing you were out there somewhere.*

*Please do not ever think badly of your mother. She was a young
girl on her own. She was frightened and she did the best she could.
Please do not ever think that you were unwanted. Please do not ever
think that you were unloved. Please do not ever think you were forgotten, either. I have loved you, with all my heart, since the day I
found out that you were in this world. I have thought about you
every day and wondered what you are doing and whether you are
having the kind of life that you deserve.*

*I have always hoped to meet you one day. More than anything. To
hold you in my arms and tell you how much I love you and have always
loved you. I hope that you have lived a life of joy and happiness. That
you have blossomed and become the person that you want to become.*

*If you are reading this letter, then it means that I am probably
no longer here. It was my greatest wish to meet you, but I console
myself in knowing that I can tell you how I feel with these words.*

*My greatest wish for you is that one day you will find a love like I
had with your mother. That you will have a child one day and love
it as I have loved you. Live your life as if it is your last day. Be brave
and strong, pick yourself up when you fall. Be yourself and let no
one tell you who you are. Surround yourself with love and kindness
and joy. But most of all, I hope that you love yourself and are proud
of who you are and who you have and still can become.*

*You were loved every second of every day and always
remembered.*

Love, your bampas

(dad)

My heart pounded. Tears streamed down my face. The stabbing pain in my rib cage was almost too much to bear. I turned the note over in my hands. Something else fell out, and I reached down to pick it up. It was a photo of my dad and my mother holding on to each other and smiling. I looked at it through blurry eyes...they looked so happy. They looked so in love. My dad was so handsome, too. I smiled slightly and ran my fingertips over his face. I looked at my mother and started to cry. She looked so young. Just a girl. I thought back to myself at eighteen and I remembered how I was; there was no way I would have been able to care for a baby; I could barely care for myself. My heart broke for her and an outpouring of empathy followed.

"I'm sorry," I whispered. I'd always judged her so harshly. Always hated her for the choices she had made that had affected my whole life. I'd carried around the consequences of her decision with me from the moment I had been born—and I had not asked for that to be put on my shoulders, but it had. But looking into her eyes now, I felt the start of forgiveness. She must have been so frightened and heartbroken when she couldn't be with the man she loved. I could not let my past, her past, dictate who I was any longer, and forgiving her was the key to letting it all go. I heard a small knock on the door and turned to see Kalli standing in the doorway holding a bottle of wine in one hand and two glasses in the other.

"May I?" she asked.

I nodded and opened the door for her. She stepped onto the patio and placed the wine down on the table.

"Did you find what you've been looking for?" She gave the letter in my hands the briefest look. I nodded. I had gotten what I wanted. His words were exactly what I had been longing to hear.

She pulled another letter from her pocket and passed it to me. The word *Phoebe* was written on the envelope.

"He always wanted you to give her this."

"Me?" I took the letter in my hands and looked at it. Holding her name in my hands was such a bizarre feeling. "No. I don't think so."

"He hoped you would have a relationship with her," she said as I put the letter on the table. "He hoped that you would forgive her for letting you go."

"Why have you all been so nice to me?" I asked.

"Dimitri…" She paused. "*Your father* used to speak of you so often that we feel like you've been a part of our lives this whole time. Every Christmas around the table he would make a toast to you. Wishing you health and happiness and love, wherever you were. On his birthday I know that when he closed his eyes and blew out his candles, he only had one wish."

The tears started falling again. The idea that I had had a family all the way across the world, and hadn't even known it, touched me.

"The day Alexandra was born, he wouldn't hold her." Kalli's voice stuck in her throat. "He felt so overwhelmed with guilt that he had never gotten to hold you. He said that he felt like he was betraying the memory of you if he loved another daughter."

A whimper escaped my mouth, and Kalli reached out and rubbed my back. "I'm so sorry to hear that, I would never want to be the cause of—"

She cut me off quickly. "No. Don't worry, soon he couldn't put her down. He loved Alexandra with all his heart. I just wanted you to know how much he loved you, too."

Kalli opened the bottle of wine and poured us two glasses. "He'd been saving this for a special occasion."

I glanced at the bottle and was shocked to see that it came from the exact same winery that Dimitri and I had visited only days before.

"You know what he would have regretted most about not meeting you?" she turned to me and asked.

"What?"

"He was so passionate about his country. You could say it was his other great love, and he always hoped he could share that with you one day."

"Really?" I sipped the wine slowly and started remembering what Dimitri had done for me these past few days. How he had taken me to all the places my father had loved and visited...he'd tried to show me my father.

"He really loved this place and its people...and he really loved your mother, too."

To hear her speak of my mother like that caught me off guard. Kalli walked over to the railing and looked out over the town and the sea below. "We had a great life together, it was filled with so much love and laughter. Every day that we were together was a gift. And he did love me very much, but...In Greek, we have almost ten ways to describe love. What your father had for your mother was the most powerful love of all. Eros. He loved me, to be sure, but he never quite loved me with the passion that he had for your mother."

She turned and smiled at me. "But I knew that the day we got married. He never kept his love for her a secret; besides, it was a story that everyone knew. After Phoebe told him about you, he was so brokenhearted that he just took a boat out one day and didn't return for years. He told me he'd just sailed around, from island to island, as if he was searching for something he knew he couldn't find." There was such sadness in this woman's voice.

No one had been left untouched by my parents' relationship. It had certainly changed my life forever, altering and shaping it just as it had Kalli's and Alexandra's.

"To Dimitri," she turned and said with a feeble smile, raising her glass for me to clink. "The funniest, most adventurous, biggest-hearted man I ever had the privilege of loving."

"To Dimitri," I said.

After that, we stayed up talking about him. Alexandra joined us and they both told me stories of my father into the early hours of the morning. Each story brought me closer and closer to knowing him, and closer to knowing them, too. They answered all my questions, even the silly ones: Did he also hate pickles? Was he also allergic to cats? All those things might seem banal and pointless to someone who wasn't adopted, but to me the tiny details were everything. We laughed together and cried together over the loss of him and they invited me to stay the night with them. When we finally stopped talking it was three o'clock in the morning. I glanced over at the port, and Dimitri's boat was still there, waiting for me.

* * *

I woke up the next morning in the small pretty room that had been made up especially for me. It was a surreal experience waking up in my father's house, even more so because he wasn't there. Breakfast that morning was a massive affair, almost as if everyone had come just to meet me. I met my grandparents, aunts, uncles, nieces, and nephews. They were all so unlike my family. They were loud, and a constant laughter filled the air. They filled me in on my father even more, telling me all the details that Alexandra and Kalli couldn't. How he'd been a quiet, thoughtful, and serious child sometimes. (He sounded a lot like me.) How he'd been bright at school, but bad at sports. How he'd broken his arm in three places when he'd fallen from a tree... all the little things that helped me shade him in. Helped me turn the idea of my father into a real living, breathing person that now existed in my head.

I spent the rest of the morning getting to know my half sister. She was the one person who was probably my strongest link to him. I could see a lot of myself in her—and it wasn't just the eyes. I instantly liked her, and talking to her made me realize that this is what I had been missing: having a sister to talk to and share things with. And when she'd told me about a boy at school that she had a crush on, and then asked my advice on how to tell him she liked him, my heart swelled and drew her in. I loved her. It was big and unconditional and sisterly, and it felt amazing.

Later that day I took a stroll up to my father's grave again. I wanted to be there alone this time. I walked through the beautiful, quaint town and noted how totally different this was from my life back home. The people here were loud and friendly and so warm and welcoming. As I reached the top of the hill, my phone buzzed in my pocket. I pulled it out and the word MOM illuminated my screen. I also saw a voice message, which I listened to.

"Dahling. Is everything okay? You haven't called. Anyway...I bought you a lovely blue dress—you can finally throw away that horrible yellow one. Your sisters and I want to make an appointment for the spa when you get back—I'm sure you didn't have that pedi—they also do fantastic brow shaping there. So I just wanted to know when you are coming home—" beep

Trust my mother to have too much to say to fit it all into one voice message.

"Why do they make the time so short? It's annoying. Anyway, I've been feeding your fish, but one day he looked a little pale so I took him to the vet. Did you know that vets don't treat goldfish by the way? And he's not very friendly, either, can't I buy you a kitten or a puppy? And please don't hate me but I did repaint that wall in your bathroom where the paint was peeling—" beep

A massive smile swept over my face. She cared enough to take my goldfish to the vet? I listened to the last message.

"I can't leave you messages like this! Call me. I have so much to tell you. We haven't spoken in days."

There was a long pause on the phone and I stopped walking and held the phone to my ear tightly.

"Jane, I hope you haven't decided to stay in Greece. I'd miss you too much. Please call me so I know you're okay. I hope you find what you're looking for and come home soon. Bye. We are all waiting for you."

Tears welled in my eyes. God, I was crying a lot these days. My family might not be as demonstrative as everyone here was, or as warm and welcoming, but in my mother's own special way she did care. She wasn't very good at talking about emotions but then again neither was I. I'd never really told her how I felt growing up.

Somewhere along the way we had agreed upon this unspoken law that we would never speak about our real emotions. And I guess her only real way of expressing them now was by redecorating my life. (I actually appreciated the new paint in my bathroom—it had been that awful rust color. I could do without the dating profile and sequined bikini, though.)

I heard a noise behind me and turned. A father and his young daughter were crossing the road talking and smiling. I stopped to watch them, but instead of thinking about Dimitri, I started thinking about my dad, my *real* dad. He'd fetched me from school every day, no matter how busy he was, and I'd go back to his practice and do my homework and read. I had been so lonely there by myself while my sisters were off having fun together.

I turned around and continued walking, but a thought stopped me dead in my tracks. It was more than a thought; it was a kind of epiphany about my whole life leading up to this point... and Dimitri had been right about a lot of it.

A sudden memory of my sisters trying to get me to join in their games and playing rushed in. They'd been so upset when I continued to refuse, and our relationship had started going downhill from there. A profound thought rocked me: They hadn't excluded me, I had excluded myself. *I* was the one who hadn't wanted to participate. I hadn't been excluded by anyone; I had always put myself on the outside.

I suddenly tried to imagine what my life would actually be like without them all. Or what it would have been like growing up here. I continued to walk up the hill; the only sound was the gravel crunching under my feet.

I reached my father's grave and looked down at it again. I felt like I should say something, but what does one say? I stood there for ages looking out over the endless sea in front of me, wondering if this journey had all been for nothing. A tear rolled down my cheek and splashed onto my father's gravestone and Dimitri's words ran through my mind.

"You didn't really come here looking for your father; you came here looking for yourself."

I bent down and rearranged the flowers around the gravestone—it was the only thing I had ever done for him as a daughter. I laid my hand on the cold stone and said a soft, quiet good-bye before turning around and walking back down the hill. I was suddenly overcome by a desire to go back home. *To my real home.* As great as it felt being with this family, I didn't really belong here with them.

After a series of very long good-byes, and promises of returning to visit for Christmas and Easter and bringing my family, too, I left my father's home. I was sad to say good-bye to my new family, but I was also excited to go back and see mine.

I walked back down to the port slowly, and with each step my dread at seeing Dimitri grew. I wondered if I would be able to find someone else to take me back to Santorini.

When I arrived Dimitri was sitting on the boat, waiting for me. He immediately jumped off and helped me onto it—and for a moment, as we stood and looked at each other, he opened his mouth as if to say something, only he didn't. I sat down in silence and watched as the boat started and the small island got farther and farther away. As soon as we were in the open sea, Dimitri cut the engines and let the boat float calmly across the water. He moved tentatively and sat opposite me. I looked up and waited for him to say something, not knowing what I felt for him right now.

"When I found out he was...*I'm so sorry*, Jane. When I found out he was dead I knew you would never be able to meet him, but I didn't want you to leave without knowing him at all, so I did the only thing I could think of, and tried to show you him through the places he'd been to and loved. All the places he visited all those years ago that had inspired me so much. I wanted you to see them all. And like you said the other night, you've never felt closer to him. And that's what I hoped would happen on this journey."

"You knew this entire time that my father was dead?"

"Yes, as soon as I put the pieces together, I made a few phone calls and..." His voice caught in his throat like he was about to cry or something. "I'm sorry. But I didn't want you to leave Greece without finding what you really came looking for."

"So you decided not to tell me. You made a decision on my behalf without even considering what I might have wanted." I felt pure, unadulterated anger rise inside me. "I came looking for my father," I yelled. I hadn't even been aware that my voice was capable of that volume.

"You came looking for yourself. And when I saw you that morning before you left for the airport, I saw that the piece you were looking for was right there, and I had to help you find it, even though I knew I couldn't help you find your father."

"This whole time, you were lying to me?"

"I only lied to you about helping find your father. Everything else has been real."

The anger dipped, giving way to a nauseous feeling as I tried to understand all of this. But I couldn't. I didn't. Nothing made sense. My father was dead.

"Jane. Look at me." I didn't have the strength to look him in the eye. All I could do was shake my head softly.

"What happened between us is *real*. It's not a lie." He tried to touch me but I flinched. "I'm sorry I lied to you. I thought I was doing the right thing. And I was going to tell you, but when we arrived and you saw the boat, I didn't have a chance to. But I'm not sorry about coming on this journey with you and watching you fall in love with Greece...and with me."

I was speechless. My stomach clenched and my eyes burned as the tears flowed. My throat tightened. The pain inside was so great that it felt like a part of me was dying.

"You lied to me," I repeated. "You did the worst thing possible, you gave me hope. Hope that I would find him even though you knew I wouldn't. I hoped, and wished, and all this time you *knew*."

Dimitri looked pained. It was etched across his face. "I know, but don't you see that we were meant to find each other? I'm the Dimitri you came looking for and you are the woman I've been looking for my whole life. Can't you also see that this was your father's last gift to you, that we found each other? If it wasn't for him, you wouldn't have come to Greece. And if it wasn't for the stories of all his adventures, we would never have met."

He tried to reach out and touch my shaking knee, but I jumped up as if a red-hot poker had just burned me, and glared down at him. He looked up and our eyes met. "Please take me home. I want to go home."

"You *are* home." He looked anguished and desperate and his

words sounded like a plea more than a statement. I almost felt sorry for him.

I shook my head wildly. It hurt. "No. This is not my home. I don't belong here."

Dimitri jumped up and moved toward me. "What we feel for each other isn't a lie."

"Ssshhhh." I held my finger up to my lips. I couldn't bear to listen to him. "Take me home, please. And don't say another word." I ran inside and into the bedroom with Dimitri following me. He came up behind me and wrapped his arms around my waist, locking me in his tight grasp.

"Please, Jane. Please." I wiggled out of his clutches and then sat down on the bed holding my head in my hands. "Can we talk about this?"

"*No!* I am so fucking angry with you right now I don't even know what to do." I slammed the bed with both my fists; it was all I could do to stop myself from hitting him, or maybe the wall.

"I don't think you're angry with me," he said. "I don't think you're angry at all."

"I am! I assure you. I am *very* fucking angry."

He shook his head. "You're hurt but it's too much to deal with now, so instead you're angry. You're angry with the universe, the world, the injustice of it all, everything. But I can take it, Jane. I'll take all the anger until you're ready to feel the other feelings, and then when you are, I'll still be here for you. I'll take as much of it as you throw at me, just please, *please* don't give up on what we have."

"Please stop speaking and just take me back. I really, *really* want to go home."

I sat on the bed in silence and prayed that there would be a flight out of here tonight and that there would be space on it. But I had to hurry up and book a ticket if I wanted to get out of here—easier said than done in the middle of the ocean. I needed someone to book it for me. I pulled my phone out and saw one small bar of reception, so I decided to call the one person that I now knew wanted me to come back home, maybe even more than I did.

"Hi, Mom. It's me..."

CHAPTER THIRTY

*I*t wasn't long before we reached Santorini and arrived back at Dimitri's house. He hadn't tried to speak to me or apologize again. I wasn't sure how I felt about that. I'd told him not to say anything else, but a part of me wanted him to beg and apologize. For a few brief moments I'd never felt anything like I had felt with him. *For* him. I'd never felt so loved and in love and so sure about anyone before. But he'd lied and I was angry and confused and everything and nothing made sense anymore. In fact, the world made less sense than it had nine days ago. I felt lost.

My mother had managed to book me a ticket and had sent the flight details to my phone. I finished packing my bags and walked back out into his living room only to find that he had taken up position in the middle of the room and looked like he was about to deliver a speech.

"I know you said that you didn't want me to speak to you again"—his words flew out like a shower of arrows—"but please just give me one more chance to explain and make this right." He looked desperate again, and I almost felt sorry for him.

"Fine." I put my bags down on the floor and crossed my arms protectively across my heart. It already felt so completely shattered, I didn't know how much more it would be able to take.

"I believe," he started slowly and deliberately, "I have *always* believed that things happen for a reason. And when I asked you to stay, I lied about the investigator and I'm sorry. But can't you see that this"—he gestured between us—"this was meant to happen. *We* were meant to happen."

"You've said that already!" I snapped.

"And I'll keep saying it until you hear me," he pleaded. "I'm in love with you." He walked up to me. "That isn't a lie."

I shook my head hard. "I can't do this. I just found out that my father, the person I came looking for, is dead, and I...I...I don't even think there is a name for these feelings. I don't know if I should be angry, or sad, or hate you, or love you, or..."

"Love me. Stay and love me and I'll spend every day making it up to you. Please."

"No, no, no..." My head was racing. "I can't. No." My heart was pounding.

This was all so overwhelming. I sat on the edge of the couch and buried my face in my hands. "What you did to me was...And I don't think I can ever forgive you."

I felt him sit down next to me. He was so close that I could feel the heat radiating off his body. "What should I have done then, Jane? Should I have picked you up from the airport that day and taken you right there so you could find out that your father was dead? Then what? You would have turned around and left without ever seeing the places he loved, doing the things he loved to do, experiencing the kind of life he led, even the foods he'd eaten... You would have left heartbroken, and worse, you would have left with nothing of him. And I didn't want that for you."

"That wasn't your decision to make," I whispered through my fingers.

"I thought I was helping you, Jane. But"—I thought I heard his voice crack again like he was fighting back tears. *Was he crying?* I almost felt sorry for him—"I was wrong."

He shifted in his seat and suddenly I became very aware of his body pressing against mine. A part of me just wanted to lean against him and forget that this had all happened. But a bigger part of me was longing to go home and get back to something familiar that made some kind of sense.

"Just take me to the airport." I got up and straightened my clothes. "I want to go home."

* * *

I had hoped that Dimitri would stay in the car when we pulled into the airport; this good-bye was going to be hard and confusing enough as it was. But he got out of the car and carried my bags all the way through the airport. He stood to the side and watched me as I stood in the check-in line. I tried very hard not to look at him. Because when I looked at him all I saw was his face in front of mine when we'd made love—and it *had* been love. But then I saw his other face, the face he'd been wearing when he'd told me that he was lying. Two such contradictory faces. How could someone be so perfect in one minute, and then so totally wrong a moment later?

I moved closer and closer to the front of the line and just as I was about to check in, he grabbed me. He yanked me into his arms and pulled me into a kiss. For a second or two I didn't react, and then I pushed him off me.

"How dare you?" I said, wiping my mouth with the back of my hand. I'd said it loudly enough that a few people were looking at us now.

"Because I love you," he said as all the people who'd been watching stepped closer.

"That doesn't give you the right to—"

He pulled me into another kiss and for a few seconds there, I let him. It was hard and hungry, and then I reciprocated. I wrapped my arms around his neck and kissed him angrily and desperately. He wrapped his arms around me and pulled me in closer. I wanted to keep kissing him so badly, but another part of me hated him. I tried to pull away and Dimitri grabbed me by the back of my head and pulled my ear to his mouth. "Come back with me and let me prove to you how much I love you. Give me another chance. Please..."

I pulled away and shook my head, and the tears came again. Dimitri looked at me with such desperation in his eyes. He looked like he didn't know what to do next—but there was nothing he could do. I had made up my mind.

"Here." He took the photos out of his pocket and handed them over to me. "These belong to you."

I took the photos and turned and walked away, and this time he let me go. I kept on walking without looking back. I checked in without looking back but just before I disappeared around the corner, I turned to see him one last time. He hadn't moved. He smiled at me, a small sad smile that broke my heart all over again, and he said,

"Tha se periméno giá pánta."

Then he turned and walked away. *What did he say?* I ran up to the nearest Greek-looking person.

"Sorry, what does *tha* . . . um, *se periméno giá*"—shit, what was the last word?—*"pánta*, I think it was *pánta*. What does that mean?"

The woman looked at me and smiled. "It means, 'I will wait for you, always.'" And then she turned and walked away.

My heart raced in my chest before it broke all over again. And then I turned and ran away, as fast as I could.

CHAPTER THIRTY-ONE

*M*y mother was at the airport waiting for me, and I'd never been happier to see her in my entire life. I ran over to her and threw my arms around her. She drew me into a hug, and it felt so good to be held by her.

"You look amazing," she said, holding my face between her hands. That was all the cue I needed to burst out crying. I didn't care that I was in an airport full of people.

"What's wrong?" Her face clouded over and she started wiping my tears away.

"He's dead," I managed to whisper. "He's *dead*."

My mother grabbed me in her arms again and held on to me. She didn't say another word; what can one say to that? We stood there hugging each other for what seemed like ages. I was aware of people walking past and looking at us, and aware that time had passed, but I didn't want to let her go.

I finally peeled myself away from her, and we started walking to the car together. This journey had made me think about so many aspects of my life, and I had questions that only she could answer. They were the questions I should have asked years ago, but I hadn't found the strength or courage to, until now. "Mom, can I ask you something?"

"Anything," she said, loading my bags into the trunk. We both climbed in.

"Are you disappointed with me?"

"What?" Her head snapped around and her eyes widened.

"When I was growing up, did you wish I was different? That I was more like you and Dad, or Janet and Jenna?"

"No. God, no," she said quickly.

"So you don't regret adopting me?"

"What? Why would you think that? Why would you ever, ever think that?"

I shrugged. "I just always thought that you preferred my sisters."

And then something strange happened: Tears welled up in my mother's eyes. I'd never seen her cry before.

"When your father and I couldn't have children, I was devastated. I wanted to be a mom so badly, and when you came along, all my prayers were answered. You were my miracle child."

"I was?"

She took my hands in hers. "I remember the moment I first held you in my arms and you looked up at me with those big mismatching eyes. I said to your dad right there and then that you were special. A one in a million."

I was floored. My mother had never told me this before. But I had never asked, either.

"And when I found out I was pregnant with your sisters, I actually didn't know how I was going to love them. I loved you so much that it felt like I didn't have space in my heart for anyone else."

"Then why did you always try to change me?"

"Oh, Jane. I never wanted to change you. Ever. Do you remember that day you came home crying from school? You were about ten years old and that stupid Lance kid, who I could have killed, teased you because you looked different from us and told you that we didn't love you as much because you were adopted?"

"How could I forget?" I said.

"Well, I cried myself to sleep. For the first time I saw how unhappy you were with yourself and how desperately you wanted to be someone else. It broke my heart, and from that day onward I decided that I would do everything I could to help you fit in and make you feel like you were one of us. That's all you ever wanted to do."

I nodded slowly. "I thought you did all that because you were trying to fix me?"

My mother squeezed my hands hard. "*Never.* You've always been perfect, just the way you are. Maybe your father and I should have helped you more, maybe we should have tried to understand what it was like for you a bit better, maybe we should have gone to family therapy and discussed it more openly in the house. Maybe we should have told you every day how much we loved you and how you were part of us. Maybe we failed you."

"I...I..." Pain constricted my throat. "I never knew you felt that way."

"I'm going to tell you something, Jane, and it's not to make you feel bad. But you were the one who put yourself on the outside, not us. You pushed us all away. Your sisters looked up to you so much when they were young. All they wanted was for you to play with them, but you never wanted to."

My throat tightened again. "I was always so jealous of them." I hung my head and looked at my lap. I thought of the conversation with Dimitri again. He had been right about so much, but that didn't take away from how angry I was with him, and how betrayed I felt.

I arrived home and my mother offered to stay with me, but truthfully I wanted to be alone. There was so much in my head that I needed to sit with and sort out. This had been the most emotional journey of my life. It had been both the best and the worst thing I had ever done for myself. On the plane I had reread my father's note over and over again, and every time I did the most amazing feeling had filled me. My whole life I'd thought I was unwanted; that I had been given away because I was worthless and unlovable.

But the truth was that I had been loved and wanted, and just knowing that made me feel so much better about myself, about who I was, and the choices I had made. But this feeling was hard to hold on to all the time. I alternated between the most intense joy and then the worst pain imaginable.

I'd gone searching for my father, and although I hadn't found him in person, I'd found the words he had left behind for me. Through them he'd helped me see my self-worth, and had given me the greatest gift of all: the feeling that I was good enough.

But I had also found Dimitri there, I had fallen in love with him, and for the briefest moment I had been happy. But that love bubble had so painfully and cruelly burst, and I didn't know how I was ever going to get over what he'd done to me. How would I ever be able to forgive him? It was true that Dimitri had been a big part of this whole thing—and I'd never be able to erase the role that he'd played. If it wasn't for him, none of this would have happened. The outcome of his lies had been good, and something really special had come from them, but I still couldn't erase the feelings of betrayal.

I went to bed that night mulling over these conflicting feelings, trying to focus on the good things that had come from my journey, but my thoughts kept returning to Dimitri and kept me awake. Although perhaps it was better if I stayed awake with the thoughts of Dimitri than if I fell asleep with them . . .

CHAPTER THIRTY-TWO

I'd been home a week before I finally called my friends over to read the note to them.

"It's the most beautiful thing I've ever heard," Lilly said, wiping away a small tear that was rolling down her cheek.

Val looked at me and nodded. Tears were also running down her face.

I turned my attention to Stormy. She was sitting in total silence and I suddenly felt terrible for reading it to her. She really had been unwanted by her mother. Her story reads like the plot of a science-fiction film but is completely true. Her parents were both strange traveling hippies of sorts, and when she was born, her mother ran away to join a cult. True story.

"It's the most beautiful thing I've ever heard." Stormy looked up at me and smiled. I'm sure it took a lot for her to smile through the pain I could see reflected in her eyes.

"So what should I do about the other letter?" I asked them. The letter for Phoebe had been sitting on my bedside table, where I had spent countless moments staring at it, resisting the urge to rip it open and read.

"You have to take it to her," Stormy said.

Val nodded. "You have to. It's your duty."

"You have to," Lilly echoed.

I glanced down at the letter. I knew I had to. But that was easier said than done. Meeting her and showing her the letter would be among the hardest things I'd ever have to do—and she didn't want to see me, so I would have to convince her, too. Maybe she didn't even want the letter?

After a few more minutes of catching up, the girls left and made me promise that I would get the note to Phoebe. So that left me no choice, but I wasn't feeling very positive. The last time I'd tried to reach out to Phoebe, she hadn't been very forthcoming. Still, I had to try.

And the first step would be to call the adoption agency and ask them to pass on the message once again. I picked up my phone and saw that I had three text messages from Dimitri. I immediately tossed the phone on my bed and moved away from it, as if it were a coiled snake about to strike.

I didn't know what to do. I wanted to read them, but I didn't. I wanted to love him, but I couldn't.

Oh, who am I kidding? I grabbed the phone and went to my messages.

First one:

Jane. I'm sorry. I love you.

The next one must have come only a few seconds later:

Actually, I'm not sorry because I got to watch you change and become this amazing, strong, beautiful woman that I knew you were from the moment I met you.

He must have been typing them one after the other:

But I am very sorry that I hurt you. I hope one day you'll be able to forgive me. I love you.

I put the phone back down on the bed and pondered. He was right: I had changed. Pre-Greece Jane wouldn't have been that harsh and unforgiving with Dimitri. She would have reacted in some self-deprecating way and blamed herself and forgiven him on the outside, but quietly hated him inside, letting yet another destructive and negative emotion eat her from within.

But I wasn't that Jane anymore—and I wasn't the Jane that would take no for an answer, either. Phoebe was going to meet with me whether she liked it or not. And so I picked up the phone and dialed the adoption agency. This time I would entice her: I would tell them to pass on the message that I had an urgent letter for her.

CHAPTER THIRTY-THREE

I sat in my car staring at the coffee shop. I couldn't see inside, so she might not even be here yet. I think I had forgotten to breathe a long time ago. My body had certainly forgotten how to work: It was frozen to the car seat.

I was clutching the letter in my hands. I had been holding it so tightly and for so long that I had crumpled it, and it was damp with the sweat coming from my clammy hands. I laid it on my lap, ran my hands over it in an attempt to straighten it, and then slipped it back into my bag. I looked at myself in the mirror, fixed my hair, cleaned the lipstick from the corners of my dry mouth, and opened the car door.

My heart pounded as I walked across the parking lot toward the coffee shop. I was assaulted by nerves so overwhelming, I had to stop walking for a second and take a deep breath. I had been so confident over the phone. I had been firm. But right now all of that was gone.

I reached the door and paused. I didn't want to do this. Every single cell in my body screamed that I didn't want to be here doing this. If I had learned anything in my life so far, it was that things didn't always go according to your own carefully laid-out plans. Instead, life was filled with painful lessons. It was full of dashed hopes and expectations that had crashed in a head-on collision with that thing we call reality. But I had also learned that once you survived the collisions intact, armed with the lessons you acquired, reality could also be beautiful. *Life* could be beautiful.

Finally, having mustered as much positivity as I could, I pushed the door open and walked in. Each step felt like I was wading through thick mud. I scanned the restaurant and...

I saw her.

She had her back to me, but I knew it was her. Don't ask me how I knew, I just did. For a few seconds I simply stood there and studied her, trying to get a sense of what she was feeling and thinking. But the only thing that offered me any insight was the frantic tapping of her foot on the ground. Clearly she was as nervous as I was.

I approached her slowly, like someone approaches a dangerous wild animal that has been let out of a cage. But the closer I got, the more the sick, strange, panicky nerves gripped me. The heat of the coffee shop ovens and the soaring temperatures outside coalesced into a suffocating blanket that made it difficult to catch my breath.

This was a bad idea. This was the worst idea ever. But I felt duty bound. I had never been able to do anything for my father while he was alive; this was the only father-daughter act I could complete, and because he wanted this to happen, I would do it. But only for him.

I reached the table and was just about to walk around it when she turned and looked at me. We locked eyes and it was as if we stared straight past the physical and into each other's souls with an intensity that froze my gut. It reminded me of what Stormy had told me once, the true meaning of the word *namaste*—my soul recognizes your soul. That was exactly what it was.

This was the first time we'd seen each other in twenty-five years. We were essentially strangers, yet we were a part of each other. We'd shared the most intimate bond any two humans can share. She'd carried me inside her body—connected to her, feeding off her, entirely dependent on her. She had *created* me, together with that magical bond that was meant to be unbreakable, and yet it had been broken. She had broken it. We shared the same DNA, yet we knew nothing about each other.

How could two people be so similar and yet so far apart at the same time?

Neither one of us said a word as I walked around the table, pulled out a chair, and sat down.

You might have imagined this playing out a few ways. Maybe in your fantasy, in mine even, my biological mother would see me and throw her arms around me. She would hold me to her bosom and she would weep from the sheer joy of being reunited with her child. I had long since given up on this expectation, though. If she were the kind of woman who would have done that, she would have been the kind of woman who wanted to meet me years ago. I knew now that this was less about me and more about her, and not being able to deal with her own pain.

So I wasn't expecting anything from her today. I wanted to give her the note and then leave. I no longer needed anything from her; my father had told me all I had wanted to know. And the rest of it I had found out for myself—inside myself. The waiter came up to our table and broke the awkward staring silence.

"Can I get you anything?" he asked me.

"Water, please." My words came out stilted, mirroring the strange way my thoughts were playing out in my head. The waiter turned and looked at my mother—*mother*, what a strange thing. She shook her head.

"No thanks," she said in a voice that I had heard every day of my life. She sounded exactly like me. The waiter left and we went back to looking at each other. One of us needed to end this, and since I had been the one to call this meeting, and hadn't taken no for an answer, I would have to be the one to do it.

"Like I said…I just came back from Greece a week ago," I said slowly. I was still trying to order my thoughts. "I went looking for Dimitri, my father, and…" I was coming to the part where I needed to say it out loud. That I hadn't found him, that he was dead. But I couldn't. So instead, I pulled the letter out of my handbag and pushed it slowly across the table. "This is for you. He wanted me to give it to you."

I looked up at her and saw the color drain from her face as if she had just seen a ghost. Her hand came out to take the note; it was shaking so badly that I didn't think she was going to be able to hold it. She clutched the note as if it was the most precious thing she owned. Her eyes teared up and a small smile started to tug on her lips.

"How is he?" she asked. Her question knocked me in the stomach like a mallet. I can't even begin to explain how offended I was. She hadn't asked me anything about myself, she hadn't spoken a word to me yet, and this was all she could say?

A feeling of anger—no, *rage*—rose up in me again. I thought I had put the anger away, but I think some wounds are so old and deep, they take more than a letter and a week to heal.

"He's dead." The words came out flatly and coldly and I stared at her, waiting and watching to see what her reaction was going to be.

"He's...?" Her eyes pleaded with me. She was willing me to say something different. She looked hurt; devastated even. But it was the fucking truth and I'd had to deal with it. In that moment, all my rage and anger and hatred toward her flooded me. How dare she get this upset over him when I was here in front of her? I was her daughter and I was sitting across the table from her and she had barely acknowledged my presence. I wanted to hurt her now as much as she had hurt me, and I had the power to do so for the first time in my life. I leaned in across the table and met her eyes.

"He's dead," I whispered with venom. "Dead."

She took in a sharp breath. A loud one. And then another, and another, and soon she had clasped her hands to her chest and it looked like she was struggling to breathe. Her elbow knocked over a glass and a few people turned to look as her breathing got worse and more erratic. It deteriorated quickly, until she looked like a fish that had been pulled out of the water opening and closing its mouth frantically.

"Mom . . ." I said instinctually. I reached out across the table. Was she having a heart attack? "I'm sorry, I didn't mean to . . . Mom?" The waiter rushed over and someone else came forward claiming to be a doctor.

"It's the heat," he said loudly. "Bring me some cool towels and a paper bag." He moved my mother to the floor and laid her out on her back. He started trying to calm her and coach her into a better breathing rhythm. And then everything became chaotic.

An ambulance arrived, and she was rushed off to the hospital, and I was ushered along for the ride. I found myself in the back of the ambulance, sitting next to her while an oxygen mask was placed over her face and she was given something to calm her.

"It might help her calm down if you hold her hand." The medic looked at me expectantly and I froze. This was all happening too fast. A moment ago I was angry and I hadn't quite recovered from it yet.

My mother turned her head slightly and looked at me.

I looked down at her hand and then reached out. The second I touched it she grabbed it so hard that my fingers crushed together. She pulled it all the way up to her chest and laid it on top of her. She looked down at my hand with something that resembled awe and I wondered if she had held my tiny hand in hers after I was born and looked at it like that. And then she closed her eyes and drifted off to sleep.

CHAPTER THIRTY-FOUR

As soon as we got to the hospital it was even more chaotic. I was ushered to the side as they guided my mother's gurney down the hall. I stood and waited until one of the nurses came and took me into the waiting area. I spent the next few minutes pacing up and down the corridor, barely able to process what had just happened. I didn't know what to do. I had to talk to someone, to make this all less surreal and to get a better grip. So I took out my phone and called my mother.

She came rushing over and the two of us sat together in the waiting room. It was a lot like the moment in the airport. We didn't speak. I didn't need to explain to her what had happened. I didn't have to explain how I felt. She just had to be there. I looked up at her face—and that's when I realized I had never seen my mother looking so nervous in my entire life.

"If I can, I want to meet her," my mother said to me. "I want to thank her."

At some stage Phoebe's family, her *real family*, arrived. I'd remembered her saying that they didn't know about me and I didn't want to overstep my boundaries, so I continued to sit in the waiting room wondering if I should even be there at all. I'd given her the note, I was free to leave. My duty to my father had been done. But just as I was ready to leave, she asked for me.

I walked into her room apprehensively. She was seated in a chair looking out the window, and she was holding the open letter in her hands. She turned and gave me the faintest smile.

"They said it was a panic attack brought on by stress, and also the heat made it worse. I haven't eaten or slept in two days...I've been nervous for this," she said in a small voice.

I nodded and sat on the edge of the bed awkwardly. "I've been nervous, too."

And then she burst into tears. "I was so scared you were going to hate me," she said. "Hate me for giving you away and then hate me even more for not agreeing to meet you all those years ago, too." She looked down at her hands and played with the note.

"I did hate you," I said faintly.

She looked up at me briefly and gave a small nod of acknowledgment. "I'm sorry," she said.

"I don't need your apologies. That's not why I came. I came to give you that note."

She looked back down at the note, and her hands started shaking again. "He was the love of my life, you know." She smiled in a way that made her look many years younger. "I have never loved anyone like that again..." She paused. "Not even my husband."

There was a silence in the room, and all I could hear was the faint ticking of the clock.

"We had this plan, we were going to get married and have children and live this life full of love and laughter and...but I was only eighteen, I was still at school, and my parents, well...I've never really forgiven them for that."

There was another silence, but this time it was so full I could almost hear her thoughts and feel her feelings.

"You have his eyes, you know." She finally looked up at me again. "I'm sorry I didn't meet you earlier, it was just too painful."

"It's fine. It was meant to happen this way." If I had met her all those years ago, I never would have gone on my journey. I never would have found those parts of me or my father, or his words that had spoken to me from beyond the grave. And I never would have met and loved Dimitri, even if it was only for a few moments. Loving him had changed me in many ways. It had made me realize that I was not the unlovable person I once thought I was and that I did, *I did*, deserve to be loved by someone amazing one day. Even if that wasn't going to be Dimitri.

"I've never been a mother to you. But can I give you one word of motherly advice? If this is the only thing I ever give you that means anything...Never let go of true love. Fight for it. No matter what the odds are and no matter how hard it is. Never, ever give up on that kind of love. If you do, you will regret it every single day for the rest of your life."

She stood, walked over to me, and wrapped her arms around me. "I'm really sorry I never got to be your mother. But I can see your parents have done a very good job, and for that, I don't regret giving you the life you deserved. I would never have been able to give you that."

And with that, she let go of me and walked out of the room. I glanced after her and watched as my mother, my *real* mother, the woman that had loved and cared for me, walked over to her. The two women looked at each other for the longest time, and then Phoebe joined her family and left. She walked out of the hospital and out of my life for the second time. But this time, I was happy to see her go. I didn't belong to her. I wasn't hers, and she was not mine.

I was Jane. I was loved and I had a family and friends that I wouldn't trade for anything. I was right where I was meant to be. I was *who* I was meant to be, and it had taken me twenty-five years to figure that all out.

* * *

My mom took me back to my parents' place and made me a cup of sweet tea.

"Honey, I've got a roast that I could pop into the oven. Do you feel up to a family dinner? I know your sisters are dying to see you."

And strangely, despite the long day, a family dinner sounded like exactly what I wanted. I smiled at my mom and nodded.

That night at dinner I was struck by how different it all felt. I was so much more relaxed. For once I allowed myself to take part in the conversation. Not to sit as a bystander and vaguely hear my sisters talking about some new interest of theirs. And I could see how happy they were to see me. They tossed one of their usual invitations out to me, for me to come to this new amazing place that served "vodka sushi" (whatever the hell that meant).

And for the first time ever, instead of brushing the idea off I said:

"How's this Friday night?"

The sound of the cutlery being put down was audible. My sisters looked at me with shock and they both started nodding slowly.

"Are you sure, I mean, would that suit you?" Jenna said. "You can bring your friends if you want."

"Even that Stormy-Rain," Jenna quickly added. God, they really wanted me there. They hated Stormy—well, *hate* is a strong word. I think she frightened the living daylights out of them.

I shook my head and smiled at these strange blond creatures that were my sisters. "No. Just us would be nice." The shock on their faces was palpable, but it was very quickly replaced by glee. I even noticed a smile from my dad, who had been very quiet throughout dinner except for right at the end when he hugged me and simply said,

"Welcome home, Janey. It's good to have you back at work."

I went home and lay awake that night with Phoebe's words ringing in my head over and over again.

"Never, ever, give up on that kind of love. You will regret it every single day for the rest of your life."

But what if that real love had hurt me? Even if his intentions had been good, and even if I had gotten exactly what I needed from him? He'd helped me meet my father. He'd helped me find what I was looking for.

It was late, and I had survived yet another emotional day—they were starting to become pretty common. I needed to get some sleep. I dug in my bag for my mobile phone, and just as I pulled it out, I noticed something shining in my bag. I reached in and grabbed the sweet from the wedding in Greece. I held it in my hands and gazed at it, almost as if I was trying to size it up.

Oh what the hell, what harm could it do? And I slipped it under my pillow once more.

* * *

The next morning I called an emergency conference. I had messaged all my friends and told them to come to my house for lunch. I needed their urgent advice. I needed something, anything. After last night's strange dreams, I needed someone to slap me silly. To intervene and give me clarity, to tell me what to do so I would not have another mental breakdown.

It was noon and they diligently started arriving. Lilly, always on time, was first. Annie, who was living a fabulously glam life in LA, was Skyping in. Val arrived looking frazzled and beside herself—*what else is new?* She had probably been kept up again all night by the sounds of her neighbor having sex with his new fiancée. He had just proposed. (That would not be the worst thing, but add in the fact she was madly in love with her neighbor—and had been for the last two years—and listening to him in flagrante delicto was devastating.) She made a beeline for the wine and started commiserating with Annie.

We all sat patiently waiting for Stormy to arrive. No doubt she would come barreling through the door like a wild storm; as her name suggested, subtlety was not her strong point.

And as predicted, a loud knock on the door, followed by what sounded like bells jingling, rang out. I opened the door to find Stormy, wearing something that looked like it had been stolen from a dead hippie, complete with bells hanging from the sleeves and shells sewn into the hem. Her hair was bright purple and she wore earrings that looked like recycled bottle tops. She burst in carrying a massive book under her arm—I recognized the book immediately. If you knew Stormy, you knew the book. She launched herself at the carpet dramatically and started.

"So"—she flipped the tome open—"I consulted the numbers this morning." She meant numerology. "And they said some interesting things."

Despite myself, I found myself being drawn to this information. "What?"

"They said this is a favorable time to follow your dreams."

"Really?" Despite myself, despite the fact I didn't believe in this kind of stuff, I wondered if it referred to the dream I'd had last night. Dimitri, in his cardboard cutout form, had stood there and repeated over and over again, "*I will wait for you, always. I will wait for you, always.*" That was it. The dream had been on a loop the whole night and it had thrown me, hence the need for this emergency friend meeting.

"What else did they say?" I asked.

"Nothing else." She shook her head. "Jane, is that organic cheese?" She got up and wandered over to the table, examining the food.

My heart pounded in my chest. I know this sounds totally

stupid, but as my dream had progressed, I had started to forget why I was even angry with Dimitri. I had started to remember how much I loved him. I think the real reason I'd called my friends over was that I needed one of them to tell me it was okay to feel this way, and that I didn't need to hate him anymore. I needed someone's permission to climb back onto the next flight to Greece and go to him. Because right now, that was all my heart was telling me to do. My heart was screaming so loudly, it had completely silenced my head.

"I don't know what to do, guys." I sat down at the table and looked at my friends.

"What do you want to do?" Lilly asked.

"I still love him. Everything he did, even though he lied, it was meant to happen. If he hadn't done it, I wouldn't have stayed in Greece and I never would've found my father. I think I want to go back to Greece. I think I want to be with him. *I don't know!* I just wish someone would tell me what the hell to do. I wish there was some kind of sign or something."

At that, there was a knock on the door. Everyone turned slowly toward it.

"It can't be," Val whispered.

"No. It can't be," Lilly echoed.

We all stared at the door in silent shock as there came another knock. We all glanced at one another with wide eyes.

"It's impossible," I said, my voice trembling.

"Everything is possible in this multiverse," Stormy said with a massive smile as she rushed to the door. I followed behind her as she pulled the door open, revealing a pizza deliveryman. My heart sank, even though it was all totally crazy and illogical—*of course Dimitri isn't standing behind that door.*

"Did you guys order pizza?" he said, looking at Stormy with a slightly confused expression on his face. A usual reaction to her.

"No," I said. "You're probably looking for number one. This is ten—the zero fell off and the landlord needs to put it back on."

"Is your name Dimitri?" Stormy suddenly asked with a mysterious-sounding voice.

The guy looked confused. "No. It's Brad. But I did go to school with a Dimitri once."

"*Aha!*" Stormy exclaimed triumphantly and looked at me. She turned to the others. "You hear that?" She sounded excited.

"Oh come on, Stormy, this is a stretch, even for you," Lilly said from behind us.

"Stormy. Really?" Val said as Annie laughed.

"I'll prove it to you." Stormy flashed us all a smile. "What's on the pizza?" she asked.

The deliveryman looked even more confused now, and perhaps a little scared. "Um, pepperoni, mushrooms, and olives."

"Olives! Olives!" Stormy exclaimed loudly. "Olives are practically the Greek national food."

Annie squawked from the screen, "Stormy, you're not being serious. Olives are a common topping."

"Oh my Goddess!" Stormy screeched so loudly that the man stepped back. "And his pants are blue and his shirt is white. Blue and white, that's the Greek flag!"

The man with the pizza started backing away as Stormy became more and more excited. She then closed the door and looked at me excitedly.

"How much more of a sign do you need?"

"You think?" I asked. Stormy nodded meaningfully, like she was in possession of the keys to unlocking the mysteries of the universe. I wanted this to be a sign so desperately that for the moment I was willing to abandon all logical thought and go with it. A bubble started rising in my stomach. Intellectually I knew this was the biggest load of bullshit ever, but I wanted to go so badly that I didn't care.

"Okay!" I said.

"Okay what?" Lilly asked.

"Okay, I'll go."

"What?" my three friends said at the same time.

"I'm going, guys. And it's not about signs and shit like that, I'm going because I love him. Oh my God that feels good to say. I love him. I love Dimitri." I jumped up and down crazily. "I'm going to go and pack a bag right now."

"Wait!" Stormy yelled, bringing the whole room to a dead stop. "Don't pack. Stay."

"What?" I looked at her with total confusion just as there was another knock on the door.

"No, we did not order pizza or Chinese or Indian curry!" I shouted as I walked to the door and opened it. But it wasn't the pizza delivery guy this time... It was Dimitri.

Chapter Thirty-Five

A gasp rose out from the room behind me. My mouth fell open and I blinked a few times to make sure I wasn't seeing things.

"You're…you're not bringing us curry," I stumbled and just looked at him stupidly. God, I had forgotten how devastatingly, breath-stealingly, panty-looseningly hot he was.

He smiled at me. Fuck, I had missed that smile. That sweet sexy smile. "No," he said.

"Okay," I replied and stood there. I stood and I stared and I didn't move. I think I was in total shock. I heard someone clear her throat from behind me.

"Aren't you going to invite him in?" Stormy said. "He's come all this way to see you."

Suddenly a thought hit me. "But how did you know where I lived or when I would be…" I turned and looked at Stormy, who was smiling like a Cheshire cat. "You?" I looked over at her.

"My neighbor helped me send those i mails."

Annie burst out laughing. "Emails."

"I, e, a, b, c," she said with a shrug. "Dimitri and I have been 'chatting.'" She gestured some air quotes with her fingers.

"Really?" I smiled at her. She was so fucking weird, and I was totally grateful for her right then. My strange friend who had taken it upon herself to intervene behind my back.

"So…" she pressed. "Ask the guy in. Don't make him lurk in the doorway like a dog burglar."

"Yes. Yes. Of course." I gestured formally with my hand and he walked in. Dimitri was in my apartment.

I followed him in. "Guys, um, this is Dimitri, and Dimitri, these are…uh, they are…um…" Mind blank. What the hell were my friends' names again? Oh yes…

"You've met Stormy-Rain, obviously," I said, gesturing toward her. He stuck a hand out for her to shake and she took it.

"Nice to meet you in person," he said.

Stormy looked him up and down for a moment and then opened her mouth. "You know, you're so *not* my type, at all, all macho model vibes with muscles and good hair and your jaw is very chiseled."

I briefly looked over at Dimitri as his brow started to furrow in what I could only assume was absolute confusion.

She continued. "But you're really hot. Jane told us how hot you were, but still you are hotter that I thought you would be, taking into account some of Jane's previous choices in men."

"Stormy!" Lilly chided loudly. I just shook my head. Dimitri looked at Stormy for a second or two and then smiled a friendly smile. He strode off and extended his hand again. "And you…"

"Me? I'm…I'm Lilly?" she said, looking a tad dazed and

confused. Clearly he was having the same effect on my friends as he had on all women. She shook his hand and was bordering on gawking at him.

He waved into the computer. "Hi."

Annie waved back. "Hi. I'm Annie. I'm not really here, as you can see."

He turned and looked at Val. She was still tearstained and clutching the wine. "Val. Hi," she said flatly. Dimitri gave her a cautious little wave. "Can I ask you something?" Val said.

I sighed. She basically asked everyone this. "Do you think guys and girls can just be friends? No romantic feelings. Just friends?"

"Um…" He looked stumped and then his face lit up. "That's a really good question. But I think I once read a study that stated it has been scientifically proven that members of the opposite sex can in fact just be platonic friends. The study was conducted with eighty-eight undergraduate students and—"

Val wailed loudly and slumped into her chair, looking completely defeated. Dimitri looked up at me and I shook my head.

"It's a very long story," I whispered to him.

Stormy tisked loudly and dramatically. "How many times do I have to tell you that you are not meant to be with that stupid neighbor of yours?" Stormy was always telling us about our love lives— how she hated Annie's ex, how I was meant to find Dimitri, how Val was not meant to be with Matt. So ironic, since she was the one who really, *really* couldn't figure out her own love life.

"Okay!" Lilly suddenly exclaimed loudly. "I guess that's our cue to leave." She blew a kiss to Annie and closed the computer and then nudged Val, who was now drinking wine out of the bottle.

"Jane, do you mind if I take some food?" Stormy asked. "Is it vegan, though?" She reached for it.

"Vegan, free range, gluten-, wheat-, and sugar-free." I smiled at her. It was a total lie. Stormy scooped up the food and rushed out with Lilly and Val. They closed the door behind them and suddenly Dimitri and I were alone.

We stood in awkward silence. In my fantasy this would have been playing out differently. Why weren't we running into each other's arms, crying, kissing, and declaring undying love?

"May I sit?" he asked, gesturing to my sofa. It sounded so formal.

"Sure."

He sat down and looked so scared. I'd never seen him like this before. I sat opposite him and we both looked at each other. Silence. And then more silence. The silence stretched out before us and there seemed to be no end to it when he finally spoke.

"I had this whole thing worked out, this big, logical argument about why you need to forgive me and be with me. And then I planned on delivering this massive speech that was supposed to win you back. It's romantic and emotive and I practiced it in my head the whole flight here, I even..." He reached into his pocket and pulled out a crumpled note. "I even wrote the main points down so I wouldn't forget anything. But..." He crunched the piece of paper in his hands and dropped it to the floor. He got up, walked across the room, and sat next to me. My body responded to him instantly. He reached for my hand and when I let him take it, he smiled.

"I always imagined your father as a pirate searching the seas and the islands for this treasure chest. A chest that contained the most important, valuable thing in the world."

I stared at him, bewildered, not sure where this was going.

"I was always desperate to know what was inside it and why it was so special." Dimitri took my hand and placed it on his chest. I could feel his heart pounding beneath my palm.

"But I know what it is now. *It's you.*" His heart pounded even harder and faster. "You're the treasure. You are what I have been looking for this whole time."

I inhaled sharply. "What?"

"I've always felt restless. I've always felt like I needed to keep moving, go places, see things, and now...all I want to do is stay in one place...*with you.* I've found the thing I have been looking for, and it's you. And your father is the person who brought us together. That's how I know we are meant to be."

Tears immediately sprang to my eyes. My biological mother had told me to never let go of true love. To fight for it, no matter what. She hadn't been there for me my entire life, but her words were with me now.

I'd gone on this journey and had seen firsthand the pain of regret. It can consume an entire life, and it affects everyone around you. My biological mother and father had been separated, and they had both regretted it for the rest of their lives. They had never been fully happy or fully alive without each other.

And I wanted to be alive and happy. I wanted to die with no regrets, knowing that I had loved and been loved. *I deserved that.* I was worth it.

"Yes," I said as the tears escaped my eyes.

"Yes what?"

"Yes, I love you and I forgive you and I want to be with you. I love you." Dimitri threw his arms around me and buried his face in my neck. I reciprocated and we held on to each other as tightly as we possibly could.

I'd gone searching for my father and instead, I had found the love of my life...

And I would never, ever let him go.

Turn the page to read an
excerpt from Lilly's story,

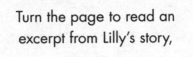

PROLOGUE

I'm sorry, I can't.

I'm sorry, I can't.

I'm sorry, I can't.

No matter how long I stared at the scribbled note, the meaning stayed the same. I held it up hoping, praying that the sunlight would illuminate the other words that had been written in magic invisible ink.

But nothing appeared.

Just those four tiny little words...and yet they had the power to bring my whole world crashing down around me in an instant. Splintering and exploding into a million little pieces.

I finally managed to pry my eyes from the note and found myself staring into the terrified faces of my stepsister and two best friends. They were looking at me as if I was about to have a celebrity melt-down, shave my head, and then poke someone's eye out with an umbrella. They looked very concerned. Like I was a ticking time bomb waiting to explode.

And they were right.

I was.

Tick. Tick.

I was teetering on the brink of insanity. I could feel it trying to suck me in like an all-consuming black hole. The tug was almost too hard to fight.

Did I even want to fight it?

But what would happen if I let go? I knew I was in shock right now, drenched in a sort of numb, detached feeling. But I could feel the other hostile emotions bubbling their way to the surface and fighting to take control.

I blinked. My eyes were stinging.

I tried to open my mouth and speak.

It was dry and nothing came out.

I looked at my best friends Jane and Val, my rocks, the two people I could always rely on for help...But they said nothing. Not a word. Just terror plastered across their faces.

I shifted my gaze to my stepsister Stormy-Rain. Unlike her name, she was a ray of tie-dye-wearing sunshine. She had the ability to turn even the most terrible situation into a positive. *Again...nothing.* Just stupefied horror plastered across her now-ashen face.

I looked down at my shaking hands; they were crunching the corners of the note. My heart felt like it was going to break through the safe confines of my rib cage, taking my stomach and lungs with it.

Rage combined with shock and gut-wrenching sorrow, and I snapped. It overwhelmed me, rising up from the most primitive part of my soul where logic, rules, and intellect wielded no power. This was a place of red, raw, uninhibited emotion.

And so I screamed at the top of my lungs until my voice went hoarse and my throat was raspy.

"Get me out of this dress. Get me out of it. Get it off!"

My desperate fingers frantically ripped at my wedding dress, a dress that had taken my two friends ten minutes to get me into, thanks to the intricate crisscross ribbons of the bodice. But I was trapped.

Jane and Val sprang into action, simultaneously grabbing at the stubborn ribbons, but it was taking too long. The air around me became too thick to breathe, and I felt like I was drowning.

"I can't breathe. I can't breathe. It's too tight."

Val made a move for the knife that had arrived earlier with the room service, and, without hesitation, she sliced through the intricate satin ribbons. The sound of the serrated knife eviscerating them was like fingernails down a blackboard; it made my skin crawl. But I could feel the bodice getting looser and looser, until it finally slipped down my aching body and pooled lifelessly on the floor.

I was finally free.

And then the tears came. Hot, wet tears streaming down my cheeks and streaking my flushed skin with angry black mascara lines. The tears turned to sobbing.

I looked at my dress, reduced to a pathetic puddle of ribbons, satin, and beads at my feet. But I still felt trapped. *My hair!* The perfect updo, held together with delicate pearl clips. Suddenly, it felt like every strand of hair was tightening around my head, like a boa constrictor going in for the kill. My fingers ripped, desperately trying to free it from its pearly captives.

I wanted to get the pearl clips removed. Gone. Off. Out. I wanted to rub every single trace of the wedding away.

I pulled out my earrings and grabbed the nearest tissue, rubbing my red lipstick off until my lips hurt. It smeared across my face like an ugly rash.

If someone were standing outside the window looking in, they would have pegged me for a crazy person. And I wouldn't have blamed them. Because somewhere in the back of my now-estranged rational brain, I knew I looked like a lunatic escaped from a mental asylum in desperate need of a straitjacket and drastic electroshock therapy. But how the hell else should I be…

Because he…

Michael Edwards—fiancé of one year, perfect boyfriend of two—had left me, Lilly Swanson, just ten minutes before I was scheduled to walk down the aisle. The bottle of perfume that he'd wanted me to wear today, insisted I wear, because "it was his favorite," mocked me from the dressing table. So I picked it up and threw it against the wall, watching it shatter into a million pieces, just like my life. I was hit by the sweet smell of jasmine and felt sick to my stomach.

What was I going to tell the five hundred guests who were sitting in the church waiting for me? Some had even flown here to South Africa all the way from Australia.

"Hi, everyone. Thanks for coming. Guess what? SURPRISE! No wedding!"

A wedding that my father had spent a small fortune on.

A wedding that was going to be perfect.

Perfect, dammit. Perfect!

I'd made sure of that. I had painstakingly handled every single tiny detail. It had taken months and months of meticulous planning to create this day, and now what?

Things went very blurry all of a sudden. I vaguely remember my brother James bursting into the room, screaming insults and then vowing to kill him. He even punched the best man when he claimed to have no knowledge of Michael's whereabouts. My rational, logical father tried to find a legitimate motive for Michael's behavior, insisting we speak to him before jumping to any rash conclusions. Hundreds of phone calls followed: Where was he? Who had seen him? Where did he go?

At some stage the guests were told, and the rumor mill went into full swing…

He'd had an affair.

He'd eloped with someone else.

He was a criminal on the run.

He was gay.

He'd been beamed up by aliens and was being experimented on. (Hopefully it was painful.)

People threw around bad words like *bastard*, *asshole*, and *liar*. They also threw around words like *shame*, *sorry*, and *pity*. They wondered whether they should take their wedding gifts back or leave them. What was the correct protocol in a situation like this?

While the world around me was going mad, I felt a strange calm descend. Nothing seemed real anymore, and I began to feel like a voyeur looking at my life from a distance. I didn't care that I was sitting on the floor in my bra and panties. I didn't care that my mascara and lipstick were so smudged I looked like Batman's Joker. I just didn't care.

Some minutes later my other brother Adam, the doctor, burst in and insisted I drink a Coke and swallow the little white pill he was forcing down my throat. It would calm me, he said.

Shortly after that, my overly dramatic, theater-actress mother rushed in to give the performance of her life.

"Why, why, why?" She placed her hand across her heart.

"What is this, a madness most discreet? A stench most foul?" She held her head and cried out, "Whyyy?!"

"For heaven's sake, Ida, this isn't some Shakespearean bloody play." I could hear the anger in my father's voice. Even after eighteen years of divorce, they still couldn't be civil to each other.

"Lest I remind you that all the world is a stage," my mother shouted back, the deep timbre in her voice quivering for added dramatic tension as she tilted her head upward and clenched her jaw.

"There you go again with your crap! Clearly you still haven't learned to separate fantasy from reality!"

"Well, I managed to do that with our marriage!"

Adam jumped between them. "Stop it. This isn't the time!"

And then all pandemonium broke out.

The priest came around to offer some kind of spiritual guidance but exited quickly, and very red-faced, when he saw my state of undress. Some inquisitive relatives stuck their heads through the door, painted with sad, sorry puppy-dog looks, but they, too, left when they saw me spread-eagled on the floor.

An enormous ruckus ensued when the photographer burst in and started taking photos of me—no one had told him. The ruckus became a total freak show when my favorite cousin, Annie, who had designed my dress for free as a wedding gift, saw the state of her "best creation" lying crumpled and torn on the floor. She looked like she was about to cry.

Then the room went very blurry and the noises around me combined into one strange drone.

I closed my eyes and everything went black.

ACKNOWLEDGMENTS

As an adoptee, this was a very hard book for me to write. And there were many, many, many times I didn't think I could continue. I didn't expect it to be so hard. I thought that after all these years it was a subject I could easily write about—I was wrong. I would never have gotten through it if it wasn't for my amazing husband—as always—who supported me all the way to the very last word. Also my therapist (seriously)—who said in one of those therapeutic voices, all soft and hushed, that it was a good thing to write this book, no matter how it turned out. So I wrote it! And I finished it! I need to thank Jessica Smit, who has helped me with every book I have ever written. She's been there right from the very beginning. She was there when I wrote the very first word of *Burning Moon*, and I really appreciate all her feedback, and she makes my books better. Amy, my editor, also makes them better—even though I hate editing.

ABOUT THE AUTHOR

Jo Watson is an award-winning writer of romantic comedies. *Burning Moon* won a Watty Award in 2014. Jo is an Adidas addict and a Depeche Mode devotee.

You can learn more at:
Twitter @JoWatsonWrites
Facebook.com/JoWatsonwrites